# Barossa Street

## Rob McInroy

Ringwood Publishing

Glasgow

Issued in 2022
by
Ringwood Publishing

Flat 0/1 314 Meadowside Quay Walk, Glasgow
G11 6AY

www.ringwoodpublishing.com
e-mail: mail@ringwoodpublishing.com

ISBN: 9781901514-41-4

British Library Cataloguing-in Publication Data
A catalogue record for this book is available from the
British Library

Printed and bound in the UK
by Lonsdale Direct Solutions

Front cover photograph courtesy of Perth Museum &
Art Gallery, Perth & Kinross Council.

# *Praise for* Cuddies Strip

'It is very much a contemporary novel. It deals with misogyny, it deals with institutional corruption, it deals with the problem of policing. I highly recommend it.'
**Val McDermid**

'I read this wonderful novel with a tear in my eye. I could hardly bear to read the ending but it was beautiful.'
**Cathi Unsworth, Novelist**

'How much I enjoyed this book. Feelings of frustration and anger went alongside thoughts of how far women in society have progressed, combined with how much further there is to go! So, it led to some stimulation for the grey matter, as well as being a page-turner. Thanks so much Rob, you should be proud.'

'What a page turner, I enjoyed every minute of it. I can't wait to read the sequel!'

'A wonderful and harrowing account of the true crimes committed in Perth in the 1930s - hard to believe it actually happened!'

'So addictive I couldn't put it down, thoroughly enjoyed it, very well done. Can't wait for the next one.'

'The best book I've read in years.'

'The pacing of the story is brilliant, but the most striking part is definitely how memorable the characters are, and this story will definitely be sticking with me. It was also interesting to read something set in Perthshire, and there are references to local sites throughout.'

'Great read, really captures a picture of what you'd imagine Perth and society was like in the 30s.'

'This is a perfect crime book... I give it a whopping five.'

'I really enjoyed Rob McInroy's narrative and felt he got the personalities of the characters across so well that I felt myself getting angry and frustrated at the way the investigation was handled by some of the officers, and felt sympathy and liking for others.'

'An enthralling book for true crime lovers. A well-written story that will keep you fully immersed until the end.'

'Tests the patience and strength of a human spirit and shakes the reader thoroughly.'

'I had high expectations for this book and it definitely did not disappoint. It was a delight to read as the story telling was sublime, the characters are all unique and well formed and the story itself was believable and more importantly felt human and real.'

'I loved this book, especially the Scottish dialect throughout, and would recommend it for anyone who likes the idea of a police procedural with a difference.'

# Part One

# January 1936

# Monday 20<sup>th</sup> January

## *A Day of Death*

Bob Kelty sauntered past the City Police Headquarters in Tay Street. He had no reason to be there but he enjoyed the sensation of being able to pass the recessed front door without having to enter. Slush from heavy snowfall two days before covered the pavement. The River Tay was pulsing to his left. He nodded as an ageing couple walked past, wearied by the shopping they carried. He smiled as he turned onto the High Street and passed the Salutation Hotel. No more Saturday night fights to break up in there. No more drunkards and arguments. Last Friday had been his final day as a constable in the Perth City Police and now he had a week's leave before a new career beckoned, library assistant at the Sandeman Public Library. Peace and quiet and a chance to do something useful.

'Excuse me, Constable.'

Bob looked round. Approaching him, smiling, hand outstretched, was Richard Hamill. Bob remembered Hamill from when he was arrested – wrongly – for the murder of Danny Kerrigan and the rape of Marjory Fenwick the previous August.

'I was hoping to bump into you,' Hamill said.

'It's no every day someone tells me that.'

'I'm worried. About a friend.'

'Right.'

'Hugh Smithson.'

'Right.'

'Barossa Street.' Hamill waited as though expecting Bob to confirm the location. Bob looked at him but said nothing. Hamill was a handsome man, a little older than Bob, perhaps twenty-four or twenty-five, with sandy-coloured hair and fine features. They walked through the slush. 'I left him a note a couple of days ago, to say I'd be coming round last night. He didn't answer when I knocked on the door.'

'Maybe he was oot?'

'He never goes out. He's a bit of a recluse. Odd, you know? Never leaves the house, never speaks to anybody.'

'Except you.'

'I run errands for him. Shopping, paying his bills ...'

'I'm sure there's an ordinary explanation. There usually is. Maybe he was busy. Sunday – havin his weekly bath.'

'I think something's happened to him.'

'How?'

'Because it's not like him.'

'How old is he?'

'Don't know. Late sixties, maybe.'

'And how's his health?'

'So so. Emphysema. Hellish cough.'

They turned onto Scott Street and walked its length until it became Kinnoull Street and they arrived at the Sandeman Library: brown sandstone, enormous windows, pillars either side of wide double doors. Bob looked at it with pride.

'I start there next Monday,' he said.

'You've not left the police?'

'I have. Last Friday.'

'That's a damned shame. You were one of the good ones.'

'There's no many of my former colleagues would agree wi you on that.'

'You always listened to people.'

'We all listen.'

'Yes, but some of you don't hear. Even so ... Will you come with me? To Barossa Street?'

2

Bob sighed. 'Aye, I suppose so.'

At the far end of Barossa Street was a row of two-storey houses, most looking over a building site for the new school. It was an eyesore, open land running uphill to Stormont Street, rubbish and detritus everywhere.

'Two years overlooking a building site and then forever a school playground full of shouting bairns,' said Hamill. 'Who'd want to live here?'

'Handy for town, though.' Bob rapped on a brass doorknocker in the shape of a griffin and stepped back and waited. No one answered. He peered through the window to the left and saw a darkened sitting room. The fire was dead in the grate. A pipe rested on a table beside an armchair next to the fire. A copy of *The Courier* lay on the armchair. Bob stared at the scene in silence. Looking through windows held a particular horror for him, since the day he looked through his own kitchen window, aged thirteen, and saw his father dead on the floor, the shotgun he had used to end his suffering beside him on the flag tiles.

'Well?' said Richard Hamill.

'You should call the polis.'

'I did. You.'

'I'm no the polis anymore, thank God.' Bob tried the door, but it was locked. The window was bolted on the inside. He crossed the road and stood on the opposite pavement and tried to gauge how far they were from the end of the street. Forty yards, maybe. It was worth a try.

'Come on,' he said. He checked his pocket-watch. Four-thirty. As they turned right, the North Inch was arrayed before them, River Tay bounding it in the near distance, Scone beyond.

'Where are we going?' said Hamill.

'Here.' Bob stopped at a dark green door on Rose Terrace and knocked on it three times. After some moments they could hear footsteps approaching and the door was opened by a young woman in a maid's outfit.

'Bob!' she said. 'Whatever's the matter?'

'Hello, Annie.' Bob smiled shyly. 'I wonder if you would be so kind as to ask Mrs Conoboy if I could gain access to her garden?'

Annie stared at him, perplexed. 'Why?'

'Police business.'

'But you're ...' She shook her head and closed the door. They heard her retreating into the house and a couple of minutes later she reappeared.

'Please come wi me,' she said. Bob and Hamill followed her down a neat and bright hallway into a broad, book-lined study and through into a drawing room. There was a garden beyond, and a high wall, and behind that wall was the rear of Barossa Street.

'Robert. What a lovely surprise.'

Seated beside a low-burning coal fire was Bella Conoboy, wife of Victor Conoboy, police inspector and, since the death of Bob's father, informal guardian.

'You're looking very well, ma'am.'

'And you. You're on police business, I understand.'

'Yes.'

'But ... '

'Mr Hamill ...' Bob pointed to Hamill. 'He requested my assistance, ma'am. We need to get access to a house in Barossa Street. Mr Smithson's. To check that he's in good health. Mr Hamill is worried about him.'

Bella tutted with concern. 'Of course. At once.'

Annie unlocked the back door and Richard Hamill exited into the garden. Bob made to follow but Annie grabbed his hand and quickly, daringly, reached up and kissed him on the lips.

'I'll call for you later,' Bob said.

'Grand.'

Bob joined Hamill in the garden and again tried to assess

how far along the street they were. 'Just aboot here,' he said, pointing to the far corner of the Conoboys' garden. From close up, the wall bounding it looked ominously high.

'How will we get over that?' said Hamill.

'I'll gie you a bunk up. Then you can pull me up.'

Both of them knew that was entirely unfeasible but they stood dutifully at the foot of the wall, staring at it.

'You'll be needin a ladder,' shouted Annie from the back door. 'In the shed. Fred Irons uses it to clean the windaes.'

Bob sighed with relief, collected the ladder and fixed it against the garden wall. He looked at Hamill. 'Aye, well,' he said, and started to climb unsteadily, unwillingly. He had no head for heights. At the top, he clambered onto the wall and started to pull the ladder up.

'Hey, don't do that.'

'I need it to get doon the other side.'

'Yes, but let me get up first, or I'll be stuck this side.'

'Oh aye.' Bob watched as Richard Hamill climbed the ladder. He was as ungainly as Bob had been. When both men were perched on the top of the wall, they looked around.

'That's it,' said Hamill, pointing to an unkempt garden below them.

'He should have got that grass cut in September. He'll be needin a flock o sheep to sort it come April.'

They pulled the ladder up and eased it down into Hugh Smithson's garden and descended with relief. They crossed the sodden grass to the house and Bob peered through a grimy window into a squat and dark kitchen. A kettle sat on the hob, a bottle of milk on the sideboard. A loaf of bread was beside it, and a knife ready for cutting. Bob frowned.

'Can you see anything?' said Hamill.

'I don't like the look of it.'

'I told you.'

The window was locked too, and Bob looked around for something to break it. He found a hefty stone by the side of the door and lifted it. Beneath was a key.

'What's the point of leavin a spare key there?' he said. 'You cannae get in here except through the Conoboys' garden.'

'Well, at least you've saved the expense of a broken window.'

Bob unlocked the door and stepped inside and halted, not sure what he was waiting for. Inspiration? Courage?

'Hello?' he shouted. 'Mr Smithson, are you in?'

He went into a narrow hallway filled on either side by prints of mawkish Victorian art in cheap frames, angled haphazardly as though hung by a drunkard. At the far end he could see the front door. The key was in the lock. To his right was the living room he'd observed from Barossa Street. There were four empty bottles of McEwan's 80/- lying on the floor, the Laughing Cavalier staring up at them. The ceiling was stained brown with nicotine. Next door, the room was a mirror image, cramped and untidy, smelling of staleness, still air and tobacco. It was empty.

He turned to the stairs and gripped the banister. 'Hello?' he shouted again as he began to climb. Fear pulsed in his throat and ears. Richard Hamill followed closely, barring any possibility of retreat.

'Which one's the bedroom?' Bob said.

'No idea. I've never been up here.'

Bob tried the first door. A boxroom. He tried the second door. A tiny bedroom, empty but for a wardrobe and a wooden chair. They retreated to the landing and he opened the third door.

They smelled it immediately, harsh and acrid, and both of them knew this was the smell of death. Hugh Smithson's room appeared empty, everything neatly in place except for the bed, where the bedclothes were rucked up as though someone had thrown them there in a hurry. And then Bob realised it wasn't only bedclothes he was seeing.

There was something in the bed.

'I think we've found Mr Smithson,' he said. He eased the top blanket back. Beneath was a sheet and he removed that too, to reveal the head and shoulders of Hugh Smithson.

'Dear God,' said Richard Hamill. Smithson was lying in a foetal position, hands fisted against his mouth, eyes wide open. Bob was about to cover the body again when he noticed blood on one fist. Slowly, he pulled back the blankets to reveal a bloodied mess. There were knife wounds to the stomach, the side, the arms, the thighs, so many of them Bob couldn't count. The mattress was vermilion, deepening to black. The only part of Hugh Smithson's body that seemed unscathed was his face.

The two men stared in stunned silence. Bob swallowed. 'I don't suppose he has a telephone?'

'No.'

He nodded. 'Could you go back to the Conoboys', please, and ask them to telephone the Police Station and advise them of a murder. I'll wait here.'

Bob looked round the bedroom while he waited for his former colleagues to arrive. It was spartan, nothing extraneous, nothing unnecessary. A comb rested on the dressing table. A grey alarm clock on the bedside table had wound down and showed six forty-five. Bob saw something underneath it and picked it up. A postcard, presumably the one Hamill said he had placed through the letterbox. It read: "It will be in your interests to see me at six o'clock tomorrow, if you will kindly leave the door open."

*Somewhat abrupt*, Bob thought. Hamill said he'd delivered it two days ago. Why would Smithson have brought it upstairs and left it by his bedside? Did he bring it that night, going to bed? Or maybe only last night? In which case he might not have seen it in time. Did that explain why he didn't leave the door open? Or was he already dead? Was it the murderer who left the postcard under the clock, and if so, why? The room was orderly, not obviously the scene of such an atrocity. There was no blood outside the bed. How was that possible? So many wounds? He pulled the rumpled bedclothes taut. There were slits in the blanket where a knife had penetrated. The first blows, at least, were through the bedclothes. Smithson had been in bed, possibly asleep, when the attack happened. Bob thought about the beer bottles on the living room floor. He was probably out for the count.

'What a way to go.' This was the third violent death Bob Kelty had witnessed in his twenty-one years. First his father, then Danny Kerrigan, shot dead on the Cuddies Strip last August when he was out walking with his sweetheart. Now Hugh Smithson. It got no easier. The emotions Bob felt, though, were not of horror, or revulsion, or even fear. Rather, a bleak sadness fell over him. Life lost, hopes elided, terminus. Hugh Smithson, sixty-odd years of struggle to get here, sixty-odd years of consciousness, unique distillation of perception and experience, a human being, spirit made tangible. Now gone. The calamity of death.

'I'm sorry.'

Sudden banging on the front door pulled him from his reverie. He ran downstairs and opened the door to reveal two police officers who stared at him in amazement.

'Kelty? What the hell are you doing here?'

'Afternoon, Sergeant. I found the body. With Richard Hamill.'

'Who?'

'It was him who telephoned for you. I waited here.'

Sergeant Petrie turned to Constable Macrae and laughed. 'Would you credit it? First day off the force and he finally does some real police work.' He shooed Bob aside and stepped into the hallway. 'Where's the body?'

'Upstairs. On the right.'

'Have you touched anything?'

'No.'

8

They turned at the sound of the front door and saw Richard Hamill joining Constable Macrae in the hallway.

'Man, you got here fast. You beat me to it.'

'You must be Richard Hamill,' said Petrie.

'At your service.'

'Well, kindly be of service by sitting quietly in the kitchen while we see what's happened here. You,' he pointed to Bob, 'follow me.'

Upstairs, Petrie inspected the body. Bob pointed out the incisions in the bedclothes. 'Murdered while he slept,' he said.

'Aye,' said Petrie noncommittally. He picked up the postcard and read it. 'What's this?'

'Hamill sent it. Wanted to speak to him.'

'And he had to send a postcard?'

'Aye.'

'Sounds a bit threatening. "In your interests". What does that mean?'

'Mr Smithson was eccentric, I believe. It wasnae easy to get to speak to him. You had to leave a message, make an appointment, like.'

'Maybe.' Petrie looked round the room. Macrae, Bob noticed, had remained outside and would not look at the body. Bob recognised that fear, understood.

'How well d'you know this Hamill?'

'No that well. We arrested him last year. The Kerrigan and Fenwick thing.'

'So why would he ask you to come with him?'

'Nae idea.'

'Aye, well, I need to speak to him.' He marched downstairs and Macrae followed, leaving Bob alone with the body once more. On impulse, he opened the narrow wardrobe. A threadbare suit and two shirts hung on hangers. There was a pair of old but gleaming brogues and a bag of shoe brushes in the far corner. Meagre belongings for sixty years of living. Beside them was a tin box. He recognised it, Princess Mary's chocolate tin sent to soldiers in the Great War at Christmas, 1914, with the names of the allied nations surrounding an image of the Princess. Bob opened it. Inside, neatly folded, was a bundle of old bank notes. He counted them. Over £100, more than a year's wages. He stared at the unseeing eyes of Hugh Smithson for some moments, then went downstairs and handed the money to Petrie.

'Looks like robbery's no the motive,' he said. 'That was just lyin in the wardrobe.'

Petrie frowned and put the tin in his pocket. He pulled out a cigarette and lit it. 'I tell you,' he said, 'this is the last damned thing we need. The King's not going to see the day out and we'll all be dragooned into marching in parades and ceremonies and the like for the rest of the bloody week.'

'Last night's bulletin was more hopeful,' said Bob. 'Said he "passed a quiet day".'

'Have you not heard this afternoon's?' Bob shook his head. 'His strength is "steadily diminishing".'

'Oh.'

Since last Friday there had been twice daily bulletins about the health of King George V, initially reporting he was suffering from mild bronchial catarrh and signs of cardiac weakness but gradually becoming more pessimistic in their outlook.

'Oh, indeed,' said Petrie. 'And now we've got a murder to deal with.' He turned to Macrae. 'I hope you didn't have any leave booked, son.'

'No, Sergeant.'

'Right then, go and fetch Doctor Murphy. Then get back to the Station and see if you can find someone who knows how to use the camera. Ask Sergeant Hamilton to contact Glasgow. We'll need their fingerprint boys to look at this.'

Macrae sped off as instructed and Petrie turned to Bob and Hamill. 'You two, hop it. I'll be in touch tomorrow to interview you.'

Bob and Hamill exited onto Barossa Street and Petrie watched them go before entering the house again, pulling the door behind him and locking it. Bob looked up at the bedroom window and closed his eyes, trying to will away the memory of what lay behind.

*

He still felt disconnected by the time he got to his home on Jeanfield Road. 'Gran?' he shouted. 'I'm hame.' He went into the living room. Gran was in her chair by a cold fireplace, a shawl wrapped round her. She was shivering. 'I left you some coal there,' he said. 'You only had to put it on.'

'As if you care if I freeze to death.'

There was still the barest trace of embers at the back of the fireplace and Bob rolled up a couple of pages of yesterday's *Courier* and tied them in a knot. He threw them on the fire and lit them and when the fire had taken hold he placed a few pieces of kindling on top, and then some coal. He waited for a few moments to make sure the fire didn't die, staring at the leaping flames and marvelling, as he always did, at their ethereal beauty. Fire was not from the same world as human beings.

'I'll mak your tea,' he said. 'Macaroni cheese, aye?'

'I had that yesterday.'

'No, you didnae, Gran. It was Sunday yesterday. We had biled beef, like always. The carrots werenae cooked enough. Mind?'

'I mind that. Bloody useless cook. Like your mither. You'll pooson me one of these days.'

Gran's illness had grown worse over the past few weeks. Annie's mum, Mrs Maybury, came in every morning and afternoon to look after her, and she warned Bob of Gran's increasingly erratic behaviour. 'She was washin the dishes in the bath this afternoon,' she said one day. On another, she reported: 'She had every damned thing out of the wardrobe and lyin on the bed.' And again: 'She's started leavin lit cigarettes all over the place. Walks away and forgets aboot them. She's goin to burn the hoose doon.' Bob knew it could only grow more serious, and that at some stage they would need to take action, but for now he tried to manage her chaotic ways as best he could. The thought of being alone was too frightening.

*

Later that evening, Bob sat in the living room of Victor and Bella Conoboy, nervous as always in their company. Victor Conoboy had been the investigating officer in charge of the Kerrigan and Fenwick case which Bob had solved through ingenious detective work, but it was a bittersweet outcome for both of them, unsatisfactory in that the killer of Danny Kerrigan was not convicted of the crime, the jury recording a verdict of "not proven". Disillusioned, both Victor and Bob had resigned their commissions. Victor had three weeks until retirement. He was ready for it and the thought of yet another murder in Perth reinforced his view.

'So if it wasn't robbery,' he said, 'what could have been the motive?' He sat in his armchair beside a high fire. His expression was sombre, an intense frown drawing his bushy eyebrows down and closer together.

'I couldn't say, sir.' Bob nursed a cup of tea on his thigh. Beside him on the settee, Annie Maybury, still in her maid's outfit, did likewise. Bella Conoboy, the fourth participant, sat in an armchair on the other side of the fire. 'Mr Smithson was a bit of a hermit,' Bob continued. 'Never spoke to anyone. Hardly ever went out. Carcary's delivered his groceries. He didn't let people in the house, unless by appointment.'

'So how could the killer get in?'

'Maybe he had an appointment?' said Bella.

'Richard Hamill had an appointment,' Bob replied. 'He

still didn't get in.'

Victor tapped his cigarette into an ashtray on the circular table beside his armchair. 'Could it be Hamill? He's the most obvious suspect.'

'If so, why would he ask me to accompany him?'

'Cover. Make it seem like he's genuinely concerned. Trying to get help.'

'Wouldn't it be better to just wait till the body was discovered? Not draw attention to yourself?'

'But when would that be? If Smithson's a recluse? Would anyone notice there was anything wrong?'

'Joe Carcary, sir. When he didn't open the door for his groceries.'

Victor nodded. 'Yes. But that could be three or four days.'

'I don't think Richard Hamill's the type, sir. I know I only tend to see the good in folks, but I've spoken to him a few times since we arrested him. He's always seemed a decent sort to me.'

The clock on the mantelpiece chimed once for nine-thirty. Victor leaned over and switched on the wireless. A newsreader was speaking in a solemn voice.

'The King's life is moving peacefully to its close.'

The Conoboys, Bob and Annie looked at one another in silence. Change was coming. The world was turning.

# Tuesday 21st January

## A Day of Questions

A harsh clanging resounded through the house, and it took Bob some moments to understand what it was. In the nine months since he had installed the telephone it had rung only once; the morning Marjory Fenwick was reported missing. The memory of that day, the overwhelming sense of failure, replayed in his mind as he ran downstairs.

'Perth 312,' he said.

'I have Perth City Police for you,' the telephonist said. Bob waited until the connection was made.

'Kelty? Sergeant Hamilton. Get yourself to the Station quick as you like. You're late.'

Bob stared at the telephone in confusion. 'I've left the force, Sergeant. Last Friday.'

'No, you haven't. You went on leave last Friday. You don't officially leave the force until *this* Friday. Correct?'

Bob faltered. That *was* correct. But ...

'And, unfortunately for you, with the death of His Majesty and the murder in Barossa Street, all leave has been cancelled. Ergo, get your useless bulk back here, immediately. Luckily for you, we didn't get round to throwing away your uniform.'

'You can't ... '

'Twenty minutes. Or it'll be a disciplinary.' The line went dead and Bob was left staring down the hallway. Through the opaque glass of the front door, he could see snow was falling.

'They can't ...' he said. But he knew they could. In the

14

kitchen he filled the kettle and set it on the range. This was going to be difficult. It had taken him weeks to explain to Gran that he was leaving the police. With her memory loss she couldn't retain the thought for long. Only in the past week had she shown signs of understanding and remembering. The news, of course, made her furious.

'Givin up a good job, good pay, for what? It'll be that hussy who's at the root of this. Stupit, like your faither.'

Now he was going to have to explain he was returning to work, if only for a few days. And then, next week, he would have to start over again, explaining he had left the force.

'Mrs Maybury will be in at nine,' he said as he laid a cup of tea on her bedside table. 'Careful when you go out to the toilet. It's snowin again.'

'Awa, ye useless laddie. A bittie snow never harmed onybody.'

As Bob rounded the corner of Tay Street and saw the entrance to the City Police Headquarters, a familiar dread tugged at his insides. His mouth went dry. His hands tingled. He pulled himself erect and entered, wiping snow from his suit.

'About time,' said Sergeant Hamilton without looking up. 'As soon as you get your uniform on you can turn round and go straight back out. Get yourself to Barossa Street. Sergeant Petrie's in charge while we're waiting for Inspector Mathieson. Door-to-door enquiries.' Finally, he looked up, as though astonished the object of his attention was still there. 'Off!' he shouted.

The snow had stopped by the time he reached Barossa Street, but the sky remained ominous, low and heavy. Policemen were at every door in the street, listening or taking notes. There were perhaps a dozen of them and Bob knew, from when he had undertaken door-to-door enquiries before, that they would be experiencing a curious combination of excitement and boredom. A big case, a murder, but their part

15

was mundane, the likelihood of them finding anything useful remote. He reported to Sergeant Petrie, who laughed when he saw him.

'Well, if it isn't the library assistant.' He instructed Bob to begin enquiries on the adjoining Barossa Place. 'Don't forget,' he shouted as Bob began to walk away, 'I want to speak to you later.'

'Aye, Sergeant.'

The first few houses Bob visited yielded nothing. At three there was no reply, and in the others, no one saw anything. All felt the need to say how shocking it was, a crime like this in a place like Perth, and Bob tried to reassure them this was an isolated instance. Perth was still one of the safest cities in Scotland, he told them. Was it, though?

He knocked on a matte black door and through the opaque glass of the window he could see a form shuffling towards him. A youngish woman, pretty but harassed, answered, wiping strands of hair from her face. She looked Bob up and down.

He introduced himself and explained his business. 'Aye,' said the woman, 'I've been waitin for somethin like this to happen.'

'How?'

'Yon man, Hamill, you cannae trust him.'

'Richard Hamill?' She nodded. 'What's he got to do with this?'

'I couldnae say. I've nae proof.'

'But?'

'Saturday mornin, I was passin Smithson's hoose, takin the bairnie to my mother's.' She indicated behind her to a large, black pram in the hallway. 'An I saw Hamill in the upstairs windae.'

'What time was this?'

'Eleven, eleven-thirty.'

'Right.' Bob jotted down the information in his notebook.

Hamill had told him yesterday he'd never been upstairs in Smithson's house. 'Are you sure it was Richard Hamill?'

'Aye. And what's more, I saw him Sunday an a, in the doonstairs windae.'

'What was he doin?'

'Just standin there.'

'And was Smithson wi him?'

'No that I could see.'

'What happened?'

'He came oot of the hoose. Locked the door. Took his bike and cycled away.'

'Where?'

'Intae town.' She gestured behind her in the direction of the city centre.

'You're sure he locked the door?'

'Aye.'

Bob frowned. 'And what time was this?'

'Aboot the same as the day before.'

'Eleven, eleven-thirty?'

'Aye.'

'Right. Anythin else you want to tell me?'

'No, tha:'s all I ken.'

'You said you expected somethin like this. How?'

She folded her arms. Behind her, a baby started crying. 'Well,' she said, 'that type, you ken?'

'How d'you mean?'

'His mammy was a tink. That makes him a tink an a. Just cause he lives in a hoose now doesnae mean he isnae. It's in the blood, ken? And you cannae trust thae bloody tinks. Murder you soon as look at you.'

Bob had no idea whether or not Richard Hamill was descended from travelling folk, and he didn't much care. Whatever might be in the blood, being a murderer wasn't.

*

17

At lunchtime, Bob walked home and made a piece and jam for himself and one for Gran. She glared at him across the kitchen table. 'You never went to Fraserburgh, did you?'

Bob blinked. That meant nothing to him. 'No,' he said hesitantly.

'I kent you wouldnae.' She chewed her piece, staring at him all the while. 'Would have been a grand job, that. Erchie Harrison's wife telt me. The fairmer, he's guid tae his men.'

'Aye, well,' said Bob. 'Maybe next year, eh?'

'We could be deid this time next year.'

Bob wondered what year Gran was currently in. Not this year, anyway. Possibly not even this century. He smiled and patted her hand. She pulled it away like she'd been scalded.

'Stop pawin me.'

*

The moment he walked into Police Headquarters, Sergeant Petrie beckoned him and led him to the interview room.

'Tell me everything,' he said. 'Every move you made yesterday, however stupid.'

Bob knew he wasn't stupid. What's more he knew *they* knew he wasn't stupid, but somehow he had been cast in that role and nothing he did changed the fact, not even solving the Cuddies Strip case. He ran through the events of the previous day and then explained his recent conversation about Hamill.

'Interesting,' said Petrie. 'I was suspicious about him from the word go. I thought he must be a tink, right enough. Got that look about him. Big-faced, ken?'

'To be honest, I'm no sure she's a very reliable witness. I mean, it's a bit of a coincidence, she just happened to be passin when he was there two days in a row. And he even came out of the hoose one time. She's layin it on a bit thick, d'you no think?'

'We've no reason to disbelieve her. What was her name?'

Bob stopped. He opened his notebook and flicked through the pages, but he already knew the name wasn't there. He looked up at Petrie.

'You didn't ask her name?'

'I ken where she lives. I can get it frae the directory.'

'Jesus Christ. The Sandeman Library's welcome to you.'

'D'you want me to do some more door-to-door?'

'No. Desk Sergeant Hamilton wants you. "Want" being a relative term, obviously.'

Bob retreated from the interview room with relief and reported to Sergeant Hamilton at the front desk. 'You wanted me, Sergeant?'

'Sergeant Petrie's finished sharing his pearls of wisdom with you, has he? I bet you feel better for that?' Bob shrugged noncommittally. The two sergeants didn't like one another and tended to project their animosity onto whoever they were speaking to. It was common practice not to take sides. Hamilton sniffed. 'The good sergeant has taken Macrae off my rota. Which means there's no one walked the Muirton beat the day.'

'You want me to walk the Muirton beat?'

'We'll make a detective out of you, yet. Back here at three.'

Bob liked the Muirton beat. For one thing, it took him past Muirton Park, home of his beloved St Johnstone Football Club. For another, he liked the people who lived there. Muirton was a newish estate and there were lots of young families, people making their way in life. There was a vibrancy to the place, a community spirit. He spent two hours walking the beat and saw no signs of disturbance, spoke to a handful of people and ruffled the hair of a couple of children and even the cold wind didn't bother him. Days like this, he could almost enjoy being a policeman.

On his way back he took a detour to the Sandeman Library and climbed the stairs to the reference library. He nodded to

Mr McKerchar, the reference librarian – and, from Monday, his new colleague – and opened *Kelly's Directory* on a bench beneath the window over Union Lane. He scanned the names of the residents of Barossa Place. Eliza Kinnell. That was her. He made a note in his pocketbook, saluted to Mr McKerchar and skipped downstairs. He was in a fine mood when he returned to the Station. The mood didn't last.

'There's good news and there's bad news,' said Desk Sergeant Hamilton. 'The good news is that Sergeant Petrie is no longer leading on the Smithson case. We've a new man helping us while we wait for Inspector Mathieson. Specially seconded from the County force. He wanted to see you the minute you got back.'

'What's the bad news?'

'That was the bad news. You'll see.' He turned away but Bob was sure he spotted a smirk on the older man's face.

He knocked on the office door and entered cautiously. The man sitting at the desk, poring over a series of files arrayed in front of him, looked up and Bob's heart lurched in his chest.

'Kelty, hope the Muirton beat was kind to you.'

'Sergeant Braggan,' said Bob. 'Nice to see you again.'

'I very much doubt that.' He gestured to Bob to approach and Bob stood to attention before the desk. Detective Sergeant Braggan was from the Perthshire County force, the highest-ranking CID officer in the whole of Perthshire and a man of dubious professional integrity. Bob had worked with him on the Cuddies Strip case and, although hating people was not in his nature, with Braggan he made an exception.

'So it was you discovered the body?' said Braggan.

'Aye.'

'Two murders in Perth in the past ten years, and you were first on the scene for both of them. Mr Lucky, aren't you?'

'Quite a coincidence, right enough.'

'Enough to make you question your faith in the all-knowing God. I mean, Jesus, why you?' Bob made no reply. 'I understand I don't have you for long?'

'Till Friday. That's my last day on the force.'

'For which we can all be grateful. Right.' He stood up suddenly and crossed to the coat stand in the corner. 'Take me to Barossa Street. Let's see what we have here.'

*

'Tell me about this witness you don't know the name of,' Braggan said as he stomped through the hallway of Hugh Smithson's house from the kitchen towards the stairs, bumping Bob out of the way as he passed.

'Eliza Kinnell. She's called Eliza Kinnell. Barossa Place.'

'Well done.'

'It wasnae hard to find.'

'Would have been a bloody sight easier if you'd just asked her in the first place.'

As they climbed the stairs, Bob filled Braggan in on Eliza Kinnell's evidence. He shared his concerns about her reliability. Braggan turned on the upstairs landing.

'If the man's got tink blood in him there'll be something wrong somewhere. Stands to reason. They cause trouble everywhere they go, those bastards. Tinks and knives go together, as well.'

'Mainly because they'd never get a gun licence.'

'As of now he's our number one suspect. I want him in for questioning.'

'He was in this morning. Made a full statement.'

'To whom?'

'Sergeant Petrie.'

'There you go then. That'll be worth heehaw.' He entered the bedroom and studied the bed. 'So how did you find the body?'

'In the bed just there. Under the blankets. Like he'd been fast asleep.'

'Or covered up.' Braggan lifted the blankets to reveal the bloodstained sheet. He studied the knife marks in the blanket and gauged their length with thumb and forefinger. 'Jesus,' he said, 'there must have been some blood.' He returned downstairs to the kitchen and peered into the Belfast sink beneath the window.

'Have you touched this?' he said.

'No.'

He looked at Bob. 'That knife would have been dripping with blood. And it must have been huge. You can tell by the size of those cuts in the bedding. There's no knife been washed in this sink. It's totally clean.'

'Aye, Sergeant.'

'Make sure we ask people about seeing anyone carrying a knife when we're doing door-to-door.'

Bob felt sure that seeing a man with a knife dripping blood was probably evidence people would offer up of their own volition, but he said he would.

'Right, I've seen all there is to see here. Let's go.'

'I wonder if I might stay on, Sergeant, have another look round.'

'Why?'

'Well, the initial inspection was undertaken by Sergeant Petrie, and …'

'Aye, say no more. Be back in an hour.' Braggan headed for the door but turned back. 'And remember to lock up behind you, for fuck's sake.'

Bob returned to the kitchen and leaned into the sink and studied it. As Braggan had pointed out, it was very clean. Suspiciously so, given the condition of the rest of the house and the foodstuffs left lying on the kitchen top. Hugh Smithson did not seem a man much given to domestic routine. He opened the sideboard drawers, looking for cutlery. In the second drawer he found a tray of knives and forks, all thrown in randomly. Among them was a large carving knife. Bob took out his handkerchief, lifted the knife and took it to the window where the light was better. The knife was perhaps nine inches long, a good inch wide at the base, and very sharp. That seemed a reasonable match with the wounds on Smithson's body. Where the blade joined the handle there was brown staining that could have been blood. The new forensic science they were developing could surely analyse that and determine if it was human. He wrapped the knife in his handkerchief and took it back to the Station.

*

Braggan appeared less interested in the knife than Bob had anticipated. 'I thought,' Bob said, 'we could get the experts to test it for fingerprints and for the blood.'

'If it is blood.'

'Aye. And if it's human blood. It could be from when he was makin a casserole or somethin.' Bob cursed himself. *Stop running down your own argument, you fool.* 'Shall I organise some analysis? I think the Glasgow fingerprint guys are due on Thursday.'

'Leave it with Sergeant Petrie to organise. I need you to go and get Hamill here, now.' He brandished a couple of pages of foolscap. 'I've got my questions ready.'

Bob sauntered to Paul Street and knocked on Richard Hamill's door. He had the strongest sense of being watched, of a hostile emptiness around him.

'Constable Kelty,' said Richard Hamill when he opened the door. 'I've been expecting you.'

'Aye, well, if you wouldnae mind comin doon the Station wi me.'

'I'll get my coat.'

The two men walked back down Paul Street and Hamill nodded to windows behind which watchers watched. 'If you wouldn't mind, next time you visit could you come round the back entrance? Especially if you're in uniform. Folks round here ...'

'Aye, so I see.'

Outside Police Headquarters a few people, mostly men, stood in groups, watching, awaiting developments, but there was nothing like as many as there had been the last time Bob was despatched to bring Richard Hamill in for questioning. Then, both men had been manhandled and punched as Bob tried to usher Hamill into the safety of the Station. As they now turned onto Tay Street, they each remembered that day with trepidation, but this time their progress was unimpeded.

Bob stood at the rear of the interview room as Sergeant Braggan strutted in, papers under his arm. He spread them on the table in front of him and settled in a wooden chair that was palpably too small for him and confronted Hamill.

'Sergeant,' said Hamill, 'such a pleasure to see you again.'

'Richard Hamill, I am questioning you in connection with the murder of Hugh Smithson. Do you understand?'

'This is the fourth murder I've been questioned about now. Haven't been guilty of any of them, I might add.'

'No smoke without fire.'

'Careful, Sergeant, or it might sound like you've already made up your mind.'

'Restrict yourself to answering my questions, Mr Hamill. And stop being a smartarse.' Braggan picked up the first of his foolscap sheets. 'I have twenty-six questions to ask ...'

'How precise.'

Braggan raised his palm in front of him, '... which will, I think, get us to the truth of this matter.' He turned to Bob, and in a chummy manner that was obviously false, he said: 'Did you read the letter in the PA today from our MP? About layabout young people, loafing about on the streets, not looking for a job, terrified they might get one. As long as they can spend their dole on tobacco they're like pigs in shite.' He turned round again. 'Do you work, Mr Hamill?'

'Is that one of your twenty-six questions or just small

24

talk? Just so I can keep count.' He raised his left hand with his thumb outstretched and the fingers folded against his palm.

'Answer the question.'

'Well, I'm flattered you might consider me a young person, since I'm twenty-five, but no. I was made redundant at Pullar's recently. There's a recession ... '

'Where were you on Sunday, the day Mr Smithson was murdered?'

'You're sure it happened on Sunday?'

'Answer the question.'

'Only I wouldn't want to waste your time giving you an alibi for a day that wasn't the day of the murder.'

'Answer the question.'

'It could have been Saturday.'

'Your postcard, which you claim you posted on Saturday, was on his bedside table.'

'Anyone could have put that there. The murderer, for example.'

'Or you. Answer the question.'

'On Sunday, I was at home writing three job applications. I spent Saturday morning in the Sandeman Library researching the companies I applied to. I can give you their names. I'm sure they can confirm receipt of the applications.'

'Any witnesses to that?'

'The reference librarian will no doubt remember me.'

'That was Saturday. What about Sunday?'

Hamill paused for a moment, then shook his head.

'No alibi,' Braggan said aloud as he wrote it into his notebook.

'In the afternoon, I walked along the Inch watching the Tay. I love it this time of year ...'

'Witnesses?'

'No.'

'No alibi.'

Bob studied Hamill's face. The man was a model of composure, but on both occasions he'd been asked about witnesses, he'd hesitated. Only for an instant, but there was a perceptible shift in his demeanour. Bob would have liked to probe deeper but Braggan rampaged on with his questions.

'Evening?' he asked.

Hamill continued his evidence. 'At six, I went to Mr Smithson's as I had advised, but there was no reply. I went home and spent the evening listening to the wireless. Mr Donald Campbell from Pitlochry was on, if you're interested. A wonderful baritone. On the Empire broadcast.'

'You were alone?'

'I was.'

'No alibi,' they said in unison. This time, Bob thought, Hamill had managed to compose himself again.

'Question three?' Hamill said.

Bob, watching in silence, admired Hamill's confidence, but at the same time, he knew that antagonising Braggan was not a wise strategy. He could tell from the stiffness of Braggan's posture that the Sergeant was growing angry.

'Your mother was a tink, I understand?'

'One of the Lindsays, indeed. Travelled all over Perthshire and Aberdeenshire in search of honest occupation.'

'What was your relationship with Mr Smithson?'

'I run errands for him. Do things. He's a recluse ... '

'Was.'

'Was a recluse. Never went outside. Never let people inside.'

'Except you.' Hamill nodded. 'So why you? Why did he trust you?'

'Are they questions five and six? Or the same question asked twice?'

'Mr Hamill, I'd advise you to take this matter seriously. You're this close to being charged with murder.'

Those words, or perhaps Braggan's expression, seemed

to have an effect on Hamill. He nodded and lowered his head slightly.

'He knew my father. They worked together at Bell's. Dad was a warehouseman. Mr Smithson was, too. As a boy I used to place bets for the pair of them at Jock Handley's in the High Street. At one point, Mr Smithson became reclusive and he started to use me for other messages as well.'

'Why did you wish to see him on Sunday?'

'I got laid off recently – I told you. So money's a bit tight. I thought, I'm doing all this work for him. And he's got plenty money. He could afford to pay me a little for my time.'

'So you were planning to extort money from him?'

'No, a fair pay for a fair day's work.'

'What happened? Did it go wrong? Did he refuse?'

'I never got to discuss it with him.'

'And, when he refused, did you lose your temper?'

'I never saw him that night.'

'Did you take the knife with you or use one from the house?'

'I never saw him that night.'

Bob wanted to ask about the knife in the drawer. He shifted his position until he could see the notes in front of Braggan. The exchange between the Sergeant and Hamill had sounded like an ordinary conversation but Bob could now see that every question Braggan asked was written down. He was reading his twenty-six questions in order, without following up with any supplementaries. The next was: "Do you have a key to the house?"

'Do you have a key to Smithson's house?'

'No.'

'If we search your house, we won't find one?'

'No.'

'So how did you get in on Sunday?'

'I didn't. There is only one front door key. Mr Smithson

told me that often. He didn't trust anyone. Wouldn't have more than one copy made. He was fanatical about security.'

*What about the back door*, Bob wanted to ask. *With the key under a stone in the yard. That didn't sound like the action of a man fanatical about security. Ask Hamill about that.*

'When you entered the house with Kelty on Tuesday,' Braggan indicated behind him in the direction of Bob with a jerk of his thumb, 'who went in first?'

'Constable Kelty.'

'And how did you get in?'

'Through the back door.'

'It was unlocked?'

'No. The key was under a stone.'

*You see?* Bob thought. *Find that odd. Ask about it. Ask how we got into the yard in the first place.*

'What did Kelty do when you got inside?'

'Checked the rooms downstairs. Then we went upstairs.'

'Him first. You following?'

'Yes.'

'Did you put the key in the front door when Kelty wasn't looking?'

Both Hamill and Bob looked up in surprise. Bob blinked. Was that possible? He tried to remember the scene, walking from the kitchen down the hallway. He remembered seeing light from outside through the window. Did he see the key in the door? He certainly saw it at some stage, but was it then? Or later?

'I doubt very much,' Hamill said, 'whether I could have done that without Constable Kelty seeing me. He's very sharp. That's why I asked him to accompany me ... '

'I'll come to that. You say you posted the postcard through the door?'

'I did.'

'But you don't think he could have received it? What you

28

said to Sergeant Perie.'

'Only because he didn't answer the door as I requested.'

'So if he never received it, how did it get on his bedside table?'

'I don't know.'

'And how did it get blood on it?'

Bob started again. Did it have blood on it? He tried to recreate the scene but, yet again, his memory failed him. He cursed. Braggan shuffled through his papers and pulled the postcard from among them. He positioned it in front of Hamill and pointed to a smudge on the bottom left corner.

'Is that your blood?'

'No.'

'How do you know it's not your blood?'

'Because after I posted it, I never touched it again. And there was no blood on it when I posted it.'

'Why did you seek out Kelty to accompany you?'

'I didn't seek him out, exactly. I was hoping to bump into him because I seriously thought something was wrong and I wanted someone to assist me. I know Constable Kelty from before, and I know him to be an excellent policeman.'

'You didn't use him as a dupe? To make you sound genuinely concerned?'

'I haven't the imagination for something as fanciful as that.'

Braggan's chair creaked as he sat back quickly. He crossed his left leg over his right and lit a cigarette.

'Richard Hamill, did you murder Hugh Smithson?'

'I did not.'

Braggan inhaled deeply. He wore the expression of a man who wanted to arrest him here and now but knew he didn't have the authority. 'This interview is concluded. Mr Hamill, do not leave town. Do not do anything. Stay where we can find you. You can expect another call from us very soon.' He stood up. 'Kelty, see him out.'

Richard Hamill smiled. He was trying to look brave but Bob, a man accustomed to such acts of bravado, recognised the insecurity in his features. Hamill lifted his hands, four fingers showing, six folded over. 'I only counted twenty-four questions,' he said.

'Then you miscounted.'

# Wednesday 22nd January

## A Day of Snow

At eight o'clock Bob awaited instructions in the spare bedroom of the Conoboys' house. 'Are they sure about this?' he said to Annie.

'Aye, they seem to be.'

Floorboards creaked on the landing, heralding Victor's arrival. 'Thank you for this, Robert. I'll try not to make you late for work.'

'It's fine, sir. Happy to help.' They both looked at the wooden bed against the back wall of the bedroom.

'It was Tom's,' Victor said. 'Bella and I talked about it the other night. There was a programme on the wireless. About this terrible recession. People can't make ends meet. Can't afford to buy food, let alone anything else. And we've got all this stuff going to waste. That bed hasn't been slept in since 1918. What on earth are we keeping it for? So we agreed we'd give it to the Salvation Army to donate to a family in need.'

'Mrs Conoboy is happy to do that?'

'It was her idea.' Tom Conoboy, Bella and Victor's only son, was killed in the last days of the Great War and Bella, unable to process the grief, had developed agoraphobia, never leaving the house until a few weeks before, when she walked the Cuddies Strip with Marjory Fenwick the day after the trial of John McGuigan. Mention of Tom had been forbidden and none of his possessions had been touched in eighteen years. Bob couldn't hide his surprise at this new development.

'How are you doing?' Bella herself appeared in the doorway, a tight smile on her face. 'You'd best hurry. It's looking like snow again.'

Taking an end each, the two men turned the bed sideways and slid it onto the landing. It was very heavy, much heavier than modern beds, Victorian craftsmanship. Grunting with effort, they carried it down the first dozen steps and negotiated the turn in the stairway and adjusted their grips, then made the final steps to the ground floor. A van from the Salvation Army was already waiting on Rose Terrace and they carried the bed into the street. Bob jumped inside and pulled while Victor pushed until the bed was in place. Ian McDevitt thanked them and slammed the van's doors shut and hopped into the driver's seat. Bob and Victor, and Bella and Annie, watched from the pavement as he drove off, waving his arm at them through the open window, the tyres of the van throwing slush a yard into the air.

Bella shivered and pulled her coat around her. The first new flakes of snow were starting to fall. 'Are you all ready for tomorrow?' She asked Bob. 'Are you in the parade?' The proclamation of the new King was to take place at eleven the next morning, preceded by a march of local dignitaries from Tay Street to the market cross.

'No ma'am,' said Bob. 'I'm on crowd duty. Preventing trouble, apparently, although I don't imagine there'll be any.'

'Don't be so sure,' said Victor. 'I remember when the King and Queen came to open the Infirmary, just before the War, not that anyone was expecting war then. I was still a sergeant. The Suffragettes were causing a lot of trouble and we were on high alert. There were a few incidents, right enough. A brick wrapped in *The Suffragette* newspaper nearly hit the Queen. I was on the corner of South Street and King Edward Street and, just as the royal car passed us, a woman jumped in front of me. She made for the car and was about to climb onto the step and grab the door handle when I caught her and pulled her back. The crowd started yelling and shouting at her and I'm afraid to say she got hit by a few punches. So did I. I had to get her back to the Station for her own safety.'

'And you never did charge her,' said Bella, laughing.

'No. I seem to recall the paperwork went astray. Most mysterious.' Bella and Victor smiled at one another, complicit in their own remembered history.

'What was it you told her?' Bella asked.

'I don't think I can say that here. In front of Robert and Annie.'

'Why not? Robert's not in the police any longer.'

Victor nodded. 'I said to her: "I almost wish I'd let you get to the car. I quite agree with your cause".'

'And she tried to recruit you.'

'She did. I used to see her in town quite a lot. Nice woman. Well-to-do. Her brother was killed in the War and I think she moved away. I stopped seeing her, anyway.'

'Victor! Just the person I wanted to see.' They all turned to see Lord Kellett approaching, hand outstretched. He was a portly man in his sixties in an old-fashioned black suit and a Derby hat. He and Victor shook hands warmly. 'I just wanted to make sure you were ready for tomorrow. I've been liaising with the Lord Lieutenant about the police attendees.' Lord Kellett was Chairman of the Police Committee and an influential man in Perthshire politics, second in stature only to Frank Norie-Miller himself. He raised an eyebrow at Victor.

'I wasn't planning on taking part, my Lord. I'll be retiring in a couple of weeks. I thought I'd leave it to the younger ... '

'I knew you'd say that. Not a bit of it, man. We'll be assembling at the County Buildings at half past ten. The procession will leave at ten forty-five and the ceremony will start at eleven. You'll be walking beside me, at the head of the County Police contingent.'

'Yes, my Lord.'

Lord Kellett smiled at Victor's discomfort. 'I'm not one for these sorts of events either, but needs must. You've served this city all your adult life. You should be part of it.'

Victor nodded. 'Well,' he said, 'the King was a fine enough man, so it would be an honour.'

'Indeed,' said Kellett. 'He was a unifying force in the country. We may only realise how much now that he's gone.'

'The new King seems a grand replacement. Young, but wise, so they say.'

Lord Kellett shook his head. 'Don't believe everything you read about that man,' he said. 'I foresee difficult times ahead. And with the world the way it is … Well, I worry, that's all.'

\*

The blizzard began at four, snow which had been falling steady since noon now blanketing the sky, occluding the day entirely, a driving wind forcing it almost sideways. Four inches fell in an hour. Electrical power was lost over large areas of Perthshire, telegraph lines collapsing under the weight of snow. Roads were impassable. Lorries and cars were stranded. The door-to-door enquiries about the Smithson murder were abandoned.

'In the name of God, would you look at that,' said Desk Sergeant Hamilton, standing in the doorway of the Station and looking at the white-out on Tay Street. 'What a day. The King's dead, there's a murderer on the loose, we've had to reinstate Kelty, Lanky Mathieson's meant to be in charge of the investigation and he's nowhere to be found and now we've got the worst bloody storm since the War. What next? Oswald Mosley marching on City Hall?'

'That wouldn't be so bad,' said Sergeant Braggan.

'The Dundee-Blair train's lost,' said Bob.

'How can you lose a train?'

'Should have been in Blair an hour since. Nobody's seen it since it left Dundee.'

'I tell you, I wouldn't set foot out there,' said Braggan. 'There's going to be deaths tonight, mark my words.' The telephone rang and Hamilton answered it. From his changing expression, Bob realised something was amiss. He went to the counter and waited until the conversation ended.

'Bunch of kids left Madderty Primary School at mid-day to walk home to Fowlis Wester. Haven't been seen since.'

'How many?'

'Eight.'

'Fowlis is nearer Crieff than Perth,' said Braggan. 'Can the Crieff boys not take care of it?'

'Crieff's completely cut off. Gilmerton bends one side, Comrie bends the other.'

'We could charter a bus,' said Bob. 'Alexander's. I expect they've cancelled most of their routes, so they'll have plenty spare. That way, we can go and look for the bairns and if we find them, we'll be able to bring them back.'

Hamilton nodded grudgingly. 'Get on, then.' Bob rounded the counter to the telephone. 'But,' Hamilton continued, 'you'd better follow the bus in the car. In case the bus gets stuck.'

Bob wondered what use a car would be for eight stranded children, but he said nothing. The telephone line went down halfway through his call to Alexander's and, for the second time in two days, he stared helplessly at a telephone.

'I'll have to go the bus station,' he told Sergeant Braggan. Braggan gestured expansively, ushering him out as he would an animal that had strayed from its territory. 'Could you telephone Mrs Maybury,' Bob said, 'Feus Road, and ask her to go and see to my gran? She'll need lookin after. The fire'll need some coal on it. She'll be needin her tea.'

'Aye,' said Braggan.

Outside, the blizzard had not abated and by the time Bob clambered into the Wolseley his overcoat was covered in snow. The windscreen wipers were of practically no use as he drove up South Street. He drove blind, praying no one would be stupid enough to be out in such weather.

At the bus station, Hugh Alexander was waiting for him, their aborted telephone conversation having given him enough information to know what was required. 'I've a bus ready,' he said. 'And a good driver.'

'Have you any more men? In case we have to dig our way out?'

Alexander pondered. 'Aye,' he said. 'I've a few still hangin about. There's nae work the day.'

'And shovels. If you have them.'

'Shovels. Aye.'

Bob unfolded an *Ordnance Survey* map and pointed to Madderty. 'There's a back road here,' he said, 'runs north to the main Crieff road. Then they'd have to turn west and walk the Crieff road to Fowlis. It's about four miles in all. The junction wi the Crieff road is about halfway. I think we should take a chance on the bairns havin got as far as the main road and carry on there till we find them. If we dinnae find them, we'll have to double back and go doon the back road. I cannae imagine that would be easy for a bus at any time, let alone in this, so that's a last resort.'

Alexander listened to Bob's plan. It made sense. 'Aye,' he said. 'Good.'

'I'll follow in the car.'

'What for?'

'In case the bus gets stuck.'

'If the bus gets stuck, what chance have you got?'

'Aye, well, maybe so, but my sergeant telt me. He's no a man to argue wi.'

'Geordie Hamilton?'

'That's the man.'

'You follow in the car, then.'

Ten minutes later, the blue and white Alexander's bus crept out of town, followed closely by Bob in the Wolseley. The first indication of the difficulty they would face came on the Crieff road as they climbed through Hillyland. Bob cried out in alarm as the bus slid across the road in front of him towards the adjoining fields. Beyond a blanket of snow was Hillyland Farm, soon to be turned over for five hundred new houses.

Inside the bus, the men were as apprehensive as Bob. 'Man,' said Jimmy Wright as he steered the bus back to safety, 'that's hellish oot there.'

'We've nae chance on the hill ootside Methven,' said Harry McFadyen, clutching his shovel like a comforter. 'It's twice as steep as this. And twice as long.'

'Aye, but we'll get a better run at it,' said Jimmy. 'Gie us a bit of momentum, like.'

They passed the outskirts of Perth and negotiated the steep bends past Almondbank, averaging little more than ten miles per hour. On the final straight before the hill into Methven, Jimmy thrashed the engine and the bus hurtled through a wall of snow, leaving an unprepared Bob in its wake. From nowhere, a car loomed in front of them, and they passed each other with millimetres to spare.

'Jesus, where did that come frae?' said Jimmy. He sped into the ascent at around forty-five miles per hour, pretty much maximum speed and far too fast for the conditions. The steering was light. If anything else were to approach, there would be no possibility of braking or avoiding it. Bob followed, staring at a world blurred into nothingness. The bus began to slow, thirty-five miles per hour, thirty, twenty-five. By the time they turned into the bend at the top of the hill they were barely at walking pace. Another hundred yards and they would have ground to a halt, but the hill levelled off and they began to pick up speed again. The convoy of two rolled steadily towards Methven and downhill through the town.

'Good job,' said Harry McFadyen.

'Aye,' said Pete Townhead.

'Aye,' said Johnny Gow.

On the long stretch at Burnbrae an easterly wind was gusting from behind them, driving the snow horizontally until it seemed that snow and bus were in some demented race. Everything outside their immediate line of vision was lost, as though they were hurtling through a tunnel, and this gave the impression they were going much faster than they were. Bob followed the lights of the bus, praying it wouldn't speed up and lose him. After another couple of miles, he felt sure they should have reached the junction of the Madderty Road but he could see nothing. He began to worry that they wouldn't even be able to spot the children and drive straight past them. They drove on for another three or four miles until Bob saw a light on the bus indicating a right turn. They turned off the main road and drove the short distance into Fowlis Wester. In the village, a handful of residents came out of their houses when they heard the bus's arrival at the village cross.

'Have you found them?' a fraught woman shouted.

'No,' said Jimmy, 'we didnae pass them.'

'They can't have made it to the main road,' said Bob. 'We'll have to go back. You'll never get your bus doon the Madderty Road. I'll have to go and see if I can find them. I'll ferry them back to the bus.'

He crawled down the Madderty Road at little more than five miles per hour. Most of the time, he wasn't even sure he was on the road. After a couple of miles he turned a corner and was dismayed to see Madderty ahead. He drove through the village to the primary school and the teacher rushed out, a woman of about thirty in an overcoat and tweed headscarf.

'Have you found them?' she said.

'Have they no come back?'

'No.'

'Damn.'

Bob sat back in the Wolseley, perplexed. They'd driven the stretch of the Crieff road in both directions and seen no sign of the children. They weren't on the Madderty Road. So where were they?

'Oh no,' he said. In the white-out, the children must have missed the Fowlis Wester crossroads and carried on walking. The next village was Gilmerton, another three or four miles away. They could die of exposure before they reached there. He turned the car and went back the way he had come until he reached the bus.

'You'll need to turn round,' he said to Jimmy. 'I think they've missed the crossroads and gone past Fowlis.'

Jimmy cursed. 'There's a layby up there where I can do a U-turn. You go on ahead. We'll catch you.'

Bob shut his window. His fingers were almost numb. He flexed them to recover some movement and started off again. When he reached the Fowlis crossroads, he kept on, straining to see through the almost impenetrable snow. A mile. Two miles. Just when he was beginning to give up hope, from nowhere he saw a shape by the side of the road. He stopped and stared, trying to make out what was there, and then he saw them, a couple of children waving at him. He pulled off the road and shouted.

'How many?'

'Eight.'

'You're all here?'

'Aye.'

Close up, he could see them now, a row of terrified, frozen children. He hugged each one in turn, counting as he went. Eight. They were all there. He heard the bus pulling up in front of the Wolseley and he grabbed the nearest children's hands.

'Hold on to each other,' he said. 'Form a chain. Follow me.'

He ushered them on to the bus and the drivers hugged them to try to get some warmth into their tiny bodies. In the dim lighting of the bus, they could see the children were exhausted. Bob knew they really would not have survived much longer.

'Where are we?' said one boy, the largest, probably about eleven or twelve years old.

'You got lost,' said Bob. 'You missed the Fowlis turn-off.' He walked back down the bus. 'How are you goin to turn?' he asked Jimmy.

'I'll have to drive to Gilmerton. Try and do a turn at the Sma Glen junction.'

'I'm doubtful, Jimmy,' said Harry.

'Me an a. If we cannae, we'll just have to find folks in Gilmerton to put aabody up for the night.'

'Everyone ready to go home?' shouted Bob. The children cheered.

Jimmy turned the ignition of the bus. Nothing happened. 'Fuck,' he said.

'What?'

'The diesel's frozen.'

'You're kiddin,' said Bob.

'It happens quite often. Just not usually in the middle of fuckin nowhere.'

Behind them, the children sensed something was wrong and the younger ones began to cry, two boys of seven or so. A couple of the girls tried to comfort them.

'Harry,' said Jimmy, 'is the blow-torch in the boot?'

'Aye. I had to use it yesterday in North Muirton.'

'See to it, then.'

'What's he goin to do?' said Bob.

'Take a blow torch to the fuel tank. Melt the diesel.'

'You cannae be serious!'

'Well, have you a better idea?'

The children were all crying now. 'I want to go home,' one of the younger boys said.

'I'm cold,' said one of the girls.

Bob recognised the terror in their expressions, understood the helplessness they would be feeling, the fear, the craving for safety, for home. 'Here,' he said. He strode down the bus and stood among them. 'The bus'll be ready to go in a wee minute. The mennie have just got somethin to sort out first. You ken I'm a polisman, aye? Well, here's a song aboot my sergeant. You can join in if you like.' And he started to sing:

'I know a fat policeman,
he's always on our street,
a fat and jolly red-faced man,
he really is a treat
He's too kind for a policeman,
he's never known to frown,
and everybody says that he's the happiest man in town.'

And he launched into the chorus of *The Laughing Policeman*, and at first the children listened in silence, and then they began to laugh, and when Bob finished the chorus he shouted 'Again,' and this time they all joined in. A bang on the back window alerted Jimmy that the diesel was unfrozen, and he turned the ignition and the bus fired into life. Harry McFadyen returned to a bus full of laughter.

'What the hell?' he said.

Jimmy grinned. 'Didn't you know? We've got Harry bloody Lauder in the back.'

'Well, tell him to give them an encore. We need to dig out the front tyres. Pete, Johnny, come on.'

Bob gave the children a rendition of *The Runaway Train* while the men cleared the road in front of the bus. When they were back on-board Bob clambered down the aisle.

'Right,' he said. 'I'll get the car and head back. Thanks,

lads, you've been fantastic.'

'Aye, ye've done all right yoursel, young ain,' said Jimmy.

Bob jumped off the bus and headed towards his car. Snow slathered his face, stinging his eyes, almost physical in its intensity. If anything, the blizzard was growing worse. He looked ahead but could see nothing but white. White into grey into infinity.

The Wolseley was nowhere to be seen.

'What?' he said. He looked around in bemusement and walked forward, straight into a drift, six or seven feet high. Beneath it, he realised, was the Wolseley. The easterly wind was driving the snow hard and fast and when it reached the impediment of the parked car it had settled around and over it. In the time it had taken them to unfreeze the bus's diesel, the Wolseley had been buried feet deep in a snow drift.

'Damn,' he said. He could hear the roar of the bus engine preparing to depart. 'Wait!' he shouted, running towards them, waving his arms. The bus began to move off and he yelled again. The bus struggled to gain traction and Bob ran desperately towards it. Just as he was about to slam his hand on the back window it pulled away and Bob watched in horror as it gradually picked up speed and drove off, leaving him alone in the grip of the storm. A white wall surrounded him and he had nowhere to go, nothing to do. An instant chill numbed his bones. If the bus couldn't turn in Gilmerton they would stop there for the night. And Bob would be stranded out here. He would be dead within the hour.

He spent the longest ten minutes of his life with his hands clamped under his oxters trying to keep warm. He stared in the direction of Gilmerton, counting slowly to sixty over and over, praying the bus would return, praying that Jimmy's driving skills would be sufficient for the task. He was starting to grow light-headed, almost dreamy, and he knew he was drifting off. Hypothermia could kill within minutes. When he thought he had counted to sixty a dozen times he concluded that the bus wasn't coming. Even now, Jimmy and the men would be knocking on doors in Gilmerton seeking accommodation for the night. Dizziness started to overwhelm him and when he heard the noise of an engine, he wasn't sure if it was in his head or real. He began to wave his hands aloft. His next thought was that they wouldn't see him. Just drive past him. Or run over him. At the last moment the bus lunged out of the void in front of him and ground to a halt. The door opened and Pete and Harry bounded out. They grabbed him and pulled him inside.

'Is your car under a drift?' Jimmy said. Bob nodded mutely. 'I thought that might happen. Realised just as we were pullin away. Just as well I thought aboot it. I was crawlin along lookin out for you. Otherwise I'd have flattened you. Wouldnae even have kent I'd done it.'

'Aye,' said Bob, clapping his hands to get some sensation back into them. 'I need tae dig it oot. Can I borrow one of your shovels?'

Jimmy shook his head. 'Man, there's nae way you're goin tae dig a car out of a snow drift in this. You'll be deid within minutes. You're on your last legs as it is.'

'I cannae leave it.'

'Wid you look around you. I doubt you could even find the bloody thing. Come on, before we freeze our knackers off.'

Bob slumped into one of the seats. *I've lost a polis car,* he thought. *I'm for it now.*

They drove back to the crossroads and turned up to Fowlis Wester. Once more, families rushed out of their houses at the sound of the bus and there was cheering and clapping as the eight missing children trooped off. They turned and waved at the drivers as they were shepherded into their homes by their parents.

'That's our good deed for the day,' said Jimmy.

'For the year,' said Harry.

They drove back to Perth and dropped Bob off on Feus Road and he waved them goodbye. He had a terrible headache but otherwise he was unscathed, the dizziness and light-headedness receding. It was gone eleven by the time he finally made it home. The snow had stopped, and the air was already milder. The city was bathed in a strange light, the meagre moon's reflection amplified by a dense blanket of snow. There was silence, a most beautiful silence, and Bob walked as slowly and quietly as he could so as not to spoil it.

He unlocked the door and stepped into a dark and freezing hallway. Instantly, he grew afraid. 'Gran?' he shouted. He rushed into the living room. Gran was in her chair, covered by her shawl. The fire was dead. The room was icy. He knelt beside her and felt her hand. It was frozen.

'Is that you, son?' she said.

'Aye, Gran. I'm here.' He ran upstairs and pulled blankets from the airing cupboard and arranged them around her. 'I'll mak you some tea, then get the fire goin. I'll light the fire in your bedroom, too.'

'No, ye'll no. We cannae afford the expense.'

Bob didn't argue and lit the fire anyway. Why wasn't Mrs Maybury here? He'd asked Sergeant Braggan to call her. What happened? He filled a clay pot with boiling water and rolled it up and down Gran's bed sheets to warm them and left the pot at the bottom of the bed. She drank her tea and he gave her a hunk of cheese and when she'd eaten that, he carried her upstairs to bed. He lay beside her and cuddled her and stayed like that for half an hour until he could tell from her breathing that she had fallen asleep.

When he got downstairs, he tried to play his fiddle to calm himself, but no music emerged and he sat in his chair and stared into space and felt an anger the likes of which he had never known.

44

# Thursday 23rd January

## A Day of Proclamations

Bob walked straight past Sergeant Hamilton at the desk. 'Here, I want you,' Hamilton shouted after him but Bob kept walking. Braggan was in the office, drinking tea. He gave a double-take when he saw Bob's expression.

'What did I ask you to do?' said Bob.

'The phones were down. You know that.'

'So I asked you to get in touch with Mrs Maybury and you said "aye" and you didnae even bother?'

'How could I? There was nae phone.'

Bob looked around. 'Remind me,' he said. 'Where are we? A *Police* Station? With *policemen*. Whose job it is to keep people safe.'

'Watch your tone, Constable.'

'Don't you dare pull rank on me, you useless bastard. She nearly died. I didnae get home till half past eleven. She was sat there freezin to death. Naebody to look after her.'

'Well, then ... '

Bob lunged and grabbed Braggan's jacket and pulled him close until they were head-to-head. He saw fear in Braggan's eyes. 'I'm not goin to hit you,' he said. 'Violence is for cowards. That's what you would do and I'm better than you. I'm just warnin you. I have two days left in this hellish job. In that time, you stay out of my way. Do not ask me anything. Do not speak to me. Do not even look at me.'

He released his grip and turned and walked out of the room. He returned to the main office.

'Where's the Wolseley?' said Sergeant Hamilton.

'I lost it.' Without another word, Bob walked out of the Station and turned towards the North Inch. The grass was still thick with snow, and he stuck to the path round the perimeter. He wiped snow from a bench by the river and sat and watched the water pulsing past, cresting over stones, white foam rising momentarily in the air before settling back into the viscous glide of the river. Cold air stung his cheeks. Skeletal trees stood by the bank. A single rook's nest from last season was still lodged in the bare branches of a chestnut tree, incongruous, improbably large. Suddenly, a colony of starlings began a tremendous clamour. Just as suddenly, they stopped. A woman wheeling a black pram walked past and Bob knew she would be wondering why a policeman was sitting by the river when he should be on duty. He said good morning and she returned the greeting and walked by. Ripples on the water suggested a trout had broken the surface. The ripples expanded and faded and then they were gone, and the river continued its progress, endless and perfect and untouchable. After half an hour Bob was cold enough and calm enough to return to the Station. He stood. Was this how other men usually reacted to events? Was this how they dealt with adversity? With violence and anger? They could keep it. Bob prayed for his equilibrium to return and began to walk back the way he had come.

*

'You lost the car?' said Sergeant Hamilton.

'Aye.'

'A Wolseley Viper? Six-cylinder, five-seater?'

'The snow, Sergeant. It was driftin somethin awful. By the time we got the bairns on the bus it was buried six feet deep.'

'You expect me to believe that?'

'Ask Jimmy Wright.'

46

'I've known all sorts of foolishness over the years. Lost jackets, broken truncheons. I even mind the time Peter Rogers handcuffed himself to the railings outside the Sandeman Library. Willie Powrie – the toerag he was meant to be handcuffing – made off with his cap and spent the whole night wearing it in the Sally. Rogers never lived that down. But never. Never have I had someone lose a fucking patrol car.'

'It's not exactly lost, Sergeant, it's just …'

'Is it in its bay in the compound?'

'No.'

'Which means I have to spare Macrae to drive you out to wherever you lost it to get it back. Two men down – well, one-and-a-half – on the day of the King's proclamation.'

'I'll make up the time.'

'Too bloody right you will. Make sure you're back in time for the parade.'

*

'So, you lost a police car?' Constable Macrae laughed as he turned the ignition.

'Dinnae you start.'

'I'm no complaining. It gets me out of door-to-door enquiries for a couple of hours. I tell you what, though, that snow's had a fair shift. You wouldnae believe it.'

Bob studied Tay Street and the town bridge. It was true. The pavements were still white, but the roads had already turned to slush. 'Reckon at this rate it'll be mostly gone by nightfall,' he said.

'Thank God for that. The procession to the proclamation wouldnae be much fun if we were still ankle deep in snow.'

'Are you in the procession?'

'Aye. It's goin to be quite an affair. The County boys are there, too. And the Black Watch. Aabody, in fact.'

'That's some do.'

47

'Well, it's no every day you get a new king.'

'Cannae say I'm that fussed.'

'Steady. Dinnae let Sergeant Hamilton hear you say that. He'll have you arrested for treason.'

'That's the least of what he'd like to do to me.'

'Aye, he's no your biggest supporter right at the minute. Nor's Sergeant Braggan. He wasnae half callin you earlier.'

'Sergeant Braggan is a walloper of the first order.'

Despite the rapid thaw, the Wolseley was still buried beneath a couple of feet of snow, and they spent half an hour shovelling it clear. As Bob expected, the battery was flat and he had to hand-crank the engine. After a couple of attempts, it caught and Macrae extended the choke and accelerated gently until he could feel the engine settling. Bob turned it on the road and the two cars returned to Perth in convoy, not passing a single vehicle on the way. Bob's thoughts turned back to the murder of Hugh Smithson. Was that only three days ago? The testimony of Eliza Kinnell in Barossa Place still bothered him. It was too pat. Manufactured. *"Tinks ... It's in the blood."* Bob had never understood the general antipathy towards travellers, most of whom in his experience were hard-working and honest, even if a minority had a tendency towards drunkenness and fisticuffs as a first resort in any ongoing disputes. But couldn't you say the same about most non-Tinks? Hadn't he come close to fisticuffs himself, earlier that morning? So what did that make him?

\*

By ten-thirty, a keen north-east wind was agitating the flags that flew at half-mast on civil buildings throughout the city. Patches of snow, slush and ice lay on the pavements. The gutters were full of shovelled snow, compacted and dirty. Rain fell sporadically, the kind of persistent drizzle that didn't seem heavy but still penetrated clothing until you suddenly realised you were soaked through. It was no day for a send-off. After handing over the keys of the Wolseley to Sergeant Hamilton, Bob Kelty exited City Police Headquarters and turned up Tay Street, glad the wind was behind him. It sliced across the river and drove into his left shoulder, spreading a chill through his body. At South Street, outside County Buildings, the worthies and dignitaries of Perth were beginning to congregate, among them Victor Conoboy and Lord Kellett.

'Morning, sir,' said Bob.

'Morning, Robert. Do you know where you've been posted for the procession?'

'Corner of South Street and King Edward Street, sir.'

Victor laughed. 'Watch out for Suffragettes, then.'

'I will, sir.' He spotted an extraordinarily tall man at the back of the line of waiting policemen. 'Is that Inspector Mathieson?' he said.

Victor looked round. 'It is indeed.'

'I was beginning to think I'd imagined him.'

'How so?'

'He's supposed to be in charge of the murder enquiry. But no one's seen hide nor hair of him since it happened.'

'He'll be working undercover,' said Victor, tapping his nose.

'In the Sally,' said Lord Kellett.

'More than likely.'

Bob threaded his way through policemen and soldiers and clergy and officials, all the city's dignitaries, none of them willing to move to let him pass, too wrapped up in their own importance, too scared of losing their position. King Edward Street was lined either side seven or eight deep, no room for more, and an overspill three or four deep was congregating on South Street. The watching crowds were quiet and subdued but not, Bob thought, especially grief-stricken. More curious, perhaps. This was the first new monarch since 1910 and that – before the Great War, before

Spanish flu, before the depression, before Bob was born, before Hitler and Mussolini and Oswald Mosley – seemed like ancient history.

'He hasnae got much of a day for it,' an old woman said to him, her head and shoulders draped in a black knitted shawl.

'Aye, well, it's maybe better in London,' Bob replied.

'Oh aye, the sun shines oot their arses in London.'

The procession neared, flanked on either side by a military guard, the men within marching in silence. The City Police, under Chief Constable Chadwick, headed the detachment, followed by the County Police, led by Lord Kellett and Victor Conoboy. Victor nodded at Bob and Bob saluted. Behind them walked the Perth Pipe Band, the Depot Black Watch, the High Constables, the Sheriff of Perthshire, the Lord Provost and Lord Lieutenant. Members of Parliament came next, then the Convenor of the County of Perth, Magistrates and members of the Town Council, the Sheriff-Substitute of Perthshire and members of the County Council. The commander and officers of the 51st (Highland) Division marched next, followed by the Sheriff-Clerk and Procurator-Fiscal, members of the clergy, representatives from the Society of Solicitors, the medical profession and officials from various organisations and public bodies. Mr Tait from the Sandeman Library was among them. It wouldn't do not to be seen in this procession.

As they wound finally towards the Market Cross, the crowds on either side of South Street followed in their wake, trying to get closer to the main event. Around them, every vantage point was taken. People stared out of windows on King Edward Street, some – brave or foolhardy – sitting on the ledges. On the roof of City Hall, directly opposite the Market Cross, they stood four or five deep. Young boys were perched on the wall facing the Cross, drumming their heels against the bricks. A large group of young men had colonised the red tower of the Fire Brigade Station and many among the crowd at street level commended them on their foresight.

'Best view in Perth,' said an ageing man propped against a battered walking stick.

'Bloody cauld, though,' said Bob.

'A polisman complaining aboot the cauld. What's the world comin tae?'

Directly opposite the Market Cross, a guard of honour from the Black Watch awaited the arrival of the procession, formed up in two rows, three sergeants out front, their swords raised vertically. White spats gleamed in the dullness of the day. One by one, the massed dignitaries, every one of them male, took up their places around the Cross while the ceremony's principals climbed to the platform. Hastily installed microphone equipment, of dubious reliability, was intended to relay the ceremony to the hundreds gathered. When it was judged everyone was in place, the Commander of the Black Watch gave the signal for a bugle fanfare and martial music briefly sounded out. The crowd settled in silence. Into that silence, the Sheriff-Principal of Perthshire, Mr DP Blades KC, dignified in civil dress, stepped forward. Beside him, in scarlet and ermine robes, stood the Lord Provost and magistrates and, in uniform, the Duke of Atholl, Lord Lieutenant of Perthshire, and Major-General Brownrigg of the 51st (Highland) Division. The Sheriff-Principal invited the Lord Provost forward, and Robert Nimmo read the proclamation.

'Whereas it hath pleased Almighty God to call to His mercy our late Sovereign Lord King George the Fifth, of Blessed and Glorious Memory, by whose Decease the Imperial Crown of Great Britain, Ireland, and all other of His late Majesty's Dominions is solely and rightfully come to the High and Mighty Prince Edward Albert Christian George Andrew Patrick David: We, therefore, the Lords Spiritual and Temporal of this Realm, being here assisted with these of His late Majesty's Privy Council, with

51

numbers of other Principal Gentlemen of Quality, with the Lord-Mayor, Aldermen, and citizens of London, do now hereby, with one Voice and Consent of Tongue and Heart, publish and proclaim, that the High and Mighty Prince Edward Albert Christian George Andrew Patrick David, is now, by the Death of our late Sovereign of happy Memory, become our only lawful and rightful Liege Lord Edward the Eighth, by the Grace of God, of Great Britain, Ireland, and the British Dominions beyond the Seas King, Defender of the Faith, Emperor of India: To whom we do acknowledge all Faith and constant Obedience, with all hearty and humble Affection: beseeching God, by whom Kings and Queens do reign, to bless the Royal Prince Edward the Eighth, with long and happy years to reign over Us.'

As he drew to a close, the drummers started a muffled tattoo and after half a minute, the pipers joined in and played *The Old Garb of Gaul*. The Perth Silver Band readied themselves and as the slow march finished, they played the national anthem. The Duke of Atholl stepped forward.

'Three cheers for His Majesty King Edward VIII,' he shouted, and the crowd joined in, though not, thought Bob, with as much gusto as might have been anticipated.

'Bloody parasite,' said the old man with the stick.

'I could arrest you for that,' said Bob.

'What, for speakin the truth? How much do we pay in taxes so that shower can live in luxury?'

'What did you come for, then, if you dinnae like them?'

'Mak sure the auld ain's deid.'

'Charlie Prebble,' said the woman in the black shawl, 'you've no a good word to say aboot anybody, have ye?'

'Certainly no you, Mavis MacIntosh.' The pair cackled and wandered off, bickering all the while. The dignitaries prepared themselves for the return march to County Buildings and the crowd began to disperse, a moment of history over. Who knew how long it would be before such a sight was seen again?

*

Detective Lieutenant Bertie Hammond of Glasgow City Police's Fingerprint and Photographic Division was at the Station when Bob returned, being served tea by Constable Macrae. Bob remembered Hammond from when he assisted in the Cuddies Strip case.

'Kelty,' said Sergeant Hamilton, 'Sergeant Braggan has asked that you take DL Hammond to Barossa Street and show him round. Although I'm not sure why he can't ask you that himself. I'm not his skivvy.'

'Yes, Sergeant. There's also the items here. The postcard and the knife.'

'Don't worry about them for now. DL Hammond is only here for the one day. We need to start at the house.' Hamilton walked off and Bob collected the keys to Mr Smithson's house and drove his Glasgow colleague the short distance across town to Barossa Street. Hammond was a short man with neatly Brylcreemed dark hair beneath a black fedora. He had a long, angular nose and a thin, wide mouth. He spoke with a Yorkshire accent.

'Did you no fancy bein in the Glasgow parade for the proclamation the day?' Bob asked him.

'Oh God, no. Only the important people are on parade today.'

'That's the trouble wi a wee force like ours. It's all hands on deck.'

'Were you in the parade?'

'No. Crowd control. Lookin for suffragettes and the like.' He laughed. 'You must get out and about a bit, wi your job. There's no many Scottish forces have their own fingerprint specialists.'

'Yes, it's one of the best bits of the job. I was involved in the Ruxton case before yours last year. That's going to go down in history that one. Not because of me. The scientists ...'

'Is that the one where they identified the victim from various body parts?'

'Scattered all over the Borders, yes. Amazing job. And I've been in Edinburgh and Dundee since. I have to say, this sounds a rum case, though.'

'Aye, I cannae get my head round it. A man who literally never leaves his house, hasnae done in donkey's years, is savagely murdered in his bed. Don't know how the killer got in. How he got out. No idea why he did it. I mean, how could Smithson have made enemies, if he never sees anyone?'

'Was it just random?'

'There must be easier pickings than Smithson's house. He was obsessed by security. Only one copy of the front and back door keys. And there was money left at the scene. Over £100. So I just cannae see a motive.'

'Well, let's see if we can shed some light on the matter.'

Bob unlocked the front door and walked inside. Hammond followed, carrying a battered suitcase. The day was dull and Bob turned on the gas lighting. It did not, in truth, offer much illumination but the sickly-sweet smell of gas seemed vaguely reassuring. Domesticated. Every time he'd been in this house it had been in darkness. There is something eerie about a cold and empty house. Unnatural. They went upstairs and Hammond surveyed the murder scene.

'Hmm,' he said. 'This is going to be difficult.'

'How?'

'He wasn't a very clean man by the look of things. Didn't do much dusting.'

'Won't the fingerprints show up better?'

'Aye, maybe. But they're likely to be his. How long's he lived here?'

'Twenty years. More.'

'And his wife left him?'

'Aye, about fifteen year ago.'

'Probably not been dusted in all that time. That's a hell of a lot of years' worth of fingerprints. Finding someone else's is going to be like finding a Catholic at Ibrox.'

Bob laughed. 'You a Rangers man?'

'Not me. Sheffield Wednesday. But up here I follow Celtic.'

'Aye? We're playin your lot on Saturday. St Johnstone. Scottish Cup.'

'Are you going?'

'No. I go to Muirton when I get the chance, but I've never been to an away match.'

'Maybe for the best. Saturday'll be an easy workout for the boys in green.'

'We'll see aboot that.' Bob went over to the bedside table. 'I'm thinkin, there was a postcard that Richard Hamill posted through the door on the Saturday. We found it underneath the alarm clock here. If someone else – the murderer, say – put it there, that might give us a fingerprint.'

'It's worth a try.' Hammond opened up his suitcase and pulled out his apparatus. 'Did you photograph the scene?' he asked.

'I think a few photographs were taken, aye.'

'The entire scene? The body? The room? Close-ups?'

'I doubt it.'

'It's very important. We must take a scientific approach to detection. Science is moving on so fast, and we must take advantage.' He began to dust white powder over the dark wood of the bedside table with what looked like a miniature paintbrush.

'Anything?' said Bob.

'Plenty. Too much. Mostly his, I would imagine.' Bob studied the surface of the table, on which was now a succession of fingerprints. Hammond took out a camera and photographed the revealed prints and then carefully applied a square of adhesive tape over the area to fix it and attached it to a piece of black card. He turned it to reveal a set of fingerprints. Bob looked at it in amazement.

'Wi stuff like this,' he said, 'I always wonder who first came up wi the idea. And more to the point, how? How did someone discover aabody's fingerprints are different?'

'There's quite a few people could be said to have established fingerprinting as a method of identification. Francis Galton, Faulds, Herschel. Faulds is a Glasgow man, so I like to credit him. As to how they discovered it, God only knows. How did the killer get in and out?'

'Dinnae ken, but possibly through the back door. There was a key left under a stone in the garden. Smithson would never have done that.'

'Why would the killer?'

'That's the trouble. I've nae idea. And once he was out back, I've nae idea where he went next. There's no back passage in the garden. Just walls.'

'Let's have a look.'

They went downstairs and Hammond studied the back door. 'I'll need to take this away,' he said.

'The whole door?'

'Yes. It'll take hours to get all this fingerprinted. Can you call a joiner and have it removed? Tell him he'll have to wear gloves the whole time and be careful not to touch anything unnecessarily. Don't smudge anything. And then it'll need to be transported to Glasgow.'

'Aye, I mind doin the same wi the windae at Aberdalgie.'

'It was you brought it down, wasn't it?'

'It was. A grand day oot. My one and only time in Glesga.'

Hammond studied the door handle closely. 'I expect your fingerprints are on here?'

'All oer it, I should think.'

Hammond smiled. 'I'll send you a photo of them when I'm done. Wee memento. Anywhere else you think he went?'

'I think he cleaned the knife in the sink and then put it back in that drawer.'

'What makes you think that?'

'The sink's too clean. Same as you, I noticed he wasnae much of a one for tidyin up after himsel but that sink's spotless. Cleaner than mine. And the knife had a wee bittie of what looks like blood at the base of the shaft.'

'What knife?'

'I found a knife in that cutlery drawer. It had blood on it. I think.'

'Where is it?'

'Back at the Station.'

'Right, I'll need to do that too, though there's not much chance of a print if he's cleaned it. Probably want to test to see if it is blood, though.'

'That's what I said to Sergeant Braggan.'

'And has he?'

'No.'

'Your man Braggan, he seems very certain the culprit is this chap Hamill.'

'He does, aye.'

Hammond looked up at him. 'Are you?'

Bob shook his head. 'There's no evidence. No motive.' He watched in fascination as Hammond repeated the process of dusting, photographing and taping. By the time he had finished, an hour or so later, they had another half dozen potential fingerprints.

'A good afternoon's work,' said Bob.

'I hope so.'

'I'll run you back to the Station and then get hold of a joiner.'

*

'I need you,' said Sergeant Hamilton as he walked through the doors.

*You must be desperate*, Bob thought.

'I'm desperate.'

Bob approached the front desk. 'Next week,' Hamilton said, 'it's going to be hellish. There's the King's funeral on Monday. That'll mean more processions and parades. And the Procurator-Fiscal's already on our backs, wanting progress on the murder case.'

'I won't be here next week, Sergeant.'

'That's what I want to talk to you about. Can you delay starting at the library for a week to help out?'

Fear flushed through Bob's body. He could feel his cheeks and ears burning. Confrontation always did this to him.

'I don't think that would be possible, Sergeant. The Sandeman Library, they're expecting me.'

'We can speak to them. Explain. They'll see it as their civic duty. I'll put you down for the early shift.'

'No.' Bob wasn't aware he was going to speak until he did. He felt like he wasn't in control of himself. 'I'm finishing tomorrow. I'll do Saturday if I have to, but after that I'm done.' He walked away before he could be bullied into changing his mind.

\*

When he got home, Gran was still in bed. 'Have you no got up?' he said.

'I've been up.'

'But you didnae get dressed?'

'What for?'

This was a new development. Gran was fiercely independent, and she refused to let age or infirmity compromise her standards. She still cleaned – or tried to clean – the house every day, dusting shelves, moving furniture, cleaning floors. Not getting dressed all day would normally have been a matter of disgrace.

'Are you feelin okay? D'you want me to call Dr Wishart?'

'David Kelty, will you get oot of my bloody sight.'

Bob had long known the day would come when Gran started to confuse him with his father and now it had happened. She glowered at him from the bed.

'I've got to tak that mince back to Peter Black's in Scott Street. It's crawlin wi maggots. Get me ma coat.'

'Later, Gran. I've got to go out now. Just you settle doon and hae a wee rest. I'll be back later.'

'Oh aye, on you go. Dinnae fash yoursel aboot me.'

Bob frowned as he closed the door. He didn't feel safe leaving her but he'd promised Annie he'd take her out. What to do for the best? Bob felt life constricting him again, the pressure, the fear knotting in his chest and leaving him breathless.

*

Annie was waiting for him outside The Playhouse. He waved and she smiled broadly. She looked bonnie in the new swagger coat her mother bought her for Christmas. Bob forced himself to be cheerful.

'Did you get a good view of the ceremony?' she asked.

'Aye, no bad. Halfway up King Edward Street.'

'I couldnae see a thing. Could hardly hear, either. It kept coming in waves, like the Provost was drunk.'

Bob laughed. 'That would have made a scandal, right enough.' They queued for entry and Bob paid sixpence for their tickets and they took their seats in the stalls. Bob looked around. The cinema was almost full.

'I didnae ken Will Fyffe was so popular,' he said.

'There's a rumour he's goin to do a performance after the film.' Bob looked confused. 'He's stayin in town, apparently. Victoria Hotel.' The lights dimmed and they settled back as the Pathé news reel started up, with reports of the war in Abyssinia, men in suits posturing at the League of Nations, talking tough, doing nothing. There was film of Oswald

Mosley and his Blackshirts marching in London. Bob flinched at the way the crowd, ordinary men and women, cheered and waved. The same sort of crowd he'd been among today, decent folk, honest, plain. The same sort of crowd who'd cheered Adolf Hitler in 1933, who cheered now as he dismantled a free society and replaced it with something hard and cruel, possibly evil. The speed and the ease with which the world could change worried Bob. The inability of politicians to prevent it worried him. The future worried him.

The film began, *Rolling Home*, a comedy drama in which Will Fyffe's ship's engineer was sacked for something he didn't do and ended up working on a yacht, where he became embroiled in a mutiny. Annie laughed throughout and Bob was glad she was enjoying herself but his own thoughts were on Gran and on Richard Hamill and Sergeant Braggan and Sergeant Hamilton and the Sandeman Library. Monday morning couldn't come soon enough.

As the credits rolled, Andrew Mailer, the Playhouse manager, strode onto the stage and raised his hands to shield his eyes from the glare of the projector.

'Did you enjoy that?' he shouted. The audience cheered. 'Do you want more?' They cheered louder. 'Do you want Will Fyffe?' They cheered louder still. 'I can't hear you.' And they cheered again. Bob, desperate to get back to see how Gran was, certainly didn't want Will Fyffe, but Annie, next to him, was cheering as loudly as anyone and he sat back in his seat as Mailer was joined on stage by Will Fyffe himself, natty in a light brown pinstripe suit. The audience cheered again and Will Fyffe called for calm.

'Aye, well,' he said, 'I always say that a man who takes a good drink, well, he's a man ...' He gave an exaggerated hiccup. 'He's a man, because when you're teetotal, you've always got a rotten feeling that everybody's your boss. Aye, you do.' He strode the stage, riding the laughter, and struck up a dramatic pose and began to sing:

'I'm not a politician, I don't believe in politics
But Russia says in years to come we'll all be Bolsheviks
They tell us Bonnie Scotland a republic's going to be
Except in Aberdeen and Glasgow, Greenock and Dundee.
Och, if Scotland turns republic, I'll tell you what I'll do
I'll wear a sporran round my neck
It'll look like whiskers on a Bolshevik
I'll be known as Will McFyffeski
When mysel I introduce
If Scotland turns republic, I'll buy a public hoose.'

He pulled himself from his pose and bent forward as though taking the audience into his confidence. 'Ha ha,' he said, 'can you imagine me settlin doon in a public hoose? Aye, I can just picture mysel behind the bar with a lovely set of lace curtains, throwin buns at the barmaids instead of kisses, eh? And the five years' plan too, have you heard about that Bolshy idea? Work five years for your money? I can see a Scotsman doin that for a start, especially in Aberdeen. But wait till I get my public hoose. I'll close what time I likeski. And when I've had one over the eightski will I cause any trouble and strifeski with the wifeski? Not on your lifeski, Mr Fyffeski. I'll be too busy with the whisky and the beerski. You know, I don't know much about this Bolshevism, but I hear they thought about doin away with the kings and queens. Doin away with the kings and queens? What are they goin to do with the aces and the jacks? But you know where I got my idea? I was listenin to one of those teetotal spouters the other nicht, in the park, and he was shoutin "Down with the drink". That gave me the idea of buying a public hoose. And mind it'll come in handy for the bolshies because I hear they're very fond of fighting and a man that's fond of fighting is always fond of drinking. So, you see, whatever happens, I'll be alright.'

61

And he sang another verse and chorus, then launched into *I Belong to Glasgow*, with the entire cinema singing along, Perthites made honorary Glaswegians for the duration. He performed for a good half-hour to continuous laughter and applause, and Bob thought it a peculiar show. The routine wasn't especially funny, yet, at the same time, Bob was impressed by the way Will Fyffe commanded the audience's attention. There was something indefinable, a star quality, presence. People wanted to like him, and they did. This was how Herr Hitler could be so persuasive, how Oswald Mosley could win over the crowds. They knew what to do.

'That was rare,' said Annie as they walked home afterwards. 'I've never seen anyone famous before, not in real life.' Bob reflected. Nor had he. What quiet lives they led. Quiet hope and quiet determination. He thought about Will Fyffe's song, about Scotland becoming a republic, getting rid of kings and queens. The King, "to whom we do acknowledge all Faith and constant Obedience."

Obedience?

Bloody parasite.

# Friday 24th January

## A Day of Apprehensions

'Mrs Maybury's here now, Gran.'

'I dinnae need lookin efter.'

'I ken. It's just a bit of company, like.' Bob studied her closely, the shallowness of her breathing, the laboured expression on her face. He went into the lobby and helped Mrs Maybury off with her coat. 'She seems awfae breathless this morning,' he said to her. They went into the kitchen and he poured her a cup of tea from the pot on the kitchen table.

'What kind of breathless?'

'I dinnae ken. She just seems to be strugglin to get her words oot.'

'I'll see to her. She'll have been frettin aboot somethin in the night.'

'Aye, she had it in her heid she'd got mince from Black's that had maggots in it.'

Mrs Maybury broke into a smile. 'She's no wrong aboot that. I mind that well. But it was twenty year ago. Before the War. I mind her chargin doon there and plonkin it on the counter and aabody in the queue walkin oot. Peter Black's petrified of her to this day.'

Bob laughed. He loved hearing stories of Gran when she was younger. She was feisty in a way he could never be. She was in control. 'He's no the only one,' he said.

'Away, she loves you mair than anythin in the world.'

'I ken.'

'Leave her with me. I'll mak some scones in a while.

That'll cheer her up.' She bustled up to Gran and adjusted her shawl, but Gran shook her away.

'Stop your fussin.'

'Shall we hae a wee game of cards, Agnes?' said Mrs Maybury.

Bob shook his head. 'She cannae mind the rules anymore,' he said in a low voice. 'We tried playin rummy the other night and it was hopeless.'

'What's he sayin? Aye bloody mumblin.'

'I'll put the wireless on, Agnes.'

'No, you willnae. It'll be some screchin woman. It aye is nooadays.'

Bob made to speak but Mrs Maybury shook her head. 'Off you go,' she said. 'We'll be fine.' Bob nodded and put on his coat and left for his final day at work.

*

'Sergeant Braggan appears not to want your assistance on the murder investigation,' said Sergeant Hamilton.

'No.'

'He made that very clear. Had a lovers' tiff, have we?'

'We didnae see eye to eye on somethin.'

'Just as well it's your last day, then.' He paused. 'Again.'

'What would you like me to do, Sergeant?'

'Beat. Central route. MacAdam's off wi lumbago.'

'Right.'

*

Traffic was backed up the extent of Tay Street, stretching into South Street. A motorist lowered the window of his Humber Twelve. 'What's happening?' he asked Bob.

'Nae idea.' He passed the queue of vehicles, the drivers' expressions growing increasingly impatient as he reached the cause of the delay. Three roads converged at the bridge and

64

the lead car on each road was stationary, but Bob couldn't determine why.

He breasted the rise towards the bridge, passed the lead car and discovered the cause of the impasse. A large swan stood in the middle of the road, wholly unconcerned by the fuss around him and giving no indication of being ready to move. It circled slowly as though trying to understand these strange objects all around.

The driver of the lead car on Tay Street, a Ford, leaned out of the window. 'Don't just stand there,' he said, 'move it.' Bob looked at the swan. The swan stared back impassively. This close, it was much bigger than Bob would have guessed. *How do you move a swan?* He stepped towards it and the swan advanced aggressively, hissing and flapping its wings. Bob retreated. He moved to his right and the swan did likewise and they circled one another like boxers prowling the ring. Bob was now on the other side of the swan, facing town. Somehow, he had to persuade this creature back down Tay Street and onto the river. He edged closer, encouraging it to retreat, trying not to frighten it. It was a beautiful bird. Its neck was crooked into an almost perfect semi-circle and its bright orange beak was rendered all the more vivid by a patch of black surrounding it. The webbing of its feet was the colour and texture of aged leather, and it stood proudly, studying him. Bob felt he was being evaluated. He approached again and once more the swan hissed and spat at him.

'Will you get on with it?' shouted the man in the Ford. Bob looked back at him helplessly. He took off his overcoat and turned to face his nemesis. The swan didn't move. Bob took a deep breath and advanced towards it, trying not to flap the overcoat and antagonise the bird. When he was a yard or so away, the swan reared its head as though about to attack and Bob flung the coat over it. He rushed forwards and grabbed the beast, pinning its wings to prevent it moving.

He pulled the coat over its head and waited for a moment to compose himself. All the while, the bird was screeching constantly, honking and hissing with fury, trying desperately to release itself. Bob heaved and lifted the swan.

'Christ,' he said. 'How heavy are you?'

He steadied himself and began to stagger towards Tay Street. The road banked sharply, and he struggled to keep control as the bird kept up its constant fight, hissing and seething at him. Bob's arms ached and he worried he was going to let go. Fear drove him on as he crossed sodden grass towards the Tay. On the pavement, a few yards from the low iron fence bordering the river, he stopped.

'Right,' he said. 'I've done you no harm, so no funny stuff, okay?' He sat the bird on the pavement and waited for a moment before standing quickly and whipping away the overcoat. The bird twisted its neck and raised itself high. Bob retreated swiftly and the swan, spotting the water, ran towards it and launched itself over the fence onto the smooth-flowing Tay, where it began to glide downriver as though nothing untoward had taken place. From above, Bob could hear the sound of applause. He looked up. The town bridge was lined with spectators, staring down, clapping. Behind him, people on Tay Street were doing likewise. Back on the river, the swan was now a hundred yards downstream, serenity in motion. Bob waved shyly at the watching crowds and put his coat back on.

*

Rain began to strafe the ground as he walked down Charlotte Street. Wind pulsed across the open expanse of the North Inch with a ferocity that, on a couple of occasions, almost brought him to a standstill. He checked his pocket watch. An hour before he could return to the sanctuary of the Station. He passed Rose Terrace. Annie would be at the Conoboys' now, probably making their evening meal. On impulse, he turned down Barossa Street. Opposite Hugh Smithson's house, the building site lay untouched. The County and Town Councils had recently agreed the site would be the location of the new St John's Roman Catholic Primary School, on grounds vacated by St Joseph's Nunnery after its recent relocation to Melville Street but works were yet to commence and it would be two years before they would be complete.

As he passed, he thought he glimpsed something moving in the upstairs window of Smithson's house, a shift of fabric perhaps, or someone sliding out of view. It lasted only an instant and he couldn't be sure whether or not it was real. He stared up at the window for ten minutes but, inside, nothing stirred.

He knocked on the door of the house next door and introduced himself to a harassed looking woman in a dark blue pinny.

'I've already telt you everythin I ken,' she said.

'Aye, I ken. But sometimes people mind things later on. When they've had a chance to think aboot it.'

'Well, I havenae.'

'You didn't see anythin that night?'

'Only what I telt thon other bobby.'

'Which was?'

'Just Jimmy Randall and Hammy Johnston.'

Bob waited, but the woman didn't elucidate. 'What were they daein?'

'Bein a pair of bloody arseholes. As usual. "There's ice on the grund", says Jimmy. "No, there isnae", says Hammy. "Look at it, it's gleamin". "That's just the moon's reflection". On and on. For aboot half an hoor, arguin about whether it was icy or no. Then Hammy, who was the one sayin it wasnae, decided to go hame and in the first ten strides he fell flat on his arse. "Jist as well it's no icy, eh?" Jimmy Randall shouted efter him and he started laughin like a lunatic for ten bloody minutes. An me needin my bed.'

'Right. I'm investigatin the murder of Hugh Smithson. Did you hear anythin that would be relevant to that?'

'No a thing. I just wish all these bloody sightseers would bugger aff. An you polis an a. Let us get back to normal.'

'Aye, it was a tragedy about Hugh Smithson, right enough.'

She slammed the door and Bob went to the next door house. A man answered his knock, smoking a Capstan Full Strength. 'I've telt you aathing.'

'Has anything come back to you?'

'No.' He slammed the door and Bob stared at its peeling paint for some moments. The house next door was empty and then there was a patch of bare land and a row of smaller cottages. Bob considered trying to speak to the residents there but, on reflection, he thought he'd have had more success interviewing the swan. He checked his pocket watch. If he walked slowly enough, he could head back to the Station now.

By the time he reached Kinnoull Street, the rain was coming down in sheets. His trousers were sodden. His back, too. Water squelched in his boots. His big toe had worked its way through a hole in his sock which Bob had darned – obviously inexpertly – last night. He sought refuge in the Sandeman Library, nodding to Mr Jephson, the lending librarian, as he passed through the lending library to the stairs up to the reference library. Mr McKerchar, the reference librarian, was seated at his desk in front of a window overlooking Union Lane.

'You know Richard Hamill?' Bob said.

'I know who he is. Can't say I've spoken to him much.'

'Was he in here last Saturday?'

'Yes. Most of the morning. I believe he's seeking employment. Asked me for information about various companies – Bell's, Dewar's, General Accident – then sat down and made notes about them all. I assume he's writing job applications. He was in every day last week.'

'Aye, he was made redundant the week before.'

'It's a difficult time, to be sure.'

'What's your impression of Mr Hamill?

'He strikes me as a conscientious young man. I wish him luck with finding a job.'

*

He walked the length of Scott Street and down South Street and onto Tay Street. The convoluted route ate up another few minutes. He took a deep breath and entered the Police Headquarters.

'Watch out,' said Sergeant Hamilton, 'it's the swan wrangler.'

'You heard about that?'

'The whole town's talking about it. The *PA*'s doing a feature on Tuesday.'

'I hope not.' Bob grinned. 'Did we have anyone in the Smithson house? About half an hour ago?'

'Not that I'm aware of. Sergeant Braggan is interviewing the Kinnell woman in the back. They've been in there a bloody long time, now I think about it. Why?'

'Oh ... Nothin.'

'I've been asked one last time by the powers that be ... Will you come in next week?'

'No, Sergeant.'

'Very well. I tried. I'll report back.' He turned away ostentatiously, and Bob felt sure he was missing something. He went to the staff area to remove his uniform. *For the last time*. He stared at himself in the cracked and cloudy mirror. He needed a haircut, but he hated doing it because each time he did the bald patch in the centre of his head seemed to grow larger. Twenty-one and balding. It wasn't right.

'Kelty!' Bob closed his eyes as he heard Sergeant Braggan striding towards him. It was the first time he'd come near him since yesterday morning. The expression on his face told Bob that whatever fear Braggan had felt then had more than dissipated. 'What the hell did you say to that Glesga keelie yesterday?'

'Nothin, Sergeant.'

'So how come he rang me this afternoon, telling me I should be getting the marks on the knife from Smithson's house tested?'

*So you should*, thought Bob. 'I don't know,' he said. 'I never said that. I just told him about the knife. He was lookin for likely places to fingerprint in the house and I said about the sink and the cutlery drawer and I mentioned the knife.'

'So now he's sticking his nose in and telling us how to do our investigation.'

'Are you goin to?'

'That's my business.' He leaned his arm high on the wall and pressed closer to Bob. 'And since you're so chummy with your Glasgow friends, you can be the one that takes that door to them tomorrow morning. Got it?'

'But I'm ... '

'Whatever you are, you're not. You were asked for personally.'

'By who?'

'By your new best buddy, Hammond.'

'Why?'

'How the hell should I know? Maybe he wants to offer you a job. Chief Fuckerupper.'

'Right.'

'They're expecting you at eleven.' He walked to the door. 'Try not to lose the car this time.'

Bob took off his uniform and hung it up. He wouldn't wear it tomorrow. Taking the door to Glasgow was more an act of friendship than work. He put on his own clothes and fixed his tie in front of the mirror. 'On we go,' he said.

'That'll be you done, then?' said Sergeant Hamilton as he

passed the counter.

'Aye.'

'Excuse me if we don't give you a grand send off. We did that last week.'

*It wasn't that grand*, Bob reflected. Hamilton and a couple of constables in the Sally for one round, which Bob paid for.

'Aye, well,' he said, 'it was grand working with you, Sergeant.'

'All this time working here, like George Washington with a teuchter accent, and with your final utterance you tell a lie.'

Bob laughed. 'It had its moments,' he said.

'It did, aye. You're no a bad lad, son. Useless bobby, but no a bad lad.'

'Tell that to the swan.'

*

The rain had stopped by the time he left the Station. The sky was heavy and full, the air sodden. There would be more rain soon. Bob lit his pipe and puffed until the fire took hold. He felt oddly numb. Last week, there had been elation, excitement, anticipation. But today, as he strolled towards home on Jeanfield Road, there was only an emptiness.

'Hello.'

He looked behind him. Richard Hamill was speeding to catch up with him, his hand outstretched. They shook hands.

'I suppose I shouldn't talk to you, really,' Hamill said, 'since I'm still under investigation.'

'No, you're fine. I've just left the polis ...'

'Again?'

'Aye, it seems to be a weekly occurrence. But this time for real.'

'Well done. Can I buy you a drink? Celebrate?'

Bob said no. Gran would be wanting her tea and he wanted to make sure that her breathlessness was gone. Hamill looked disappointed, and Bob had the sense that he

71

wanted to talk. Braggan had interviewed him three times now and there was no doubt he had it in for the man. Bob felt an ache of pity for Richard Hamill. He was trapped in something he might not be able to get out of. 'Ach, maybe just the one, then,' he said.

They entered the Corner Bar on the corner of High Street and Paul Street and Hamill ordered at the bar while Bob took a seat at the back.

'Thanks,' he said as Hamill placed a pint of mild on the table in front of him.

'Your Sergeant Braggan's a nasty piece of work.'

'You have to dig deep to find any redeemin features, aye.'

'I'm sure he's a very good policeman.'

'If that's so, why's he spent so much time investigatin you?'

'Ah, you believe in my innocence?'

'You didnae do it, did you?'

'No.'

'So why's he so interested in you? What's his line?'

'He has it in mind that I have a key to the house.'

'Do you?'

'Nobody does. I've told you, Smithson was obsessive about security. There was only one key made for the door. But someone "saw me in the house" apparently.'

'Aye, I ken aboot that.'

'And the second reason he thinks I'm a murderer is that my mother was Jeannie Lindsay. A tinker.' He raised an eyebrow sardonically and supped from his beer. 'That makes me a tink, too. And therefore, undesirable. "Find a tink", he told me, "and you don't need to look much further for trouble". So there you are. It's the tinks that are the cause of all our current strife.'

'I'm sorry.'

Hamill shook his head. 'It's nothing. Gypsies in Germany, they're having it much worse than me. They're in danger.

Compared to that, Sergeant Braggan's stupidity is nothing to worry about.'

Bob nodded and sipped his drink. 'Aye, Mr Eden was talkin about Germany in the League of Nations yesterday. I was listenin to it on the wireless last night afore I went to bed.'

'Hot air. The League of Nations'll do nothing.'

'You think not?'

'Of course not. The Nazis have been steadily introducing laws against Catholics, Jews, Gypsies, Socialists, anyone they don't like, ever since they got into power. Who stopped them? Now, they're doing the same thing in Danzig.'

'That's not even in Germany.'

'Exactly. What they're doing is against the Danzig constitution. Against the Court of International Justice. But so what? Mr Eden will stand up and say, "this is an unconscionable situation" and then he'll sit on his hands again.'

'From what he was sayin last night, I thought he was takin a firmer line than that.'

'*He* may be. But the League won't. They won't go against Herr Hitler. Or Senor Mussolini. The Italians bombed a Red Cross unit in Abyssinia last week. What's the League of Nations done about that? The Abyssinians requested an enquiry into Italy's conduct of the war. They asked for financial assistance. A country illegally invaded by another country. And what have the League of Nations done? Not a damned thing. The irony is that the Italians were even ready to open peace talks, but no, the League refused. They're toothless tigers. I tell you, the world will be at war within five years.'

'You really think so?'

'There's no other outcome. Fascism. It's a cancer. It infects every society it touches. And it's coming here. When it does, people like me, I've got no chance. I'm worthless.

Degenerate. Dangerous.'

'Degenerate?'

Hamill stopped talking and looked away. He appeared flustered. Bob paused for a moment before speaking. 'When Braggan interviewed you the other day,' he said, 'and he asked if there was anyone with you on Sunday ...'

'Yes?'

'I got the feeling ... I got the feeling you werenae tellin the truth.'

'Why?'

'Oh, you just started actin a bit shifty. Like you're doin right now, in fact. Like you're lyin, and the thing is, you're no very good at lyin.'

'It should be you leading the investigation.'

'It probably should, aye. But you're avoidin the question.'

'Do you know about me? What I am?'

'No.'

'But?'

'I may have a notion.'

'And would that bother you?'

'No.'

Hamill finished his drink and placed the mug on the table. 'I have a friend,' he said. 'His name is Hamish.'

'And Hamish was with you on Sunday?'

'Yes.'

'All day?'

'All day. All night.'

'And you won't tell them that?'

'What we do is illegal. I could go to jail.'

'At the moment, your biggest concern is bein hanged.'

'I have faith.'

'Aye? In Braggan?'

'No. In justice.'

Bob swigged the last of his drink and placed his mug beside Hamill's. 'I hope you're right,' he said. 'But I also hope you'll tell them your alibi. If you need to.'

'If I need to.'

They rose and left their glasses on the bar and went out into the coldness of a January evening. They walked solemnly, each thinking about their conversation, about the future, their role in it.

'Richard Hamill?'

They turned to see to Sergeant Braggan and Constable Macrae approaching.

'Officers,' said Hamill, smiling.

Braggan stepped in front of him. 'Richard Hamill, I am arresting you for the murder of Hugh Smithson. You are not required to say anything unless you wish to do so ...'

Hamill listened as his rights were read. He turned to Bob and shrugged.

'If you need to,' Bob said.

'If I need to.'

# Saturday 25<sup>th</sup> January

## *A Day of Success*

It was midday by the time Bob arrived at the Identification Bureau on Pitt Street in the centre of Glasgow, having become completely lost almost the moment he arrived in the city, despite having made the same journey only months before.

'Thought you weren't coming,' said Bertie Hammond.

'So did I. I think I crossed the Clyde half a dozen times.'

'You shouldn't have crossed it at all.'

'I ken that ...'

Hugh Smithson's back door was wrapped in old cotton sheeting and laid sideways in the rear of the Wolseley. The two men manhandled it upstairs to a large, open office where Bertie pulled the sheeting off and inspected the door.

'This is Ronnie Irons,' he said to Bob. 'Ronnie's going to do the analysis for us. Now, we need your fingerprints, so we can eliminate yours from what we find on the door. Ronnie can do the honours.' Bob allowed the man to grip each finger in turn and press it onto a tray of ink and then rotate it on a piece of paper marked out with squares for each finger. Bob studied the result. It was strange. *That's me*, he thought. *For as long as that exists, I exist. In decades to come, people can look at that and know that once it held my essence.*

'We'll have time for a spot of lunch before we go,' said Bertie.

'Go where?'

Bertie winked. 'You didn't think I dragged you all the

way down here on a Saturday just to deliver a door?' He reached into the breast pocket of his jacket and pulled out two tickets. Main Stand, Parkhead Stadium. Celtic versus St Johnstone, Scottish Cup, Second Round. Bob stared at them in amazement and reached out for them.

'Steady. Not with fingerprint ink all over your hands.' He led Bob to a sink in the corner and Bob washed his hands. 'I'm friendly with some of the directors at Celtic,' Bertie said, 'and when I heard you'd never been to an away match I thought ...'

'That's very kind of you.'

'Just a word of warning, though. You'll be among Celtic supporters, so if the unimaginable should happen and St Johnstone score, sit on your hands and look glum like the rest of us.'

Bob laughed. 'I'll do my best, but I'm no promisin anythin.'

*

Parkhead was an impressive stadium, long and rounded, with the Main Stand dominating the north edge of the playing area and a sweep of banked terraces bounding the other three sides. Bob felt a surge of excitement as he mounted the wooden steps of the stand and emerged from gloom into the brightness of a crisp January day. The pitch lay before him, an expanse of lush green still tinged white with a lingering frost. The terraces were packed, including an area set aside for St Johnstone supporters, six hundred of them waving their rattles, blue and white scarves visible above their overcoats. The area directly opposite the stand, covered in a corrugated iron roof, was the infamous Hayshed, and the noise from there was deafening. Bertie Hammond pointed Bob to his seat and sat beside him, smoothing his herringbone overcoat beneath him and removing his fedora.

St Johnstone won the toss and kicked off and after

the first five minutes, it appeared the consensus view that Saints were there to make up the numbers had some basis in truth. Celtic were camped deep in St Johnstone territory, internationalist winger Jimmy Delaney pinging crosses into the middle for Jimmy McCrory. Bill Taylor and Willie Clark, the full backs, and Percy Dickie and Harry Ferguson, the wing backs, struggled to contend with the speed of Celtic's attackers. Only James Littlejohn, the inaptly named giant at the heart of St Johnstone's defence, held strong, seeming to intercept every cross and clear it to safety.

'A matter of time,' said Bertie. Bob could only agree but, as the minutes passed, the Saints defence gradually found their feet and grew in confidence and, for all Celtic's possession, there had been little to concern Bob Wylie in the Saints goal. On fifteen minutes, though, a cross from Buchan managed to evade Littlejohn and Jimmy McCrory pounced, firing in a speculative shot. Wylie flung himself to his left and pushed the ball behind for a corner.

The corner was swept away by Taylor and St Johnstone broke downfield, their first foray into the Celtic half. Jimmy Tennant sprinted down the wing and flicked an inch-perfect pass to Hugh Adam, who headed into the path of Jimmy Beattie. With a single touch, Beattie brought the ball under control and drove low and hard to Kennaway's left in the Celtic goal. Stretching full-length, Kennaway managed to parry the ball to safety.

Stung, Celtic intensified their efforts, targeting Delaney on the left, and the next fifteen minutes saw a constant Celtic barrage. The crowd, anticipating goals, grew restless. Jimmy McCrory was as inventive as ever but, wherever he went, James Littlejohn seemed to be a fraction ahead of him. A deafening roar rose up from all corners of the ground as Clark appeared to handle a Delaney cross in the penalty area but Mr Hasburgh, the referee, waved play on.

Bob watched breathlessly. He had expected Saints to be

thrashed but now, as their defence soaked up each wave of Celtic attacks, he could dream of a draw and a replay on the wide-open spaces of Muirton Park, where Saints' usual expansive style could flourish. An incisive cross-pass from Willie Nicholson to Jimmy Tennant suddenly opened up the Celtic defence and all around Bob the Celtic-supporting crowd rose in alarm. Tennant crossed into the box and the ball was poorly defended, bouncing out to Tennant again. He crossed again and Jimmy Beattie suddenly found himself in space. He steadied himself and advanced on Kellaway and scooped the ball over his diving body into the left-hand corner of the net.

St Johnstone had taken the lead.

Bob let out a yelp of delight that, luckily for him, went unnoticed among the howls of anguish from all around. Cheers from the St Johnstone supporters in their enclave down in the terracing were drowned out by the disapproval of twenty-six thousand angry Glaswegians.

The five minutes left until half-time stretched to ten as the referee inexplicably allowed play to continue. Throughout, Celtic threw men forwards while James Littlejohn and his fellow defenders repulsed everything calmly, stoically, professionally, until finally Mr Hasburgh blew for half time.

'I can breathe again,' said Bob.

'St Johnstone's a decent team,' conceded Bertie. 'Brilliant defending, good counter-attacking.' They discussed the match for a few minutes before Bob changed the subject.

'I hear you got a British Empire Medal in the New Year's Honours,' he said to Bertie.

'Aye, for the work on the Ruxton case.'

'Did you meet the King?'

'No, I was meant to. But he had another engagement apparently, so it was handed over by the Duke of Cambridge.'

'That must have been disappointing.'

'I'm not bothered about that kind of thing, to be honest. I

just want to make policing better. More professional. That's all that motivates me.'

'Aye, I can see we need it.'

'In some places. With some people. I hear your man Braggan's made his arrest?'

'Aye.'

'And how do you feel about that?'

'As you said, we need to make policin better.'

Bertie nodded sadly. 'Diplomatically put. I'd love to get my hands on that case. It's just bizarre. No motive. Motiveless brutality is rare, and when it happens, it's generally pure chance. This was pre-meditated. Someone's worked out how to get into an impregnable house. Why?'

'I dinnae ken. So what would you do? If it was your case?'

'Well, I'm not that kind of detective. I'm happy with my fingerprints and analysis, but if it was me, I'd start again. Study whatever photographs you did take. Dig into the victim's past. There must be a reason for his murder. If he's had no contact with the outside world in recent years, the reason probably lies in the past. Did he have enemies? With grudges?'

'But why now, after all this time?'

Bertie shrugged. 'Find someone with a connection, then you'll find the answer to that.'

Cheers from around the ground alerted them to the return of the two teams. 'Forty-five minutes from glory,' said Bertie.

'If my heart holds out.'

Celtic kicked off the second half and immediately picked up where they had left off. Again and again, James Littlejohn headed the ball clear, Ferguson and Dickie nipped at the heels of the wingers and Taylor and Clark swept in to clear any residual danger. A second enormous shout for a penalty erupted as Taylor appeared to take Crum's feet away but Mr

Hasburgh was unmoved.

'That bastard'll be lucky to get out of here alive if we lose this,' said a gnarled veteran of Parkhead seated in front of Bob and Bertie.

Moments later, Crum found himself in space but blasted over the bar. Jimmy McGrory, of all people, missed a sitter. A Morrison free kick on the edge of the penalty area flew inches wide. Always, there seemed to be two St Johnstone defenders marking every attacker.

But then, from nowhere, Buchan found himself with a clear view of the goal from ten yards out. Clark and Taylor advanced towards him, but he danced through them and struck the ball past Wylie's despairing dive into the net for the equaliser. The crowd rose in relief and Bertie tugged Bob's sleeve. Reluctantly, Bob stood and applauded the shattering of his hopes. Surely now, he thought, the game would be up. One breach of the Saints defence would be followed by another, and another.

So it seemed, with another five minutes of Celtic onslaught, the crowd yelling them on, but then, on seventy-six minutes, St Johnstone unexpectedly broke down the right. The diminutive Adam floated across into the box and Jimmy Beattie, predatory as ever, strode towards it. Kennaway came to meet him and with a jink to the right, Beattie rounded him and slammed the ball into an empty net.

'Yes ... ' shouted Bob before he was silenced by a punch to the kidneys from Bertie. The Celtic fans around him seethed at this travesty on the pitch. Bertie and Bob looked at one another and laughed. Bob rubbed his side. He put his head in his hands to conceal the delight that was overtaking his face. Bertie shouted a desultory curse in the direction of the referee.

Fourteen minutes that seemed like fourteen hours followed. McCrory, in one of his poorest games all season, fired over the bar. A speculative punt from Morrison ricocheted off Taylor and narrowly skidded past the far post. McCrory, again, rattled the crossbar. The St Johnstone line held firm. Once, James Littlejohn ventured beyond the half-way line and was roundly reprimanded by his colleagues. *Wring hands. Hold breath. Count to sixty. Count to sixty again. Count to sixty again. Escort the minutes into history.* And then the last action of the game, Delaney crossing, Clark clearing high and wide into the middle of the Hayshed.

And the final whistle.

And St Johnstone had defeated Celtic in the second round of the Scottish Cup by two goals to one.

\*

It was ten o'clock before Bob got home. As he walked up Jeanfield Road his thoughts turned to Gran and he worried once more about her. Tonight, though, all was well. Annie had been round and given Gran some supper and helped her to bed. A note on the kitchen table said she had been good as gold. Gran was asleep when he looked in on her, serene, almost smiling as she lay upright in the bed, propped up on three pillows. The laboured breathing from yesterday appeared to be normal again.

He went downstairs and took out his guitar. He would have preferred to play fiddle but that was too loud for this time of night. He turned off the gas lighting and in the residual light of the waning fire, he looked out of the window at the clear night sky, Orion centremost, ready to fire his bow. He started to play *When the Saints Go Marching In*, picking the melody on the D, G, B and E strings and driving a rhythm with the low E and A. He played it over and over and the tune began to morph into something new, a blues, a rag, a celebration, until the tune was no longer about saints, or St Johnstone, or Bob Kelty, or triumph in adversity. It was about life, the lived experience, the way every moment unfolds and presents a new opportunity, the way the universal melds with the personal and creates in every human being the unique matter of their existence, for good or ill. Bob Kelty, twenty-one-years old, thirteen stone, son of David Kelty and Jessie McIvor, half of the essence of each of them, fashioned into something else, something new, some other. Bob Kelty, who loved Annie Maybury and wanted to marry her; Bob Kelty, who wanted bairns of his own, grandbairns, a future that would gradually, inevitably, beautifully become a history. Bob Kelty who, when his final breath came, surrounded by family, circling this life one final, perfect time, would say, 'Aye, but that was grand.'

# Monday 27th January

## A Day of Departures

Bob wore a black tie in honour of the King, whose funeral would take place at one-thirty that afternoon. He looked up at the double doors of the Sandeman Public Library, a full fifteen feet high. They were a symbol of permanence, gravity, learning. For Bob, they were a symbol of a new start, new opportunity. For the first time in his life, he was doing something of his own choosing. He was following his own path. Pride and nervousness jangled inside him. He knocked on the door hard enough to hurt his knuckles. Still, he doubted he could be heard in the cavernous library beyond, but a few moments later, the left-hand door opened and Mr Jephson appeared, buttoned up in a dark suit, hair slicked back, glasses low on his nose.

'Bob Kelty,' Bob said. 'I start today.'

'Ah yes, Robert Kelty, we've been expecting you. Mr Tait wishes to see you in his office, if you'll come this way.'

Bob followed Mr Jephson up the short flight of steps into the main building and then up a grand twisting staircase to the reference library and offices. The man seemed not so much to walk as to flow up the steps, as though his legs were not moving. 'This way,' he said as he led Bob across a wide landing into office accommodation at the rear. He knocked delicately on a door bearing a sign saying *City Librarian* and waited until instructed to enter. He opened the door, ushered Bob inside and closed it behind him again. Bob stood in a large, book-lined office. Before him, in front of a window overlooking Kinnoull Street, was an enormous wooden desk. It gleamed. It contained a single blotting pad and an inkwell. A man was seated behind it, studying that morning's *Courier*. He looked up as though surprised anyone else should be in the room.

'Kelty?'

'Yes, sir.'

'Approach.' Bob positioned himself in front of the desk, his arms behind his back. Mr Tait studied him for long enough to make Bob prickle with discomfort.

'You're due to begin working in the public library service today?'

'Yes, sir.'

Mr Tait reached behind him and took a cigarette from a silver case on the cabinet beside the window. He lit it and placed an ashtray next to the blotting pad, fixing the position until it was perfectly aligned.

'Am I to understand that Chief Constable Chadwick requested you stay with the City Police for a further week?'

'I was asked, sir. I doubt the request would have come from the Chief Constable himself, of course ... '

'But you were asked?'

'Yes, sir. But I advised Sergeant Hamilton that I was already contractually obliged to you ... '

'And why did the City Police make such a request?'

'I think, sir, because they are still investigating a murder enquiry, and there is His Majesty's funeral today ... '

'In which case, they made their request to you because they were short of manpower at a very difficult time?'

Bob faltered. 'As I say sir, I explained my contractual ... '

'I don't give a fig for your reasoning, Kelty. I consider this a serious matter. Quite reprehensible.'

'Sir?' Bob couldn't fathom what was going wrong.

'In my opinion this is a dereliction of your civic duty. If you had come to me last week and explained the predicament,

I would of course have approved whatever extension the City Constabulary required. That would have been *my* civic duty.'

He stared at Bob and inhaled from his cigarette, exhaling after a few moments as he nodded and tapped ash into the ashtray.

'I have decided. You're not the calibre of man we need in the public library service. You are selfish, feckless, lacking honour, lacking sense. Your contract with us is terminated.' He stubbed the cigarette out although it was only half smoked.

'Mr Jephson?' he shouted. The door opened and Bob's escort appeared once more. 'Show this man out.'

*

Bob bounced down the stairs of the library and, from the pavement, looked back at the doors, irrevocably closed. He walked towards the High Street unthinkingly but, before he reached the corner, he turned and retraced his steps and walked the length of Kinnoull Street to Barossa Street. He passed Hugh Smithson's house and looked up at the bedroom window but saw nothing untoward this time. Again, the room beyond was mired in darkness. On Barossa Place he stood outside Eliza Kinnell's house and knocked on the door.

'Hello,' he said when she opened the door. 'You may remember me, the other day ...'

'The polite bobby, aye. What are you, plain clothes the day?'

'Somethin like that. I wanted to ask, when you saw a figure in the upstairs windae, are you sure it was Richard Hamill?'

'Aye.'

'Only, it's quite a dark room. I thought I saw someone in there mysel, but I couldnae have put a face to the man.'

'Well, I could.'

'And now I think about it more, I'm no even sure if it

wasnae a trick of the light.'

'Well, I'm sure.' She leaned against the edge of the door and smiled. She appeared to be studying Bob's features.

'Right. And what time was it, again?'

'Ten, half past. I tak the bairn to my mother's so's I can get some work done.'

'Baith times?'

'Aye.'

'Right. Sorry to bother you.'

'Nae bother, darlin. Come back any time. Off duty, like.'

'Aye,' said Bob, flustered. 'I'll be away, then.'

He took a shortcut over the North Inch towards Tay Street and entered the City Police building. Sergeant Hamilton greeted him with surprise.

'Have you forgotten you're supposed to be starting your new job the day?'

'I got the sack.'

'On your first day?'

'I didnae even get that far. I never got started.'

Sergeant Hamilton picked up a pen and twirled it slowly. 'Aye,' he said, 'I feared that might happen. I tried to warn you.'

'A call from the Chief Constable?'

'I imagine so. I'm sorry, son, you didn't deserve that.'

'No. Is Sergeant Braggan here?'

'No, he's gone back to the County, thank God. Solved his case, now he's taken his ego back where it belongs.'

'Sergeant Petrie, then?'

'No. If it's about the murder, you're too late. Hamill's in court in ...' He took out his pocket watch and held it at arm's length. 'Half an hour.'

'The witness. Eliza Kinnell. She telt me she saw Hamill at eleven, half eleven.'

'Aye?'

'I've just spoken to her again and this time she says it was ten, half ten.'

Hamilton gave a genial smile. 'And what were you speaking to Eliza Kinnell for?'

'I was just curious. About something she said.'

'Are you sure it was something she said that had you curious?'

'What do you mean?'

'I don't know much about that lassie, but from what I hear it's a turnstile she needs in her house, not a front door.'

Bob faltered. *"Come back any time. Off duty, like."* He blushed instantly. Sergeant Hamilton spotted it and laughed.

'And that's why you're not a loss to the police force, son. I'll tell Sergeant Petrie about it when he comes back but I don't suppose it'll change anything. Doesn't matter what time Hamill was in the house. Just that he was.'

'But ...'

But Bob knew there was no point pursuing the conversation. He said goodbye and went outside. It was snowing again. Would this winter ever let up? He walked towards the Magistrate's Court, opposite the County Police headquarters, and stared up at the Ionian columns and double doors that were even higher than the Sandeman Library's. He walked inside.

'Morning Bob,' said Eck Thornton, the wizened old caretaker. Despite wearing a suit, he still managed to look scruffy. Bob had got to know and like him from the numerous times he had appeared in court to provide evidence. 'No working the day?'

'No. I've come for the hearing.'

'Richard Hamill? Were you involved in that, too?'

'Aye, kind of.'

'Jings, laddie, you get yourself into all the good cases, don't you?'

Bob smiled. 'Just a knack.'

'I'm surprised aboot this one, though. I ken Richard

Hamill. Kent his faither too, and his mother. Braw family.'

'Aye, I ken. There's mair to this than meets the eye. That's why I wanted to see the hearing? Is it okay?' He nodded towards the courtroom.

'Private hearing, no public allowed, but since you're on the case on you go.'

Bob smiled and tapped the older man's shoulder, then walked into the courtroom. Sergeant Petrie, seated at the far end, glowered when he saw him, but, before he could approach, a door opened at the rear of the court and two gowned men bustled in, clutching bundles of paper. Bob sat as far away from Petrie as possible, ignoring him, and watched the men go about their business, advocates for the prosecution and the defence. The door opened again, and Honourable Sheriff Substitute Duncan Macnab entered.

'Court will rise,' shouted an usher and the courtroom stood as the Sheriff Substitute glided towards his seat. It looked like a throne, crimson red upholstery and mahogany frame.

'Be seated,' he said as he took his place at the bench. 'Have the prisoner brought in.'

The doors behind the dock opened and Richard Hamill emerged from stairs running beneath the court. He wore the same suit he had on Friday, his tie hitched to one side, as though it had been put on without the convenience of a mirror. His sandy coloured hair was not as immaculately combed as normal. His eyes were dull. He was handcuffed and Bob was dismayed to see Hamill's usually confident demeanour had been replaced by something like fear. *Don't buckle now, Richard. You're goin to need your strength yet.*

'Richard Spion Hamill, you are charged that on or around Sunday the nineteenth of January, 1936, you entered the house of Hugh Smithson and there you did murder him by stabbing him repeatedly with a knife. How do you plead?'

Hamill gripped the wooden rail surrounding the dock.

'Not guilty,' he said, his voice clear but thin.

Mr Campbell, the defence solicitor, rose. 'My client intends to mount a strong defence against this preposterous charge. He is a man of sound character and good standing and I request that bail be granted.'

'Not granted,' said Sheriff Substitute Macnab. 'The accused will be remanded in Perth Prison until trial in the High Court at a date to be determined.'

Richard Hamill lifted his head and stared directly at Bob Kelty.

*

When Bob emerged from the courtroom, South Street was blocked by dignitaries once again, all dressed in mourning, readying themselves for the procession to St John's Kirk. Victor Conoboy hailed him, and Bob thought to pretend he hadn't spotted him and walk on, but Victor waved again and they made eye contact and a precious opportunity for solitude was lost.

'Morning, sir,' he said.

'You look a bit down, Robert. I thought you'd be over the moon, with St Johnstone's victory on Saturday.'

'Aye, that was grand, sir.'

Victor sensed immediately all was not well. He had known Bob for nine years or so and knew how fragile his confidence was. He could always detect, sometimes before even Bob himself, when a difficult passage was approaching. He peered into his eyes. 'What is it?' he said.

'My job, sir, at the library. I lost it. I think the Chief Constable ...' He stopped and looked around him, aware that Chief Constable Chadwick of the City Police would be among those gathering for the parade. He saw him in the distance, talking to the Procurator-Fiscal. Both men were watching him. 'I think the Chief Constable put in a bad word with the library, sir. He was annoyed I wouldn't extend my service with the force ...'

'After you'd resigned your commission?'

'Yes.'

'And what will you do?'

'I don't know.'

He sounded and looked desolate, and Victor knew from experience it would not be wise to leave him on his own. 'Listen, come with me. To the church ... '

'I couldn't, sir. I'm not dressed ... '

'Hang it, you're wearing a black tie. Join me. Then we'll go home and have afternoon tea and we can talk this through. Bella will know what to do.' Bob started to disagree but Victor waved his hand. Leaving Bob to his own devices at this moment was not a viable option. 'No argument,' he said. He, too, looked round for Chief Constable Chadwick and spotted him on the pavement outside the court buildings. The two men stared at one another in silence.

At one o'clock, the hour when the King's body was due to be transferred from Windsor Railway Station to St George's Chapel in Windsor Castle, the procession was called to order and they solemnly made their way up South Street onto St John's Street and then St John's Place. There were hundreds of people queuing for entry outside St John's Kirk. For all the size of the crowd, though, there was almost silence. The procession made its way inside. Already, there were around two thousand mourners in the kirk, and they watched the procession enter and take their places at the front. Bob and Victor took a seat in the third row. Stewards encouraged people to bunch up and identified vacant spots which those outside could fill. All side passages and vantages were filled and still there were hundreds outside as Reverend Cumming began proceedings by leading the mourners in singing Psalm 103. Dr Lee of St John's knelt to offer the first prayer, praising the manifold gifts with which the late King was endowed. They sang *O God Our*

*Help in Ages Past* and ministers from the sundry churches of Perth took it in turn to read a lesson. Reverend Shillinglaw prayed for heavenly blessing and comfort for the new King. 'Grant succour, in all his perplexities Thy guidance, that he may rule for the comfort of his people and the glory of Thy holy name.' The service drew to a close with *How Bright These Glorious Spirits Shine*, after which pipers from the Black Watch Depot marched down the main transept and played a lament. Bob closed his eyes to tears he struggled to prevent. He cared not a fig for the King but the solemnity of the occasion, the obvious upset of so many of the mourners, the stateliness of the pipers' lament, opened his heart to the pains of the world. Richard Hamill came into his head at that moment, his penetrating stare, his pleading eyes. *Help me. Help me.*

*But how can I?*

When the pipes were stilled, the organ started up and played Handel's *Death March in Saul*. As the notes echoed into eternity the congregation rose and sang the *National Anthem*. At one-thirty precisely, the maroon was fired and, as happened in every town and city and village across the land, the city of Perth observed two minutes' silence.

Afterwards, Victor Conoboy lit a cigarette on the cobbled street outside the kirk. 'Come on, let's go home,' he said.

'Aren't you still on duty, sir?'

'I'm retiring in a couple of weeks. What does it matter? Just wait there a moment.' He crossed St John's Place and tugged Chief Constable Chadwick's arm and the two men exchanged words briefly but vigorously. Victor returned and nodded to Bob.

'What did you say, sir?'

'My piece.' He walked in silence and Bob followed. Bella Conoboy greeted them like prodigals returning when they arrived at Rose Terrace, calling for Annie to make tea and bring cakes. At Victor's prompting, Bob repeated the story of his experience at the Sandeman Library. Bella's mouth was pursed.

'I knew David Tait when he was a boy,' she said. 'He was a sneaky little brat then and he's a sneaky guttersnipe now. Doing the Chief Constable's dirty work. And having the gall to accuse you of a lack of morals. He's the one who's not to be trusted.'

'Yes, ma'am.'

'You won't see it now, of course,' she said, 'but this may be a blessing in disguise.'

'I suppose so. At least I'm not in jail.'

She looked at him curiously. 'How so?'

He explained about Richard Hamill, the magistrate's hearing, Richard being bound over pending trial at High Court, the changing testimony of Eliza Kinnell. 'She's another one who's not to be trusted, ma'am,' he said. He chose not to relate Sergeant Hamilton's suspicions about her other activities. He didn't know if they were true and, even if they were, it was none of his affair. But he did know she was inconsistent, at best, in her testimony, and her motives were questionable.

'I'm convinced he's innocent,' he said.

'Very well,' said Bella, putting her teacup on the saucer in front of her. 'In that case, you must do something about it. You must contact Mr Hamill's defence. Give evidence.'

'Against the police case?'

'Against the police.'

\*

Gran was sleeping again when Bob got home, propped up in bed and breathing heavily. Normally the lightest of sleepers, she didn't stir as Bob moved about the room, tidying distractedly. He shook her hand lightly.

'Gran,' he said. 'D'you want somethin to eat?'

She began the process of coming round, a grimace on her face and then her eyes opening, then shutting again, then opening again, and her mouth opening as she pulled in a series of shallow breaths.

'D'you want anythin to eat?'

She closed her eyes. Her head was lowered, chin resting heavily against her throat. She raised up suddenly and tried to take another breath and coughed and fell into a choking fit for some moments. Bob patted her back, then gripped her hand and squeezed.

'A nice cup of tea, maybe?' he said. She gave a feeble nod, her eyes rheumy, unfocused. Bob got up but Gran held hold of his hand.

'Dinnae leave me, son.'

'I'm just goin to make some tea.'

'Dinnae leave me.' She was wheezing now, struggling for breath, and Bob realised with horror that she had deteriorated in a matter of moments.

'Gran,' he said, 'I think you're havin a heart attack.' She shook her head again, but her breathing was too laboured for speech. She retched and barked like a seal. The retch was dry and was followed by another, and another, and she hung over the bed as though ready to vomit, but nothing came.

'I need to telephone the doctor,' said Bob. 'Wait there. Dinnae worry. I'll be back in a minute.' He eased his hand from hers and stared at the grimacing old woman in the bed, fear in her eyes. He ran downstairs and with a breathless voice requested to be put through to Doctor Wishart. He relayed the symptoms and Doctor Wishart confirmed the likely diagnosis.

'I expect she's already had the heart attack. This is the aftermath. I'll be there in fifteen minutes,' he said.

'Is there anything I can do?'

'Keep her upright. Stay with her. Leave the front door open. I'll come straight up.'

As he hung up, Bob could hear Gran coughing again, the harshest, hardest sound. He took the stairs two at a time and rushed into the bedroom. Gran was almost out of the bed, retching impotently and gasping for breath. Bob pulled her back and propped her up. She stared at him, and her spindly hand reached out and took his. She gulped for air two or three times and retched again, then gulped for air and this became a pattern, each time the pain etching itself deeper into her expression.

'I love you, Gran. I love you. The doctor's on his way. He'll have you right as rain.'

Gran stroked his hand. 'No, son.' She tried again to suck air into her lungs, but the fluid that had gathered there made it impossible. Bob was helpless. He cradled her against his chest and rubbed her back, gripping her left hand and stroking the back of it with his thumb. He could offer nothing else. The worst of the attack appeared to be over – for now, anyway – but she was still wheezing and fighting for breath. With relief, he heard the tread of footsteps on the stairs.

'The doctor's here, Gran.'

'Now then,' said Doctor Wishart, sweeping into the room and laying his bag on the bed. 'How are we, Mrs Kelty?'

Gran didn't reply. She concentrated on trying to gain her breath as Bob stood aside and the doctor took his place beside the bed. He pulled back the sheets.

'Yes,' he said, 'the ankles are very puffy. Has she been retching?' he asked Bob.

'Aye. But nothing comes out.'

'That's the fluid on the lungs. Makes it hard for her to breathe.' He turned to Gran. 'Are you in pain, Mrs Kelty?' Gran nodded. 'I'll give you something for that.' He opened his bag and took out a syringe and filled it from a glass vial. 'Morphine,' he said to Bob.

'Will that help?'

'With the pain, yes.'

'With ...?'

The doctor bent over Gran and raised the sleeve of her nightgown and administered the morphine into her arm. She lay back on the bed and stared up at the ceiling and after a few moments she closed her eyes momentarily, then opened them and stared straight ahead, as though frightened to keep them closed. She was still short of breath and gasping for air, but she was no longer fighting against herself.

'She'll rest now,' said Doctor Wishart. They went onto the landing.

'Will she be okay?' Bob asked.

'It's doubtful she'll see the night out, I'm afraid. I can call an ambulance and have her taken to the Infirmary, but I fear there's little to be done. It's a question of palliative care.'

'Could I have done something earlier? Would it have helped?'

'No. Her heart is just giving out. It's a muscle. It's tired. She's worked hard all her life. She hasn't got the fight anymore.'

'But ...'

'Honestly. Don't blame yourself. She's had her time. She's had enough. She's ready.'

They agreed not to take her to hospital. The strain of the journey would probably cause another attack, Doctor Wishart said. She'd prefer to be at home. Bob saw him out and went upstairs. Gran was conscious but not alert. He cradled her once more and stroked her hair and rocked her gently. He began to sing, his voice hoarse and cracking:

Oh! Rowan Tree Oh! Rowan Tree!
Thou'll aye be dear to me,
Entwined thou art wi mony ties,
O hame and infancy.
Thy leaves were aye the first o spring,

96

Thy flowers the summer's pride;
There wasnae sic a bonny tree
In a the countryside
Oh! Rowan tree!

Her breathing grew more shallow, the fighting for air over. He felt her warmth, felt the beat of her heart, heard her snuffling breath. He kissed her head and cradled the last trace of his blood kin as it slowly kindled into memory. At one in the morning, he fell asleep and woke up an hour later, still cradling her. She still breathed. He fell asleep again and woke at three and she was still alive, but he knew it was a final flicker. He sang one last song.

Ae fond kiss, and then we sever!
Ae farewell, and then forever!
Deep in heart-wrung tears I'll pledge thee,
Warring sighs and groans I'll wage thee.
Who shall say that Fortune grieves him,
While the star of hope she leaves him?
Me, nae cheerful twinkle lights me,
Dark despair around benights me.

And he held her tight again and kissed her downy cheek and closed his eyes and he knew that when he opened them again Gran's would be closed for ever.

# Part Two

# May 1936

# Monday 25<sup>th</sup> May

## A Day of Prosecution

The arrest of Richard Hamill and the death of King George and the death of his gran were inextricably linked in Bob Kelty's mind. Those eight days in January had melded into a single, painful expanse of time through which history marched in cruelty, leaving Bob in its wake. He scarcely knew what was real. Had he saved eight children's lives? Did he discover, with Richard Hamill, the murdered body of Hugh Smithson? Was he sacked by the Sandeman Library before he had even begun working there? The whole period formed a brutal cacophony in his mind, a fog of confusion. Over the following months he had slowly begun to recover his equanimity, largely by refusing to excavate the memories of those days. For that reason, he was dreading the next week. At the point when he needed to be at his most lucid in order to help Richard Hamill, his mind was constantly filled with thoughts of Gran and grief.

'Come on,' he said. 'Do it.' At half past eight on a fresh and clear May morning, he left his bed and breakfast in Eyre Place and made his way from the new town across Edinburgh to the High Court of Justiciary for the start of the trial for murder of Richard Hamill.

\*

Alexander Burnett was a short man, tidy and neat, precise, a caricature of the solicitor he was. His pencil moustache was meticulously groomed, his hair – almost pure silver – short

98

and thinning. Round spectacles were perched on his nose. Alongside him was his assistant advocate, Peter McKenna. Burnett smiled as he reached for a cigarette.

'And off we go again,' he said.

Bob sat in an uncomfortably straight-backed wooden chair. The man opposite him, in whose hands Richard Hamill's life now rested, was the person who had made Bob's last appearance in the High Court of Justiciary so traumatic. Then, Burnett was defence advocate for John McGuigan, the accused in the Cuddies Strip case, and Bob, as the first police officer on the scene of the crimes, was subjected to a sustained and hostile examination in the witness box by Burnett. After two hours, Bob left the stand exhausted, convinced his testimony had been so weak he had ruined Marjory Fenwick's chance of justice. He had thought Burnett dishonest, a charlatan who believed in nothing save the acquittal of a man he knew to be guilty. He could never have imaged that, within months, he would be collaborating with him. Speaking to Burnett about the previous case over the past few days had been illuminating. Burnett's recollection of events Bob had thought he remembered only too well was radically different. His justifications of his behaviour were plausible. His manner was pleasant. Had Bob changed his opinion on him? Perhaps not, but he was prepared at least to give him some lassitude.

'How do you think the trial will go?' he asked.

'I think the prosecution case is weak. Circumstantial evidence – which is all we have here, nothing concrete, nothing certain – depends on connections. A suggests B, C supports A, D reinforces C and so on. Gradually, a case is established where everything interlinks, everything rests on the base of something else, until you reach the keystone, like the building of an arch. That's what Albert Russell did so well for the Prosecution in the McGuigan case ...'

'Not good enough for a guilty verdict.'

'There was nothing Russell could have done about that. You're in the hands of the jury. They'll look for any excuse to save them having to deliver a guilty verdict, especially with a capital crime.'

'You think he was guilty?'

'Certainly.' He caught Bob's disapproving expression. 'You must understand, we advocates are also weighing evidence as the case progresses. It's new to us, too. I had my version of the story, which came from my discussions with McGuigan, and I was satisfied at the start of the case that he *could* be innocent. But in court, we hear the story from different perspectives. Yours, for example. We hear new evidence, we hear new interpretations of old evidence. Clearly, we must assimilate all that, we must consider, reflect, re-think. At the start of the trial did I think he was innocent? Possibly. By the end? No.'

'But you stood in court and summed up and criticised Marjory, criticised me, tried to turn the jury against that poor lassie. Tried to turn them towards the wrong verdict.'

'Everyone deserves a fair trial. Otherwise, we are in the realms of mob justice. We must watch out for that in Mr Hamill's case, too.'

'How?'

'There are circumstances, not germane to the case, which would be most unfortunate if they were to be revealed in court. Concerning the nature of the man. Such things may colour a jury's judgement. We had something of the same with Mr McGuigan. As with Mr Hamill, he was a man of tinker extraction.'

'And you think the prosecution will focus on these other circumstances?'

'I do. With luck, they won't succeed. Lord Chief Justice Aitchison was assiduous in closing down such avenues in the McGuigan trial, and I expect him to do so again. But there's more than just being of tinker extraction in this case.

Be prepared, if things are going well for us and badly for the prosecution, we may see Mr Maxton make allusions – never direct accusations – about Mr Hamill's lifestyle. Watch out for words like flamboyant. Or Bohemian.'

'Pansy,' said McKenna. 'Fruit.'

Bob shook his head. 'This is why I hate all this charade.'

'On one level, I don't disagree. But's it's the best system we have. Now, to business.' He stubbed out his cigarette and leaned forward, fingers splayed on the table. 'I have to tell you, you are my number one witness. Everything hinges on you. I don't say that lightly, and I don't mean to frighten you, but it's as well you know. I'm telling you this because the prosecution, if they choose to address you at all – and they may not, if they fear the quality of your evidence – will seek to diminish your words and discredit your testimony.'

'Like you did.'

'Exactly. And I saw how that affected you. I saw your confidence draining away with every question I asked. But ...' He paused for effect. 'But you held firm. You performed much, much better than you realise. In truth, I never got anywhere with you. All the same, I got the feeling as you stepped down that you'd convinced yourself you'd had a disaster.'

'Aye.'

'You didn't. Far from it. So remember that when you're in there again. You know the truth. Tell the truth. Be brave.'

*Brave*, thought Bob. *Aye, right.*

*

Frederick Maxton was morbidly obese. He rarely shifted from the dais and leaned heavily on it with both hands at all times, as though keeping himself upright. His back was bent, and his left leg was braced to take his weight. He wheezed as he spoke.

'Mr Hamill, were you at the house in question in Barossa

Street on Saturday, January eighteenth?'

'I was.'

'What time was this, and what was your business?'

'It was early, around ten, perhaps, before I went to the library. I put a note through Mr Smithson's door.'

'Was that your only visit to the house that day?'

'Yes.'

'You returned the next day?'

'I did. At six. The note I put through the door on Saturday, that was to tell him I'd be coming round.'

'You needed an appointment to see Mr Smithson?'

'He was reclusive.'

'Very well. And did he answer when you called?'

'No.'

'Did this surprise you?'

'Yes.'

'What did you do?'

'Nothing. I went home.'

'It surprised you, yet you didn't do anything? You didn't think to notify anyone? Mr Smithson, as you state, was a reclusive gentleman who never left his home. And you had arranged to meet with him. Surely it must have seemed peculiar for him not to answer? You didn't question it?'

'Not immediately. The next day, after I'd thought about it, I began to worry. That's when I ... '

'So it took you a whole evening's reflection to conclude that something was amiss?'

'No. I concluded early that evening that something was amiss. But I couldn't do anything about it until the next day.'

'Not call the police?'

'I had no evidence that anything had happened. Just a bad feeling.'

'You had a "bad feeling"? Very well. And when you had this "bad feeling", *then* you went to the police?'

'Sort of.'

'What does that mean?'

'I met a gentleman, Mr Kelty, whom I knew to be a policeman. So I asked him for assistance.'

'Mr Kelty wasn't a policeman, though, was he?'

'No. As it happened, he had resigned his commission three days before.'

'So, despite your concerns, you still did not relay them to anyone in officialdom?'

'No.'

'Let us return to the day before your abortive attempt to meet Mr Smithson. January the eighteenth. Did you enter Mr Smithson's property that day?'

'No.'

'You're sure?'

'Yes.'

'And yet court has heard a witness who places you inside the house on the eighteenth of January and then again on the day in question, the nineteenth.'

'The witness is mistaken.'

'On the first of these occasions, January eighteenth, about eleven-thirty in the morning, you were seen through an upstairs bedroom window.' He turned to the jury. 'The bedroom in which Mr Smithson met his fate.'

'That was not me.'

'And on the second occasion, the next day, again around eleven-thirty, you were seen leaving the house and climbing on a bicycle and cycling towards town.'

'That was not me.'

'Are you saying the witness imagined these events?'

'I cannot answer for the witness.'

Lord Chief Justice Aitchison stretched out his arm. A scowl of irritation had overtaken his face, as it often did. 'There may be some other possible explanation, Mr Maxton. It may have been someone who resembled the accused. Wore similar clothing. Had a similar complexion. Alternatively, a person can see an event one day and quite mistakenly transplant the whole circumstances to another day. That is the most frequent explanation for such things.'

'I'm grateful, your Honour,' said Maxton, looking decidedly ungrateful. 'Could that be?' he said to Hamill. 'Could the witness have mistaken the date she saw you through an upstairs window?'

'The only time I've ever been upstairs in that house was the day Mr Kelty and I discovered the body.'

'And could she have mistaken the date when she spotted you in the downstairs room, then departing on a bicycle?'

'She must have done. I wasn't there.'

'You're asking us to believe a witness could have twice mistaken the date that something happened?'

'What you can believe of the witness's statement is a matter for you, sir, not me.'

'Perhaps she was not mistaken at all. Perhaps she recollects perfectly.'

'I was not there. On either occasion.'

Alexander Burnett sat back and watched Maxton. The man was perspiring heavily beneath his wig, his face red and oily. Burnett was pleased with the progress. Maxton was flailing. Eliza Kinnell's evidence earlier had not gone as well as Maxton would presumably have liked. She was his first witness and he must have expected her testimony to set the tone for his prosecution. It did, but not in the way he would have hoped. The Kinnell woman was dressed and made-up as though she was going to the dancing on a Saturday night. She spoke quickly and rather shrilly and did not present as a convincing witness. Burnett had watched the faces of the jury during her testimony. There was clear antipathy on the faces of at least two of the women jurors. Most of the others looked unimpressed. Now, Hamill was beating off her accusations with ease.

'I should like,' said Maxton, shifting from his dais for the first time and taking a couple of steps to his right as he rifled through his notes, 'to present a letter written by Mr Hamill to Mr Smithson. I have a number of such letters, covering a considerable period of time ... '

'Objection, your Honour,' said Burnett, rising from his chair. 'The defence has never seen any of these letters.'

'They were put in the court documentation yesterday,' said Maxton coolly.

'Yesterday? They must presumably have been in the possession of the police since January, and I have not been given the opportunity of seeing them. If they are material to the case, then they should have been made evidence for the prosecution to allow the defence to deal with them. They cannot be thrust upon us at the last moment like this. I have not the faintest idea what they contain.'

Lord Aitchison turned to Maxton. 'I trust there will be discretion in the use of these documents?'

'Of course, my Lord.' He waved the letter towards the jury. 'This was written by Hamill on the third of January – a little over two weeks before Mr Smithson died. "I am sorry I have to write this,"' he read, '"but I think you will agree that, for a great many years, you have availed yourself of my services without compunction. I have willingly run errands for you and attended to your affairs, at little recompense for my time. In the past, I have accepted this but with the economic situation such as it is, and with the grave likelihood of redundancy, I feel pressed, once more, to insist that I receive recompense for my time."'

'Objection,' said Burnett. 'I object to this line of enquiry and I ask that my protest will be recorded in the shorthand record.'

'I trust there is a point to this, Mr Maxton?' said Lord Aitchison.

'There is, my Lord. If I may continue.' He read from the letter again. '"Lately, I have the impression that you

105

expect me to be at your beck and call, like a servant boy or an indentured labourer. You imagine you can require of me anything that takes your fancy. You are quite mistaken in this. I do not intend to become a cheap drudge. I am not yet starving. You see, when I object to your insults you make insinuations that are quite untrue. You are never satisfied, always expecting more and more of me."' Maxton turned once more to his pile of notes. 'This, as I say, is but one such letter. I have a number of similar ... '

'Mr Maxton, I believe we have understood your point.'

'Yes, my Lord.'

Lord Aitchison scratched his cheek. 'It seems to me that, if a man is unhappy with the working relations he experiences with another man, it is not at all unnatural to express those reservations in a letter.'

'Yes, my Lord, but ... '

'And I believe what you have read out expresses just such a sentiment. The jury will be able to form a view on what you have read out. I do not believe we need to hear any more such appeals.'

'Yes, my Lord.' Maxton fumbled with his notes. 'I have no further questions for this witness.'

'Lunch.'

*

'How did it go?' Bob asked. Not being allowed to view the trial was even harder than he had anticipated. He had walked the length of the Royal Mile, down to Holyrood House and back again, and studied the Heart of Midlothian on the pavement outside St Giles' Cathedral for several minutes in an attempt to pass the time but the trial was constantly in his thoughts.

'Rather well,' said Burnett, 'until Maxton pulled a rabbit from his hat.' He explained about the letters.

'Are they damaging?'

106

'I think the judge took some of the sting out of them. Said it wasn't at all unnatural to write about such a situation if it was vexing Hamill.'

'What's next?'

'My turn to question Hamill.'

'Good luck.'

'Luck has nothing to do with it.'

*No,* thought Bob, *but does justice?*

*

After lunch, Richard Hamill was returned to the dock, accompanied by two policemen. Burnett was pleased to see him looking around the courtroom with interest. Being tried for your life would test the constitution of any human being but the morning had probably been easier than his client could have imagined. The prosecution's examination was over and Hamill could anticipate a gentler cross-examination this afternoon. The court stood to attention as Lord Chief Justice Aitchison swept in from his quarters and assumed his position at the centre of the court.

'Mr Burnett,' he said, 'your witness.'

'Thank you, my Lord.' He took off his spectacles and pointed to the jury with them. 'Members of the jury,' he said, 'you heard a lot of hot air and bluster from Mr Maxton in the morning session. You heard the prosecution attempt to build a case for Mr Hamill being a brutal – possibly insane – murderer. For make no mistake, the man who murdered Hugh Smithson in his bed is not someone who could be described as normal. This was a frenzied attack, utterly brutal. Long after Mr Smithson must have been dead, knife blows continued to rain on his helpless body. I ask you to remember that. This is no straightforward killing, the mundane product of a dispute or argument, as we see only too often in this courtroom. Make no mistake, this crime takes us into the realms of evil. Richard Hamill,' he pointed to Hamill in the dock, 'Richard Hamill is a quiet man who until now, has lived an unblemished life. He worked in a dry-cleaners' until he was laid off through no fault of his own. He has no criminal record. He is educated and urbane, a modest but engaging conversationalist and companion. I ask you, members of the jury, to look at him and question whether such a soft-spoken man could, simultaneously, be a fiendish murderer. I believe there is only one answer to that question.'

He turned now to Hamill in the dock. 'Mr Hamill, we heard this morning the testimony of Eliza Kinnell, who placed you at the scene of the crime on two separate occasions, on the Saturday and then on the Sunday. You have already refuted this quite forcibly and persuasively ... '

'Objection,' said Maxton, not deigning to rise.

'Sustained. Don't over-plead your case, Mr Burnett.'

'You offered a cogent rebuttal of her claim, then. Would you agree?'

'I was not in Mr Smithson's house on either of those occasions.'

'Do you know Mrs Kinnell?'

'Yes. We lived next door to her family for some years when I was a child. We're similar ages.'

'Ah, I see. Did you play together then, being similar ages?'

'No.'

'You said that rather firmly, Mr Hamill. Peremptorily, even. Such intonation cannot be picked up in the shorthand record and so I make the point now, to record it for posterity. Is there a story behind that?'

'The Armstrongs – that was Eliza Kinnell's family's name – they didn't like our family.'

'Why not?'

'My mother. She was Jeannie Lindsay. Of the Lindsays. Travelling folk.'

'What we might call a tinker family?'

'Yes.'

'You were not living a tinker lifestyle, though?'

'No, mum married a scaldy '

'A what?'

'A non-tinker. So, we lived in a house in Paul Street. I went to school. Dad worked. Mum looked after the family. Normal.'

'But the Armstrongs took against you? Because of your mother's heritage?'

'Yes.'

'Members of the jury, when Eliza Kinnell first spoke of her suspicions to witness Robert Kelty, from whom we shall hear later, she made this accusation ...' He paused and searched among his notes for a moment, then quoted from them: '"You can't trust him ... that type ... his mammy was a tink".' He turned back to Hamill.

'Is that the kind of treatment you received from the Armstrongs when you were a child?'

'It is.'

'Did you or your family do anything to justify such a negative opinion?'

'No, we lived a very quiet life.'

'Mrs Kinnell mentioned a bicycle. On the second occasion when you allegedly visited the house. Do you own a bicycle?'

'I do not. I have a hearing impairment in my right ear. It affects my balance. I couldn't ride a bicycle without falling off.' Laughter filtered through the court. Maxton and Lord Aitchison frowned at the gallery. Burnett concealed a smile.

'What we do know – what you have acknowledged – is that you left a note through Mr Smithson's door requesting a meeting with him. Why did you do that?'

'I really wished to speak with him. My financial position was becoming dangerous. I'd been laid off and wasn't having success finding other work. Meanwhile, Mr Smithson was expecting me to work on his behalf for nothing. I believed I deserved some recompense for that work.'

'You had raised this with him before?'

'Yes.'

'Is that the subject of the letters which Mr Maxton referred to this morning? I have to ask, of course, because although I am your defence attorney, I have not yet been afforded the opportunity to examine them myself.'

'It is.'

'Was that the only topic of debate in them?'

'Yes.'

'Over how long a period did you conduct this communication with Mr Smithson?'

'The past year. My employment was looking vulnerable from around Christmas of 1934 and I suspected I would be made redundant in due course.'

'But he didn't reply to them?'

'No.'

'And wouldn't entertain the prospect of paying you for your efforts?'

'No.'

He took off his spectacles again and walked away from the dais. 'Mr Hamill, I am genuinely puzzled why, when it was obvious Mr Smithson had no intention of doing the decent thing and paying you for your enterprise, you continued to offer your support to him. If I were to put myself in such a position, I do not believe I would be so generous with my time. Why did you not just walk away?'

'Mr Smithson had no friends. He was not a bad man, just strange. I knew only too well that being different can make life difficult. If I didn't help him, no one would. He didn't deserve that.'

'Even if he had answered your query that fateful day, and had again declined to offer financial recompense, would you have continued to help him?'

'I would.'

Burnett returned to his dais and stared at his notes. 'Although we cannot be certain of the exact date or time of the murder, it is considered by the experts most likely to have happened on Sunday the nineteenth of January. Where were you that day?'

'At home.'

'All day?'

'Yes.'

Burnett bit his lip. Right up to this point he wasn't sure whether or not to ask the next question. He finally made up his mind. 'Were you alone?'

'No.'

'Who were you with?'

'A friend. Hamish Nesbitt.'

'And this Hamish Nesbitt. He can vouch for this?'

'He can.'

'So, on the day the crime probably occurred, you can demonstrate you were otherwise engaged?'

'Yes.'

'No further questions.'

Mr Maxton rose and limped across the court to replace Burnett at the dais. 'Mr Burnett has made great play,' he said, 'of describing you as a "quiet man" and "modest" and "urbane". That may be the case. By all accounts, though, you are quite a flamboyant character as well. Is that the case?'

'I wouldn't say so.'

'You're not married?'

'No.'

'Never engaged?'

'No.'

'Ever courted a young lady?'

'No.'

'Tell me, Mr Hamill. This ...' He looked in his notes,

'Hamish Nesbitt. He is a friend of yours?'

'Yes.'

'And he was with you on the nineteenth of January?'

'Yes.'

'You are sure of that?'

'Yes.'

'Of course, we don't know the precise time the heinous crime was committed. How long was Mr Nesbitt in your company?'

'All day.'

'All day? From what time, would you say?'

'Very early in the morning.'

'Very early? Eight o'clock?'

'Earlier.'

'Seven o'clock?'

'Earlier.'

'That certainly is early. And at what time did he leave?'

Hamill stared at him, then at Burnett, then at the floor. 'Seven o'clock the next morning.'

An audible gasp arose from the jury and from the gallery. Burnett studied the faces of the jurors with concern. There was no question, they had understood the inference of Maxton's questioning. The damage had been done. He stared at Peter McKenna and shook his head.

'No further questions,' said Maxton.

# Tuesday 26<sup>th</sup> May

## *A Day of Attack*

The Defence team's chambers were tense. Burnett and McKenna smoked cigarettes, Bob his pipe. The bonhomie that had typified their engagement the day before was replaced by silence.

'It was a miscalculation,' said Burnett finally. 'I shouldn't have raised it.'

'But it's important evidence,' said Bob. 'It can prove Richard's innocence. How could you not raise it?'

'Because we fell into the prosecution's trap. They can use it against us. Character assassination.'

'I didn't think Andrew Maxton would stoop to that,' said McKenna.

'Nor me,' said Burnett. 'Not this early, anyway. But he'd had a wretched day. Lost every argument. His case was slipping away from him.'

'We can only hope he doesn't continue to allude to it.'

'Doesn't matter. That cat is well and truly out of the bag and prowling round the feet of the jurors, meowing.'

'What's first today?' Bob asked, wanting to change the subject.

'Sergeant Braggan.'

'Give him hell.'

'When it's my turn, rest assured.'

\*

'You don't work for Perth City Police, do you, Sergeant

Braggan?' said Maxton. Braggan stood stiffly in the witness box. He studied the faces of the jury across the courtroom. *Too many women*, he thought.

'No, sir, I work for Perthshire County Constabulary.'

'Could you tell the court how you came to be involved in a case under the City Police's jurisdiction?'

'A murder investigation requires a huge amount of manpower, sir. The City force is quite small. They have limited numbers of officers, especially those experienced in CID work.'

'And you are experienced in CID work?'

'Yes, sir, I'm the highest-ranking officer in the Perthshire CID.'

'And you were a key officer in the successful investigation last year of the murder on the Cuddies Strip in Perth?'

'I was.'

'So I imagine the City Police were very glad of your experience and skill?'

'I imagine.'

'What were your initial thoughts when you saw the crime scene?'

'It was a brutal attack. I understand there were numerous knife wounds, too many to count at the scene. It was strangely calm, though. There was no sign in the room of a struggle.'

'Why do you think that was?'

'I believe the victim was asleep in bed when the first, fatal wound was struck. He probably died almost instantly, but the killer, in his frenzy, kept stabbing the dead body.'

'As you say, a brutal assault. Has the murder weapon ever been found?'

'We are not sure. There was a knife in the cutlery drawer in the kitchen which may have been used but we can't be certain. A fingerprint expert from Glasgow City Police examined the knife but there were no prints clear enough for an identification. The accused's premises were also searched for a weapon, but nothing was found. He may have disposed of it elsewhere.'

Burnett rose. 'My Lord, I would like to remind the court that the accused is still that – accused. We can make no presumptions about anything at this stage, disposal or otherwise.'

Lord Aitchison frowned at him. 'You appear to be doing my work for me, Mr Burnett.'

'Apologies, my Lord.'

'However, Mr Burnett is correct. Sergeant Braggan, please restrict your testimony to matters of fact.'

'Such a frenzied attack, Sergeant Braggan,' said Maxton, 'the crime scene must have been somewhat horrific?'

'On the contrary. The body had been covered by blankets and I understand at first glance, there was little indication that anything had happened. The room looked quite normal.' He looked at the jury. 'You couldn't half smell it, right enough.'

'I'm sure.'

Burnett stifled a chuckle. The jury's faces exhibited sundry expressions of disgust or distaste or amusement, according to their disposition. Talking about the smell of putrefaction was not something one did lightly – juries are as squeamish about such matters as any group of the general population. Sergeant Braggan was a coarse fellow, indeed, and it was unlikely the jury would warm to him.

'The only thing that stuck out,' said Braggan, 'was the note.'

'The note?'

'The one that the accused claimed to have put through the door. It was lying on the bedside table.'

'So Mr Smithson received the card?'

'It would seem so.'

'Yet the rendezvous with Hamill was never made.'

'Apparently not.'

'What did the note say?'

Braggan pulled his notebook from his breast pocket and opened it at a page with the corner folded down. '"It will be in your interests to see me at six o'clock, if you will kindly leave the door open",' he read.

'What did you make of that?'

'It sounded rather threatening, sir.'

'Objection,' said Burnett. 'It does not sound in the least threatening. "*Kindly* leave the door open".'

'Perhaps not threatening,' said Maxton. 'But might you say abrupt, Sergeant?'

'Yes, sir. Abrupt.'

'Was there anything unusual about the note?'

'It had a bloody fingerprint on it.'

'You're sure it was blood?'

'Yes, sir.'

'And did you manage to test the fingerprint?'

'No, sir.'

Burnett scribbled furiously in his notes. The knife and the note would make for fine points of attack when the time came. He listened patiently as Braggan proceeded with his evidence. A witness identifying Hamill as being in the house on two occasions. The discovery of a cache of angry letters from Hamill to Smithson. Hamill's repeated requests for money. Burnett already had the broad thrust of his defence prepared, of course, but fine tuning as the case progressed, in response to witness testimony, was an aspect of the job he enjoyed. Braggan's testimony was turning out to be particularly fruitful for him.

'You have no doubt as to the accused's guilt?' Maxton asked in conclusion.

'No doubt.'

'Your witness, Mr Burnett.'

Burnett strode towards the dais and settled his notes in place and turned to the jury, taking them in slowly, waiting, creating a pause, a moment of drama. He loved this part, the start of what he knew would be a crucial cross-examination.

'Sergeant Braggan, may I also offer my congratulations to you on the successful conduct of the Cuddies Strip murder – and rape – enquiry.'

'Thank you, sir.'

'I'm sure you will also wish to acknowledge the pivotal role in that investigation of PC Kelty, who is, of course, a witness also in this case.'

Braggan gave the merest nod of his head and made no reply. After all, no question had been asked.

'I mention PC Kelty because, of course, it was he who discovered the body. Although you've given us a description of the crime scene, you didn't actually see the body in situ, did you?'

'No, sir.'

'So when you said "I understand at first glance there was little indication that anything had happened", it was PC Kelty who advised you of this.'

'And Sergeant Petrie.'

'Indeed.' He turned to Lord Aitchison. 'My Lord,' he said, 'the note referred to by Sergeant Braggan is included in the evidence. I am unsure why Mr Maxton did not present it to the jury, but I would like to do so now.' There was a pause while the usher collected the item from a wooden case at the rear of the courtroom and passed it, first, to Lord Aitchison and then to the foreman of the jury. It was handed from juror to juror, while Burnett waited at the dais.

'You are quite certain this is blood, Sergeant Braggan?'

'Yes, sir.'

'How did you form that opinion?'

'By studying it.'

Lord Aitchison spoke sharply. 'Are you a doctor or an analyst?'

'No, your Honour, I'm a policeman.'

Laughter rang out once more in the courtroom. Lord

Aitchison ignored it. 'Are you aware the presence or absence of blood can be decided by science with some precision these days?' he asked.

'Yes.'

'Has this postcard been subjected to scientific testing?'

'No.'

'Why not?'

'Because I thought it would tend to destroy the character of the impression, and I thought it better to retain it in the form in which it was found.'

'It rests upon your word that this is a bloodstained postcard?'

'Yes.'

'It might be anything. It might be boot polish or the like.'

'Not likely boot polish.'

'But something else?'

'Yes, possibly.'

'My Lord,' said Maxton, rising and turning towards the judge. 'The reason why no blood test has been made was that I had been informed it would obliterate the mark on the postcard.'

Burnett interjected immediately. 'I do not accept for one moment that they could not make a test for blood on a postcard without obliterating the mark. The progress of science in this arena has been remarkable. This is a significant issue, my Lord. The presence of blood would tend to suggest that the murder happened after the note was posted through the door. It is our contention that this is not a safe presumption.'

Lord Aitchison nodded slowly, his expression sombre. 'I am not at all satisfied with the prosecution's management of this.'

'My Lord, if I may approach the bench?' said Maxton.

'Granted, Mr Maxton. Mr Burnett, please.'

The opposing advocates stepped towards the bench beneath the judge. Mr Maxton coughed. 'My Lord, I would like to request that testing is undertaken on the note to ascertain whether or not the marking on it is blood.'

'I have no objection, my Lord,' said Burnett.

'Very well,' said Lord Aitchison. 'If it is at all possible to keep that impression intact it must be kept intact.'

'Very good, my Lord.'

'I think we shall adjourn for lunch. This has not been an edifying morning.' Lord Aitchison rose and, as the usher called for the court to rise, he hurried away to his private offices. Burnett turned to Maxton. He smiled. Maxton did not smile back.

*

The lunchtime mood in the defence chambers was more genial than the morning, courtesy of their successful filibuster in relation to the bloodstained postcard. Where, that morning, they had concentrated on rehearsing details of the case, Burnett and McKenna were now content to allow conversation to stray into other matters.

'Did you see the election results in Belgium yesterday?' Burnett asked as he poured teas for all three men from a Wedgewood teapot. McKenna nodded solemnly.

'No,' Bob replied. 'I didnae see a paper this morning.'

Burnett waved a copy of *The Scotsman*. 'The queerest result. And worrying. Very large gains for the extreme left and extreme right. The country's fractured down the middle. The voice of moderation has been silenced.'

'These are worryin times.'

'When a place like Belgium is starting to embrace the extremist menace, we're all in trouble. There's a country that saw more than its share of strife in the War. How they can imagine militaristic responses will solve anything now beggars belief.'

'There's another war coming,' said McKenna.

'There is, indeed. Probably started by Mussolini. The

119

nerve of the man. Listen to this.' Burnett read from *The Scotsman*: '"If Britain acknowledges Italian sovereignty over Abyssinia, then he will "solemnly undertake" not to trespass on British empire interests in Egypt."' He threw the paper down. '"Solemnly undertake"? That lying, murdering, treacherous rogue. As if we could believe any of his solemn undertakings.'

'As if he has any right to Abyssinia,' said Bob.

'Just so,' said Burnett. 'I think Haile Sellassie is the one who has sovereignty over that wonderful country. Spent a couple of years there in my youth. I'd go back in a flash. And what's more, he has the gall to suggest Italy might return to the League of Nations.'

'Exactly,' said McKenna. 'It's like the Devil himself asking to join the Kirk of Scotland to promote observance of the holy scripture that he's spent two thousand years trying to destroy. The League is doomed.'

'Much like Freddy Maxton,' said Burnett, sipping from his tea. McKenna gave an expansive nod of his head. Talk turned to horses, the upcoming Derby.

Bob studied their complacent expressions. *Don't relax too soon*, he thought. *We're no there yet.*

*

Sergeant Braggan took the stand again at the start of the afternoon session to continue his cross-examination by Mr Burnett. He did not look happy to be there.

'My Lord,' Burnett said, 'I am advised by my honourable friend, Mr Maxton, that the note at issue this morning has now been passed to the University of Edinburgh and they promise a response by lunchtime on Thursday.'

'And the process will not destroy the item?' asked Lord Aitchison.

Maxton rose. 'We are given to understand not, your Honour.'

120

'How unfortunate this was not effected prior to trial.'

'Quite,' said Burnett. He turned to the witness stand. 'Sergeant Braggan,' he said, 'you interviewed Mr Hamill on January the twenty-first, the day you were drafted in to assist with the investigation?'

'To lead the investigation, yes.'

'I rather fancy Inspector Mathieson believes he led the investigation, Sergeant.'

'He led overall. I was in charge of the detection side of things.'

'Thank you for that clarification. Now, could you answer the question?'

'I interviewed Hamill on the twenty-first, yes.'

'You developed your suspicions about Mr Hamill very quickly, then?'

'Straight away.'

'Straight away? Really? How terribly prescient of you. On what evidence?'

'The sightings. Mrs Kinnell ... '

'Ah yes, Mrs Kinnell. Was she quite consistent in her statements?'

'I believe so, yes.'

'About matters of timing, perhaps?'

Sergeant Braggan blinked and looked downwards, suspecting a trap but not knowing what it was. 'I believe so, yes.'

'So, we have putative sightings of Mr Hamill. What else led you "straight away" to suspect him?'

'I thought it fishy the way he dragooned Kelty into it. Kelty's a nice lad, but he's naive. Easily swayed. Sees the good in people, doesn't see the bad.'

'That is witness Robert Kelty, who was a former policeman, and whose tireless endeavours led to the apprehension of the culprit in the Cuddies Strip case. Is that correct?'

121

'He was … Yes.'

'So you fancied this might be some form of subterfuge? Use Mr Kelty. Appear concerned. Throw the police off his scent?'

'It wouldn't be the first time.'

'But unfortunately for him, dogged Sergeant Braggan was on the case … '

'Mr Burnett,' said Lord Aitchison, 'is this line of questioning leading anywhere or are you merely taking the opportunity to make facetious comments?'

'I believe it is, my Lord. Sergeant, was there any specific material evidence pointing to Mr Hamill?'

'Not specific, no.'

'Any general evidence, then?'

'There was the nature of his lifestyle. That kind of behaviour – well, it tells you something, doesn't it?'

'If you could restrict your comments to evidence relating to the crime in question, please Sergeant.'

'Objection,' said Maxton. 'The sort of bohemian lifestyle the defendant has confessed to is indeed germane. It speaks of a moral failing.'

Lord Aitchison raised his hand. 'I'm sure the jury have noted well the matter of Mr Hamill's lifestyle and will consider that carefully in their deliberations. I do not believe there is anything further to be explored in that regard. Continue, Mr Burnett.'

'Thank you, My Lord. Let me repeat my question, Sergeant: was there any general evidence pointing to Mr Hamill as the culprit?'

'The blood on the note.'

'Yes, which is still in dispute, of course.' He paused. 'The note may be marked with blood.' He paused again. 'Or boot polish. Time will tell. Because no test was undertaken at the time. Was there any other general evidence?'

'No.'

'You mentioned that a knife was found in the premises?'

'Yes.'

'But an expert test for fingerprints found nothing?'

'Correct.'

'Was there not a train of thought that there may have been blood on the blade? Near the handle?'

Braggan shifted uneasily. 'It appeared to have some contamination ... '

'Which could have been blood?'

'It didn't look like blood to me.'

'And, as we know from your reasoning regarding the postcard, you have a sound grasp of the scientific principles behind blood analysis.'

'Mr Burnett,' said Lord Aitchison, 'your flippant comments are becoming wearisome.'

'My Lord, apologies. Sergeant Braggan, this knife could conceivably point to some general, perhaps even specific evidence. It is therefore of some import. Was the knife ever tested to ascertain whether there was blood on it?'

'No.'

'Why not?'

'It felt to me like a red herring.'

'But one simple scientific test could have resolved the issue. And you chose not to undertake it?'

'No.'

Burnett studied his notes as though seeking his next question but, in truth, was creating a break in proceedings for the jury to form an opinion on Sergeant Braggan and this missed opportunity. He looked up again.

'There was money found in the premises, I believe?'

'Around £100.'

'And where was it found?'

'In Mr Smithson's wardrobe.'

'So, not what you might call concealed? Easily discovered?'

'I suppose so.'

'Well, literally so. Did witness Robert Kelty not discover it within minutes of the discovery of the body?'

'I believe that's so.'

'Did you wonder why Mr Hamill, a man who, by his own admission, was in sore need of additional funds – that being, of course, the genesis of this whole unedifying story – would not have made even a cursory search of the house for money?'

'He might have done so.'

'I beg your pardon?'

'Who's to say he didn't find a bigger stash of money and make off with that?'

Burnett stared at him for some moments, allowing the jury to imagine what he might say in reply. 'You searched Mr Hamill's property, of course?'

'Yes.'

'And did you discover a "bigger stash of money" there?'

'No.'

'No.' He looked at the jury, then at Braggan. 'So, your case for arresting Richard Hamill rests on a complete lack of evidence, plus a notion that maybe he found a "bigger stash of money" and made off with it?'

'There was more than that to back up my opinion.'

'But we are yet to ascertain exactly what that is, Sergeant Braggan. One final opportunity: we have the stained note, the possibly bloody knife, a witness placing him at the scene – is there anything else by way of evidence which pointed you in the direction of the defendant?'

'No.'

'Very well. How did Mr Hamill appear during his interview?'

'Cocky. Cheeky. Like he was trying to get a rise out of me.'

'I don't suppose you appreciated that?'

'Mr Burnett,' interjected Lord Aitchison once more, 'the Sergeant is not the one on trial here. Leave his sentiments out of it.'

Burnett nodded solemnly. He studied Braggan, pompous in blue on the stand. Enough. 'No further questions, my Lord.'

Maxton indicated he, too, had no further questions. He remained seated, pensive. Burnett and McKenna nodded at one another slightly.

'Court adjourned,' said Lord Aitchison. 'Ten o'clock tomorrow morning.'

\*

Alexander Burnett bit into a buttered crumpet and mopped a slick of escaping butter from his plate.

'That went well,' he said. They filled Bob in on the cross-examination, Braggan's difficult afternoon.

'He didn't come across at all well,' said McKenna. 'Completely unable to offer any cogent explanation for why he believed Hamill was the killer.'

'Indeed,' said Burnett. 'I think we've undone much of the harm of yesterday's turn of events.' His copy of *The Scotsman* was opened at the racing page. '*Pay Up* will pay up, mark my words,' he said.

'Nonsense,' said McKenna. '*Mahmoud's* the one. 100/8. A snip. It's time for a grey. Twenty-four years since a grey won the Derby.'

'That's because greys don't make good racehorses. Too temperamental.'

'Utter rot. You don't suppose the Aga Khan would have a horse that wasn't up to the mark?'

'I grant you the Aga Khan has a fine eye for a horse, but if you want one of his, you need to go for *Taj Akbar*. Gordon Richards, greatest jockey alive.'

'Never won the Derby, though. That's the mark of a real

jockey. Charlie Smirke's on *Mahmoud*. He won two years ago. *Windsor Lad*. I made £20 that day. Looking for £25 tomorrow.'

'It's good to have ambitions.' Burnett turned to Bob. 'What about you? Who's your tip for the Derby?'

'I don't follow the horses.'

Burnett harrumphed. He tossed *The Scotsman* towards him. 'Have a look through the runners and riders. See what you fancy. I'll get one of the court lads to run out and put a line on for you.'

'I don't bet.'

'Oh, come on, don't get all hair-shirted on us.'

'I get paid a shilling an hour. I cannae afford to fritter away good money on nonsense like the horses.'

'Here.' Burnett took a pound note from his wallet and handed it to Bob. 'Have a bet on me. Then, if your horse doesn't come in, there's nothing lost.'

'Thank you, but no.'

'It's just a bit of fun.'

A body on the floor, the image that Bob saw every day of his life, the moment his childhood ended, his father dead on the kitchen flags, shotgun beside him where it fell after he used it to expunge the horror of a drawer full of betting slips. That image came to Bob now. So did the memory of bookies pursuing his gran to repay his father's debts for months after, restitution demanded from beyond the grave, across generations, without pity. Threats and recriminations. Anger, fear, loss.

'It's only fun if you've got money you don't need and won't miss,' he said. 'Otherwise, it's the gate to hell.' He took his jacket from behind his chair and swung it on. 'D'you think I'll be called tomorrow?'

'Hard to say, but you better stay in the witness room to be on the safe side. It's such a strange prosecution case, I honestly can't predict where they're going with it.'

'Aye, well, I'll see you in the morning, then.'

'Sleep well.'

Sleep well? Bob had no idea when he last had. There was too much life happening for that.

*

Through the telephone box on Princes Street, Bob watched the bustle of people on the pavement and the constant convoy of trams and buses on the road. Even at seven o'clock, everything here was so fast, frenetic. Bob could never live in such a place.

'How is it going?' Annie's voice was strangely formal, as though she were enunciating every syllable with precision. Her telephone voice.

'Burnett says well. He says he gave Braggan a right goin over. I wish I'd seen that. It's the most frustratin thing, no bein allowed into court to listen. I dinnae ken why I bothered to come, really.'

'Come hame, then.'

'I will, tomorrow. For the fitba.' Scone Thistle, for whom Bob played in midfield, had reached the final of the *Perthshire Advertiser* Cup. Bob was already growing nervous about the match, but it was a welcome distraction from being nervous about giving evidence.

'I'll maybe come along.'

'That would be grand.' Bob wasn't sure if it would, in truth. Annie had never come to see him play and he'd never encouraged her to do so.

'Will you give evidence tomorrow?'

'Aye, I think so.'

'I hope it goes well.'

Bob could hear the concern in her voice. 'I'll be fine. I've done it before.'

Strangely, he almost believed himself.

# Wednesday 27th May

## A Day of Achievement

On the third morning, the public gallery was full for the first time. Thus far, the case had not captured the public imagination in the way the John McGuigan trial had the previous December but although the newspapers were circumspect in their reporting of Richard Hamill's lifestyle, this nonetheless generated increased interest. The morning session, though, was dull. The gallery started to shift and whisper. Even the participants seemed detached. A procession of witnesses – Joe Carcary, Maisie Daniels from Miller's Dairy, former colleagues from Pullar's, a couple of neighbours, all testified about nothing of consequence. The longer Maxton went on the more perplexed Burnett grew. He kept waiting for some dramatic new evidence.

'The Crown would like to call Mr Robert Kelty.'

*At last*, thought Burnett. He sat up and smiled at McKenna. He hadn't been sure whether the prosecution would even call Bob. Maxton's fear must surely be that Bob would speak of an investigation compromised by a surfeit of certainty and a lack of leadership. Maxton was fiddling with his papers and did not evince an air of confidence. These were the defining moments in any trial, the test of whether one's evidence and one's eloquence were equal to the challenge. Bob Kelty could make or break the case, of that Burnett was certain, but which Bob would he get in the box – the capable citizen or the nervous nellie? Bob was equally adept at either role.

Bob was led to the stand and took the Bible and swore an

oath to a God in whom he did not believe in a voice that was, to Burnett, comfortingly strong. The colouring of his cheeks was raised but otherwise he appeared in control. More than he had during the Cuddies Strip inquisition anyway, Burnett reflected.

'Mr Kelty,' Maxton said, 'you were first to find the body, is that correct?' Bob said it was. Again, his voice was firm. 'Can you explain the circumstances which led to this discovery?'

Bob related the meeting with Richard Hamill, Hamill's concern, the locked door and the entrance through the Conoboys' garden.

'Whose idea was it to go through the garden?'

'Mine.'

'Mr Hamill didn't suggest it?'

'No. He couldn't have known the Conoboys lived behind the house, or that I knew the Conoboys.'

'Couldn't he?'

'Well, I see no reason why he should. We didn't know each other well.'

'And yet he sought you out to accompany him on this errand?'

'Yes.'

'Did you not find that strange?'

'He thought I was still a police officer.'

'And did you explain you weren't?'

'Yes.'

'But still he asked you to go with him?'

'Yes.'

'And you agreed?'

'Yes.'

'Very well. We may come back to that.'

Bob's skin prickled. Like Braggan before him, he recognised the setting of a trap but couldn't imagine what the trap might be. He looked across at Mr Burnett, but the advocate was stretched across his chair, seemingly unconcerned.

'You were involved in Sergeant Braggan's initial interview with Mr Hamill, I understand?'

'I was.'

'How did Mr Hamill seem in that interview?'

'He seemed very composed, sir.'

'Composed?'

'Yes.'

'Sergeant Braggan, in his testimony to the court, suggested he thought Mr Hamill was "cocky". Like he was trying to get a rise out of the sergeant. Was that your perception?'

Bob reflected for a moment. He had worried at the time that Hamill was antagonising Braggan. Was that being cocky? 'I think that may be Mr Hamill's nature, sir. He likes to make jokes. Sergeant Braggan didn't appreciate that.'

'I'm not sure I'd appreciate a man I was interviewing about a particularly heinous murder joking with me, either. In poor taste, wouldn't you say?'

'I fancy it might be Mr Hamill's way of managing his nerves, sir.'

'And did you think Mr Hamill, jesting or otherwise, offered valid answers to Sergeant Braggan's questions?'

'Yes.'

'There was nothing that concerned you about his statement?'

'There didn't seem anythin that could tie him to the crime.'

'But he could provide no alibi?'

'Not at that time.'

'Not at that time?'

'When he was questioned, he said he had no alibi for the Sunday.'

'That's not what we've heard in this court.'

'I wouldn't know.'

130

'When he was questioned, you say, he offered no alibi. That changed subsequently?'

'He later told me about the friend he had visiting that day.'

'That would be,' Maxton rummaged through his notes, although Bob felt sure he knew the name anyway, 'Hamish Nesbitt?'

'Yes.'

'And did Mr Hamill tell you Hamish Nesbitt stayed the night?'

'Yes.'

'What did you make of that?'

Bob glanced briefly at Richard Hamill in the dock. Hamill remained expressionless, his hands clasped in his lap. 'It's not my place to judge.'

'You are aware of the law on such matters?'

'I am.'

'And you have no opinion on the matter?'

'Do I need an opinion? I'm here to give evidence, not opinions.'

*Bravo*, thought Burnett. He sat up, making brisk motions, hoping Bob would notice them so they could make eye contact and he could let him know how well that had played. Bob stared straight ahead.

'Very well. You didn't think it strange that he initially denied having an alibi, only to later make one up?'

'I simply told him that if he had an alibi, he ought to use it.'

'And why do you think he didn't?'

'That's not for me to say, sir.'

Maxton turned to the jury. 'Mr Hamill told this court he had an alibi in this Hamish Nesbitt and yet, under caution, he made no such admission. Either he has lied to this court or he lied under oath in an official police interview. Given his bohemian lifestyle, you may understand his reasons for

131

doing so, but the undeniable fact remains: Mr Hamill has told a lie. If he has told one lie, how many more may he have told?' He turned back to Bob.

'When you made access to the house, where was the front door key?'

'In the lock.'

'You are sure of that?'

'When Sergeant Petrie and Constable Macrae attended the scene, I used it to let them in.'

'But was it in the lock when you first entered the house?'

Bob remembered Braggan asking Richard Hamill if he had put the key in the door when Bob wasn't looking. *Most unlikely*, Hamill had said. But was it?

'I can't be completely certain on that point ... '

'You can't be certain?'

'No.'

'So, it is feasible that Mr Hamill put the key in the lock without you noticing?'

'It is feasible.'

'Which would mean, of course, that he had access to the house all the time. Let's move on. The note that Mr Hamill put through the letter box, where did you find it?'

'On the table beside Mr Smithson's bed.'

'Did you think that strange?'

'Not particularly.'

'You don't seem to find anything strange, Mr Kelty.'

'Objection, your Honour.'

'Sustained. Mr Maxton, refrain from personal observations. Mr Kelty is in the witness box, not the dock.'

'Of course, my Lord.' He turned to Bob again. 'What did you infer from it?'

'I don't understand your question.'

'Do you think Mr Smithson put it there?'

'I couldn't say. It could have been him. Or ... it could have been the murderer. I have no way of knowing.'

'There was blood on the note, was there not?'

'Objection.' Burnett rose from his seat. 'We are still awaiting scientific analysis which will determine that.'

'Mr Maxton, rephrase your question,' said Lord Aitchison.

'There was a mark on the card which may be blood. And Mr Hamill could not account for how that mark got there?'

'No. He said there was no mark on it when he posted it.'

'Indeed. How did Mr Hamill seem when he saw the body?'

'Well, I was in a state of shock myself, sir, so I wasn't necessarily payin much attention to Mr Hamill, but I would say he was shocked too. He said, "Dear God" or something like that.'

'He looked at the body?'

'Yes.'

'Did he offer any comment on it? What might have happened?'

'No.'

'And afterwards, when you went downstairs to speak to Sergeant Petrie, how did Mr Hamill seem?'

'Concerned.'

'About what?'

Bob faltered. 'About Mr Smithson, I presume.'

'You presume? But you don't know? Perhaps he was concerned about himself? His alibi?'

'I couldn't say.'

'His alibi which, to an extent, was being provided by you?'

'Objection, your Honour.'

Lord Aitchison hitched his gown up over his shoulder. 'Let the line of questioning continue for a few moments longer,' he said. 'You may answer the question, Mr Kelty.'

'If you're askin whether Richard Hamill used me to give the impression he was a concerned and innocent man, then that is possible. I don't know. My impression was that, when

133

he asked me to accompany him, he was genuinely concerned and genuinely wanted my support. And when he saw Mr Smithson, he seemed genuinely upset.'

'A very genuine man indeed, it seems. You habitually see the best in people, Mr Kelty?'

'I try to, sir.'

'So it didn't occur to you that Mr Hamill might have been using you?'

'No.'

'But now that the matter has been raised, do you agree it is a possibility?'

Bob looked again at Hamill in the dock. He stared straight ahead, his expression a void of fear and expectation. 'It is a possibility.'

'And it's also possible that, if Mr Hamill did indeed have the front door key, then he could have effected entry to the house any time he chose?'

'I couldn't say.'

'But you can say that he chose to have you accompany him? Despite not being a police officer?'

'Yes.'

'No further questions.'

Burnett waited a moment before rising. Maxton had probably just about shaded that exchange. His plan was clearly to use Bob's innocence as a way of planting doubts in the minds of the jurors about Hamill. Was Hamill as straightforward as he seemed, or was Bob simply too nice to notice deception? Was Hamill manipulating Bob? Braggan, of course, had already called Bob naive, no doubt a pre-planned description concocted by Maxton, one of which he was now taking advantage. Naive Bob Kelty suckered into suggesting Hamill had honourable intentions just at the moment when a brutal killer was acting most dishonourably. It was a decent enough tactic, but it had a whiff of desperation about it. If you can't nail the accused, go for the witness. As a defence advocate, he'd seen this technique applied more often than he could remember.

Bob watched from the witness box as Burnett took his position at the dais. His collar was too tight. His jacket itched. He could feel himself perspiring, hoped he wouldn't start to smell. He hadn't had a bath since Sunday. The bed and breakfast where he was staying offered little in the way of amenities or comforts. Burnett nodded encouragingly.

'Mr Kelty, we have already heard you were a policeman in the Perth City force at the time of the crime, although you had tendered your resignation and were working your notice?'

'That's correct.'

'A key component of the Crown's case – indeed, I'm struggling to see any other component ... '

'Objection.'

'Sustained. I've already warned you about being facetious, Mr Burnett.'

'Apologies, my Lord. A key element of the Crown's case is the testimony of Mrs Kinnell, which placed Mr Hamill inside Mr Smithson's house on two occasions, the probable day of his murder, and the day before. It was you who took Mrs Kinnell's statement. Is that correct?'

'Yes.'

'What did you think of Mrs Kinnell's evidence?'

'I was unconvinced, sir.'

'Really? Sergeant Braggan was most convinced. It was one of the things that led him "straight away", in his words, to suspect Mr Hamill. What did you find so unconvincing?'

'Firstly, I thought it too pat. She just happened to be passin the house at the very moment Mr Hamill was there, two days in a row. That didn't seem likely.'

'No. When you put it like that, that is indeed an astute observation. You said "firstly". Is there more?'

'Two things, aye. The first time I questioned her she said

135

she'd been waitin for something like this to happen.'

'And did she reveal why?'

'She said, "because he was a tink".'

'A tink?'

'Mr Hamill's mother was from a travellin family. Commonly called tinks.'

'Commonly and pejoratively?'

'Aye.'

'So you detected an element of prejudice?'

'It was in the tone of her voice.'

'Indeed. And the other thing?'

'I questioned her again, a few days later. The first time she said she saw Mr Hamill at eleven or half past. The second time she said ten or half past.'

'And did you ask if she had misremembered?'

'Aye. She was adamant on both occasions about the time.'

'But on each occasion the time was different. Mr Kelty, accepting you are no longer a serving police officer, from your experience in the force would you have much confidence in Mrs Kinnell's evidence? Enough to immediately suspect Richard Hamill?'

'Definitely not.'

'Sergeant Braggan has been keen to tell the court he was in charge of the case. In the time you remained involved, what was your impression of the police conduct of the investigation? Was it effective?'

'Sergeant Braggan is a very confident and experienced officer. When he came in, he took over the investigation ... '

'Let me ask this differently, Mr Kelty. And please be honest, not polite. You are no longer a serving officer. Your loyalty is to the truth, and only the truth. At the time of the investigation, did you believe Mr Hamill was guilty?'

'No.'

'Do you believe him now to be guilty?'

'No.'

'Why not?'

'There is no proof. Not a shred of evidence against him. There is no motive. There was £100 in the wardrobe, untouched. We know Mr Hamill wanted to speak to Mr Smithson about money, and he had recently lost his job, but he didn't take the money that was there. He had helped out with Mr Smithson for years. Mr Smithson was a friend of Mr Hamill's father. That's loyalty. This attack, it was the work of a madman. I look at Richard Hamill and I don't see a madman. But Sergeant Braggan came into the interview with him that day with his set of twenty-six questions ... '

'Twenty-six questions?'

'Yes.'

'Already written down?'

'Yes.'

'Is that common?'

'Not very, no.'

'And he proceeded to ask all twenty-six questions?'

'Yes.'

'In order?'

'Yes.'

'As you were listening to the interview, did other questions occur to you from the responses Mr Hamill gave?'

'Yes.'

'Can you give me an example?'

Bob thought for a moment. 'The sergeant asked at one point whether Mr Hamill brought a knife or used one in the house. Mr Hamill denied even being there. Sergeant Braggan went on to his next question ...'

'And?'

'And we found a knife in the kitchen, with staining on it which might have been blood. I would have pursued that line of questioning with Mr Hamill. Did he put it there, that kind of thing.'

'But Sergeant Braggan didn't?'

'No.'

'In fact, he never deviated from his twenty-six questions?'

'No.'

'What did you infer from that?'

Bob paused. What he was about to say was the truth, but it still felt like some kind of betrayal of his former colleagues. 'He had already made up his mind that Richard Hamill was guilty.'

Burnett's lips were pursed as though he were contemplating something awful. 'On the basis of Mrs Kinnell's contradictory evidence and a note which may or may not have blood on it.'

'Objection.'

Burnett turned to Lord Aitchison and pointed at Maxton. 'My Lord, if my learned friend objects, perhaps he could remind the court what other pieces of evidence, specific or general, piqued Sergeant Braggan's interest?'

Lord Aitchison studied the advocates in turn. 'That does not seem an unfair observation, Mr Burnett. However, your defence might be better served by widening your enquiries.'

'I quite agree, my Lord. As ever, you get to the nub of the matter, so allow me to follow your sage advice. Mr Kelty, while you were part of the case, did you see any attempt to pursue different lines of enquiry? Widen them, as it were?'

'No.'

'Was anyone else interviewed in connection with the crime?'

'No.'

'Was anyone else brought under any suspicion? Even the slightest?'

'No.'

'Did any senior officers offer any dissenting views?'

'No.'

'Sergeant Petrie?'

'As soon as Sergeant Braggan was assigned to the case,

Sergeant Petrie withdrew.'

'Inspector Mathieson?'

'I never saw Inspector Mathieson.'

'You never saw him?'

'No.'

'But wasn't he leading the enquiry?'

'Yes.'

'Yet in the week you worked on the case, you never saw him?'

'Not once.'

'And did you find *that* strange?'

'I certainly did.'

'No further questions.'

Mr Maxton raised his bulk from his chair and made his way slowly to the dais. He opened his folder of notes seemingly at random and without looking up he spoke to Bob.

'Did I understand you to say you visited Mrs Kinnell on two occasions?'

'Aye ... Yes.'

'Why did you visit on the second occasion?'

'Because, as I've explained, I had some doubts about her evidence. I wanted to be sure there weren't any misunderstandings.'

'Very conscientious of you. Presumably, on the second visit, you were still a serving police officer?'

Bob took a deep breath. He smelled trouble. 'No.'

'You had already resigned your commission?'

'Yes.'

'And served your notice?'

'Yes.'

'So why did you go to see Mrs Kinnell? Do you not consider your behaviour to be unusual?'

'I ... I was sure something was amiss ... with her evidence.'

'But you were no longer a police officer?'

'No.'

'And did you appraise Mrs Kinnell of that fact before you started questioning her?'

'No.'

'So, she will have thought she was speaking to a police officer?'

'I didn't say I was.'

'But you didn't say you weren't?'

'No.'

'Do you not consider it might have been wiser to speak to your former colleagues about any suspicions you may have had and let them deal with the matter? Officially?'

'I was just curious. I didn't have anything in particular ... '

'So you took matters into your own hands?'

'I suppose so.'

'Were you already working for Richard Hamill at this point?'

'I'm not working for Richard Hamill now. I never have.'

'But you are working with his defence attorneys.'

'I am not. They requested my version of events and I gave it to them. I would have done the same for you if you'd bothered to ask.'

'I must say, I am curious,' said Lord Aitchison, scratching his florid cheek, 'why you didn't call this witness earlier, Mr Maxton. He was the person who found the body, after all. And he appears to have a more complete awareness of the intricacies of the case than any previous witness, Sergeant Braggan included.'

'My Lord, this is somewhat delicate, but since you ask, Mr Kelty had already left the police force at his own request.' He looked at Bob. 'I understand he was unable to make the grade as a police officer. That made me ... '

'That is not the case, Mr Maxton. I remember this young man very well from a particularly nasty trial last year. I thought him an exemplary witness then and I think so now. I don't think it does to denigrate people, for whatever reason.'

'I have no further questions, your Honour.'

Lord Aitchison fixed Bob with a penetrating stare. He nodded almost imperceptibly. Bob felt his skin flush.

'We shall take an early adjournment. Trial will resume tomorrow.'

*

'Well,' said Burnett, 'you certainly made an impression on Craigie Aitchison. Now perhaps you'll believe me when I tell you to have faith in yourself?'

'It was heartenin to hear his words.'

Burnett threw his hands in the air in mock indignation. 'In the name of God, man, take some praise when it's offered. Stop being so damned Calvinist.'

'I never was good at that. "Dinnae start thinkin you're onythin fancy", my gran used to say to me. "And if onybody tells you you are, they're after somethin."'

Burnett smiled. 'Yes, my mother used to say much the same thing. "Know your place."'

'"And do what you're told",' said McKenna.

Bob looked at his pocket watch. If he made the five o'clock train, he could be back in time. 'Is that me done?' he said. 'Will they want me tomorrow?'

'I shouldn't think so. The Prosecution's finished with you. We may call you again when it's our turn, but that won't be tomorrow.'

'Grand. I'll be here anyway, but I won't need to get here first thing. I'm awa back to Perth the night.'

'What for?'

'Fitba.'

*

Three hundred or so people lined the pitch at Foxhall Park in Coupar Angus as seven o'clock struck, raising a cheer and waving their bunnets and rattles as Scone Thistle and St Leonard's ran on to the pitch for the final of the *Perthshire Advertiser* Cup. This was the penultimate game of a long season, one which started back in early August of the previous year, when their precocious winger Danny Kerrigan was still terrorising defences with his speed and accurate crossing. As the players stood to attention on the halfway line while the national anthem played, Bob closed his eyes and remembered his friend Danny, remembered the night he discovered his body, remembered investigating his murder, seeking justice for his girlfriend Marjory Fenwick, standing before Lord Aitchison and giving evidence, watching justice not being done. *Win this for Danny,* he thought. *For Madge.*

The referee blew his whistle and the game commenced, a battle between two fine attacking teams in great form. Scone Thistle, already holders of the Perthshire Cup and playing for the league championship on Saturday, were on the middle leg of an unprecedented treble. In the early stages of the match, the nerves attending such lofty ambitions affected their style, made them unusually crabbed and defensive.

'Come on,' shouted Bob from his position in central midfield. 'Move up, move up.' It was the first time any of his team-mates had ever heard him speak out in such a fashion during a match. Mackie Henson took a pass from him and galloped down the right wing. When his way was blocked by a defender, instead of halting and passing inwards, on impulse he spurted forward, passing the defender with ease, and then he turned towards goal and ghosted past another St Leonard's defender. On the edge of the box, he floated a cross towards centre forward Gerry Lammin, who jumped above the St Leonard's defence and headed the ball firmly into the left-hand corner of the net. Cheers arose from the Thistle fans behind the goal. Bunnets flew into the air and rained on the ground as the players shook hands and retreated to their own half to re-start the game.

'Grand,' shouted Bob.

'Aye,' said Mackie Henson.

A couple of minutes later the score was 2 – 0 as Andy Delbridge fired in a low, skimming shot from the right-hand edge of the box, beating the flailing St Leonard's goalkeeper with ease. By half-time Thistle were in control and, although there were no further goals, the result was no longer in serious doubt.

'Captain Kelty,' said Mackie Henson as they sat in the wooden hut at half-time drinking tea and smoking cigarettes. 'Givin us what's for.'

'It worked, though,' said Gerry Lammin.

'Aye, keep up the shoutin, Bob,' said Andy Delbridge. They all laughed. Gerry Lammin ruffled Bob's hair. Bob settled the strands back into place.

Within a minute of the restart, it was 3 – 0, courtesy of an own-goal by the St Leonard's right back, Shorty Pryde. On seventy minutes Andy Delbridge beat three defenders on his own and lifted the ball over the diving goalkeeper for the fourth. The Cup was won. When the final whistle blew, the team gathered at the edge of the pitch and shook hands with each other, and then with the opposition players. They waited while a trestle table was erected on the centre circle and the *Perthshire Advertiser* Cup was placed on it and local dignitaries picked their way across the grass to gather beside it.

'Roll on, Saturday,' shouted Gerry Lammin as captain Jim Christie went forward to receive the cup from Mr Bissett of the *Munro Press*.

'Treble, here we come,' said Andy Delbridge.

'Bring it on,' said Bob Kelty.

\*

'You were grand,' said Annie. They walked hand-in-hand to the bus station. Night had descended suddenly, the deep-clouded sky affording little light.

'We were, aye.'

'No, *you* were grand. The best player on the park.'

'Mackie. Or Gerry.'

'You. Maybe I'll come and watch you more often next season.'

'Aye, well, it's no always like this. In December or January, it's gey cauld. And wet.'

'Are you tryin to put me off, Bob Kelty?' She laughed to show she was only teasing.

'No, but ... I'm no sure if I'll be playin for them next season.'

'How no?'

He faltered. 'I've telt you before, how I'd like to open a wee café and teach music in the back.'

'Aye.'

'Well, I'm just thinkin ...'

'Are you goin to do it?'

'I dinnae ken. Aye. No. Well, I couldnae afford it yet, but ...' But life goes on. Bob stared into the gloom of the evening but in his mind he saw an August afternoon, another football match, another life, and Danny Kerrigan with the ball, Danny Kerrigan with his future ahead of him, Danny Kerrigan, unaware that that future was evaporating, Danny Kerrigan, all too soon to encounter the catastrophe of death.

'Life needs to be lived,' he said, 'because you never ken when it's goin to run oot.'

# Thursday 28ᵗʰ May

## A Day of Results

Bob hurried uphill from Waverley Station to the High Court of Justiciary. The way was steep and offered a grand view of Edinburgh, with Princes Street straight and wide down below and the castle high to his right, but he was deep in concentration and saw none of this. He replayed the conversation last evening with Annie about setting up a café. Although this had long been his ambition, he had never done anything to make it reality and, the longer time passed, the more distant the dream had become. He was happy working at Alexander's bus company and very grateful to Hugh Alexander for giving him a steady job. The offer had come as a surprise when Bob had bumped into Alexander in Meal Vennel a couple of days after the King's funeral. When Alexander had enquired why he wasn't at work, Bob had explained about being sacked by the Sandeman Library.

'It surely wasn't the polis who put them up to that?' Alexander had asked him.

'Aye, I think so. They wanted me to stay on a while and I wouldnae.'

'Damn. And I only wrote to your Chief Constable yesterday, saying what a grand job you did savin those bairns.'

'Did ye?'

'Aye. My men were singing your praises. And believe me, that bunch don't usually go lavishin praise on folks. Dour, you might call them. Aye, so I wrote to your Chief

Constable. Recommended you get promoted to sergeant.'

Bob laughed. 'Well, thank you very much for that but it's no a promotion I'm needin right now. A job of any sort would do.'

Alexander had pondered for a moment. 'Right then,' he'd said. 'Start Monday, eight o'clock.'

'What, drivin a bus?'

'Christ no, I've seen you drive the Wolseley, I wouldnae let you near one of my buses. Office manager. I'm lookin to expand into Fife. I need a good man with me. Aye?'

'Aye. Monday it is.'

That had been four months ago, and the work was enjoyable. The company certainly was expanding, and Bob was kept busy planning new routes and keeping the ever-expanding fleet of buses on the road but, for all he enjoyed it, he knew this was not where his future lay. More and more, he felt the urge to teach, to nurture, to inspire youngsters in a way he had never been allowed to experience. In his heart, he had almost reconciled himself to never achieving the dream, but something in the conversation last night with Annie galvanised him. You can't wait for life to make decisions for you. Life runs its own path and you can't know where it might lead, but being passive, which Bob had been all his life, practically assured it wouldn't lead where you wanted it to. He *would* open his café. He *would* teach music. He knew that now with a clarity he couldn't explain, and the knowledge made him happier than he had been at any time since before the death of his father.

*

'And how did your "fitba" go?'

'Grand,' said Bob, ignoring, as he always did, the patronising tone of the middle classes mimicking his accent. 'We won the cup.'

'Impressive.'

146

'We've already won one cup. Chance to win the league on Saturday. No one's ever done the treble before.'

'I wish you luck.' Burnett settled his wig on his head and checked in the mirror that it was straight. 'I hope you appreciate how well you did yesterday,' he said. 'Your testimony was excellent. The jury will be making comparisons between you and Braggan. They won't be in Braggan's favour.'

'Just so,' said McKenna. 'It was obvious which of you was the professional.'

'I'm not though, am I?'

'Professional doesn't only mean the office you hold,' said Burnett. 'Professional means how seriously you hold that office, how competent you are, able. That's how you came across. Able. For that reason, I've decided I don't need to call you to give evidence again. You've said all that needs saying. We've more than enough to win this one. So you can watch from the gallery today.'

'Great,' said Bob, relieved not to have to spend another day wandering the streets of Edinburgh. The case would be resolved in a day or two and Bob was pleased to know he would be there for the denouement.

*

'My Lord,' said Maxton, 'I have heard from the University this morning. They have conducted their tests on the note. Professor Gallacher from the University is in attendance and, if the court has no objections, he is willing to be called as a witness.'

'Mr Burnett?' said Lord Aitchison.

'No objections.'

'Very well, call Professor Gallacher.'

A tall, slightly stooped man was brought to the witness stand and took the oath. He spoke with a broad Ulster accent.

'Professor Gallacher,' said Lord Aitchison, 'may I thank

147

you and the University for the speed with which you have undertaken this analysis. I understand you have an outcome?'

'I do, Your Honour.'

'Well, tell us, we're all agog. Is it blood on the note?'

'No.'

The judge could not conceal his surprise. 'Is that so? And what is it?'

'I don't know. But whatever it is, it is not of human origin.'

'And you have no doubt?'

'No.'

The judge thanked Professor Gallacher and instructed him to stand down. As he made his departure, there was a buzz in the court, the public gallery debating in whispers the importance of this evidence. Bob tried not to laugh. Lord Aitchison jotted some notes on his papers and looked up. He made no attempt to conceal his irritation. He pushed his spectacles up his nose and frowned at Maxton.

'Well,' he said. 'Whatever you wished to prove with this note, it seems to have backfired somewhat.'

'There is still the fact of it being on Mr Smithson's bedside table, Your Honour.'

'And that signifies?'

'Mr Smithson lived to see the note.'

'Even assuming that to be so, and I see no irrefutable proof either way, how does that advance your argument?'

Maxton rested his bulk on first his right leg and then his left. He did not appear comfortable. 'We only have Hamill's word that he did not gain entry to the house ... '

'By the same token, you have provided no evidence that he did.'

'Your Honour, I would like to stand down the next two witnesses and move straight to the Crown's final witness.'

'As you wish.'

'Call Mr Edward Charnold.'

148

Burnett and McKenna checked the order of proceedings, noted the witnesses who had been stood down, pondered the import of that. Someone from Jock Handley's bookmakers' and another former colleague of Smithson's from Bell's. It was hard to see anything useful having come from those two, but Edward Charnold was an unknown quantity. Burnett had assumed him to be no more than a character witness, but this sudden focus on his evidence suggested otherwise.

There was a bustle of activity in the courtroom as Edward Charnold, a man of around seventy, leaning heavily on a stick, was assisted up the steps into the witness box.

'You may remain seated if you prefer, Mr Charnold,' said Lord Aitchison.

'That won't be necessary.' Charnold stared defiantly at the judge. Lord Aitchison smiled and waved to Mr Maxton to proceed.

'Mr Charnold,' he said, 'could you tell us your occupation.'

'I'm retired, son. I used to work in Bell's. The warehouse on Kinnoull Street, ken?'

'And there, did you know Mr Smithson?'

'Aye, I was his supervisor. He was a good warehouseman, Shuggy Smithson.'

'Reliable?'

'Oh, aye. Well, maistly. He could take a drink, ken?'

'Was he a regular drinker?'

'No. Jist once in a while. He tended to make up for it then, right enough. Nae stoppin him.' There was a murmur of laughter in the gallery. A couple of the jurors, too, tried to hide their amusement. Maxton continued as though nothing had happened.

'And did you also know Henry Hamill?'

'Aye.'

'Henry Hamill,' Maxton turned to address the jury, 'is the father of the accused.' He turned back to Charnold. 'Did the two men got on well?'

'Oh, Christ no, they couldnae thole one another.'

'No?'

'Some affair years afore. They wouldnae let it go.'

'Do you recollect what this affair entailed, Mr Charnold?'

'Somethin to dae wi money. Wouldnae pay a debt.'

'Who wouldn't pay whom?'

'Eh?'

'Who owed money to who?'

'Smithson owed Hamill.'

'And they argued about this?'

'For twenty bloody year. Pardon my French, but they did my heid in, the pair o them. Aye bickerin.'

'And did they ever resolve the matter?'

'Hell, no. It got worse. Ae time, Shuggy accused Henry of breakin intae his hoose.'

'Hamill broke into Mr Smithson's house?'

'Aye, so Shuggie said. Said he had a key an let himsel in.'

'Mr Hamill had a key?'

'Well, so Shuggie said.'

'This is a vital point, Mr Charnold. You are clear in your mind that Mr Smithson told you Henry Hamill had a key to his house and on one occasion he let himself in?'

'Aye, that's what I've jist telt you.'

'Did you ever raise this matter with Henry Hamill?'

'Aye, I did say to him ae time, "what's this aboot you sneakin intae Shuggie's hoose, Henry?"'

'And what did Mr Hamill reply?'

'To be honest, son, I cannae mind that clearly. It was a lang time ago, I've had a few nips since then, ken? But I think he just said something like "Smithson's aye bad mouthin me" or that kind of thing.'

'But he didn't deny it?'

'No.'

'No further questions.'

A rustle of disappointment went through the public

gallery, who had enjoyed Mr Charnold's testimony. Much of this trial had been dry and dusty stuff, not a vintage murder case, and Charnold's fruity language and couthy manner had briefly enlivened proceedings. Mr Burnett smiled broadly as he replaced Maxton at the dais. Advocates, too, liked characters in the witness box. Especially when they had the potential to disrupt the careful planning of their opposing advocates.

'Mr Charnold, I sympathise. It is particularly vexing when staff you manage are at each other's throats all the time.'

'Aye, it was a richt scunner.'

'Quite. Do you recall when this alleged break-in took place?'

'Oh, donkeys' years ago. Fifteen? Mair. Just efter the War.'

'Fifteen years ago.' He turned to the jury. 'One is well aware of the phrase "sins of the father", but in this instance, that might be stretching matters. It is difficult to see the relevance of this testimony to the matter at hand concerning Richard Hamill. However, since this testimony has been raised, let us consider it. The fact of the key.' He turned back to Charnold. 'Did you ever see this key?'

'No.'

'You've told us that Mr Hamill senior,' he paused and turned to the jury again, 'because I urge you to remember we are talking here not of the accused but of his father, you've told us Mr Hamill senior did not deny owning a key.'

'That's right.'

'Let's turn the question on its head. Did Mr Hamill senior ever *admit* to owning such a key?'

'No.'

'And did he admit to breaking into Mr Smithson's house?'

'No.'

'Knowing Mr Hamill, do you think such a thing likely?'

'I couldnae say, son.'

'But on balance of probability, was Mr Hamill the sort of man likely to indulge in law-breaking?'

'No really. He was steady, ken?'

'And did you ever meet Richard Hamill?'

'Aye, couple of times, his faither brocht him tae the warehoose when he was just a laddie.'

'What did you think of Mr Hamill?'

'Bit of a soft lad, ken? Poncy.'

'Not someone to brutally murder an old man?'

'I wouldnae hae thocht so, no.'

'No further questions.'

Mr Maxton rose stiffly. The advocates crossed on the floor of the court, studiously avoiding each other's gaze. 'Mr Charnold, did you know Mr Smithson to be a dishonest man?'

'No, he was straight enough.'

'So, if he were to make a statement, would you tend to believe it?'

'Aye, I suppose so.'

'No further questions.' He remained standing at the dais while Mr Charnold limped out of the court, leaning even more heavily on his stick. The court was silent. Everyone was focused on Maxton. He stared at his notes for some moments.

'That concludes the evidence for the prosecution, my Lord,' he said.

Lord Aitchison's granite features were impassive. His impressive chin jutted forward. Deep lines etched into his skin radiated from the eyes. Somehow, he managed to look austere and friendly at the same time. Something in his eyes, a warmth, a humanity. He rubbed his nose and surveyed the court.

'Mr Maxton,' he said finally, 'I must profess myself puzzled by the ambiguity of the prosecution evidence. This is a capital case. A man's life is at jeopardy. The evidence you have presented has been – I must be brutally honest here – slight. For circumstantial evidence to build into a satisfactory case, there must be a degree of contingency. There must be an indication of causality. Answer me honestly, is it safe upon the evidence you have presented to this court to put anyone in jeopardy?'

Maxton stared at the floor in front of him for some time. Finally, he shook his head and looked at Lord Aitchison. 'Your Honour, my view is that it is not safe. It would be very dangerous, I believe, on such evidence as this, to put any man's life at jeopardy.'

Bob sat forward, nonplussed. For the judge to be questioning the prosecution case, even before the defence had begun their own, was highly unusual. And now Maxton himself seemed to be arguing against it. Tension was palpable in the courtroom. All the players sat stiffly, as though uncertain how to proceed. Burnett and McKenna stared at one another, dumbfounded. In his twenty years at the bar, Burnett had never once heard an attorney concede that his case was incompetent. He felt a swelling of sympathy for Maxton, a good man, and an efficient advocate, who had been dealt an impossible hand.

Lord Aitchison exhaled deeply. 'What has to be considered,' he said, 'is the quality of evidence to show that Hamill committed the murder. I submit there is none. There is the note which, we now know, is not bloodstained. What of it? Even if it were, that would not advance the case at all. One witness professed to seeing him in the house. She passed the house at the same time on consecutive days – although what time that actually was appears to be a matter of conjecture – and Hamill happened to be standing at the bedroom window on the first occasion. Then the next day he appeared again, and this time came out of the house. And rode away on a bicycle he claims not to be able to ride. The long arm of coincidence has often been referred to in this court, but really this is incredible. We heard the testimony of Sergeant Braggan, with his twenty-six questions and his unenquiring mind, a most unpersuasive witness. And now we have heard an extraordinary – and, frankly, utterly uncorroborated – story about a break-in fifteen years ago, which the Prosecution would like us to believe is germane to the case at hand.'

He turned to the jury. 'You will recall my introductory remarks about the way in which circumstantial evidence should be governed. You must build up an edifice, but you must see that it is well founded. If it is not, you may not think it safe. Very well, it is time for you to give thought to that. You have heard what counsel for the Prosecution has said about the safety of this case. If you are of the same opinion, there is an end of this matter. I request you give this question your consideration.'

The foreman of the jury, a middle-aged man with wispy hair Brylcreemed firmly across his shiny pate, turned to the other jurors and they held a rapid, whispered conversation while the court watched in silence. After no more than thirty seconds, the foreman turned to face the judge once more.

'Have you a judgement?' asked the clerk.

'Yes.'

'Do you find the prisoner not guilty?'

'Not guilty.'

'Thank you,' said Lord Aitchison. 'A most sensible conclusion, and I commend members of the jury for the speed with which they have reached it. Mr Hamill.' He turned to Richard Hamill seated in the dock. Prompted by the policemen either side of him, Hamill stood, as bemused as everyone else by the turn of events. 'We have heard the entirety of the evidence submitted by the Prosecution, and even the Prosecution's Counsel has conceded it is without merit. In my opinion, this case should never have been brought before my court. Not before a thorough police investigation had been undertaken and I am confident that such did not happen. Mr Hamill, I am pleased to tell you that you are free to go.'

*

Burnett, McKenna and Bob Kelty sat in the snug of the Clansman Tavern on the Royal Mile an hour later. They had invited Richard Hamill but Richard, overwhelmed by the morning's events, declined. He would rather be alone, he said. The advocates drank whisky, Bob a pint of mild. A haze of cigarette smoke hung in the room, and they could barely make themselves heard above the noise of the locals chattering and laughing at the bar.

'A highly satisfactory week's work, gentlemen,' said Burnett, raising his glass. 'A tricky trial skilfully negotiated.'

'Their case didnae seem to have much goin for it,' said Bob.

'No, indeed, and anything it might have had was spiked by your testimony. Well done, young man. You made it abundantly clear in your evidence that the police had not undertaken a thorough investigation and had rushed to judgement.'

'In the end,' said McKenna, 'there really was no case to answer.'

'No,' said Burnett. He sipped his whisky. 'My greatest concern, though, was keeping the jury focused on the crime, not the accused.'

'It looked bad,' said McKenna, 'on the first afternoon.'

'To be fair to Maxton,' said Burnett, 'he didn't milk it as much as he could. And when he did, Craigie Aitchison shut it down immediately. What was it he said? "I'm sure the jury have noted well the matter of Mr Hamill's lifestyle. I do not believe there is anything further to be explored in this regard".'

155

'That was a turning point,' agreed McKenna. 'I've seen trials go completely off the rails in moments like that.'

'They become witch hunts.'

'Juries lose all reason.'

'Would you have done it?' said Bob. 'Raised his lifestyle? If you were in Maxton's position?'

Burnett blew smoke from his nostrils, then inhaled from his cigarette again. 'Yes,' he said. 'I probably would.'

Bob stared at him, then studied the vivacity around him in the bar, people having fun, laughing, talking. Over the past few days, he had come to know Alexander Burnett. The fearsome individual he recalled from the McGuigan trial was revealed to be altogether different, a mild, humorous, thoughtful man. Bob's preconceptions had been changed.

And yet.

And yet the law was a lousy affair. There was no getting away from that. He had known it when Marjory Fenwick was denied justice. Now, even in the face of Richard Hamill gaining his freedom, that fact had been reinforced. Somehow, truth seemed malleable. Vulnerable. People and situations could be manipulated for particular ends. Things which didn't matter could be made to matter. Things which did matter must remain concealed.

'Aye, well,' he said, rising from his seat, 'I'd best be gettin back for my train.'

'You haven't finished your drink.'

'It was nice meetin you again. Dinnae take offence if I say I hope it's the last time. It's not you – it's just ...'

'I know what you think. And I don't blame you. But just remember what happened today. The wheels of justice, young man, the wheels of justice. Sometimes they do run smooth.'

'Do they, aye?' He put on his jacket and said goodbye and walked into the cooling afternoon air. Tourists gathered round the Heart of Midlothian. A news vendor shouted out for people to buy the *Evening Telegraph*. The news board read "Mahmoud wins Derby!" Bob had forgotten all about the race. *Mr McKenna would be pleased to pocket his £25*, he thought. Mr Burnett would no doubt chalk his failure down to bad luck. Nothing to worry about.

At Waverley Station, he sat on a bench and waited for his train. Here, in a corner where the sun never penetrated, the air was distinctly cold. Shadows and damp, even at the beginning of summer. Gradually, the platform began to fill, young women in chic hats, men in worn suits, puffing constantly on cigarettes, older couples forever studying their watches as though convinced time might somehow elude them and they would miss their train. Bob Kelty never felt more lonely than when he was in a crowd. He should be happy, he knew, and part of him was, the part who knew Richard Hamill and liked him and knew he was an innocent man. But the part of him that was Bob Kelty, lost soul in search of meaning, could not summon any enthusiasm. He lit his pipe and thought of Annie, her bonnie smile, her couthy ways, happy demeanour, and he pictured a life together, bairns, adventures, growing old, the beauty of belonging, the strength of trust, and he pictured their future, a café of their own in the centre of Crieff, somewhere that was theirs alone, their corner of the world, their refuge, nest, home, and he conjured the myriad nights of music and dance and song and romance there would be in the long years to come, and in this fashion, he edged away from the abyss which routinely awaited him and stepped back into the world of light.

'I love you, Annie Maybury,' he said.

# Friday 29th May

## A Day of Assistance

Next morning, at first light, Bob stood at the top of Kinnoull Hill and watched the world emerge. The River Tay curled beneath him. In the distance, the River Earn joined it and the two rivers became one and pulsed towards the North Sea. The fields below were green, fresh, ready for another season's growth and harvest. There were starlings chattering in an oak tree to his right. A lone magpie prowled the ground ten yards away. The air was fresh, night-time chill gradually dissipating in the light of day. This was where Bob came when he needed to think. The warp and weft of the world, its implacable teleology, could only be comprehended at such height, from such distance, at such remove. Whatever his cares or his fears or his hopes, they mattered nothing up here, because nothing did, not when measured against the grain of sand that comprised his universe within the whole universe.

Bob turned and cycled back towards town, decision made.

*

At one o'clock, during his lunch hour, he hurried down New Row to Old High Street. In Rattrays, he bought a tin of *Hal o The Wynd* tobacco to celebrate the successful outcome of the trial and then walked towards Paul Street. To avoid prying eyes, he went round the back, where there was a narrow dirt pathway running the length of the street. The entrances to the houses were on the first floor, the ground floor space given over in years gone by to livestock. Each doorway was reached by a stairway twisting through ninety degrees. The stair to the house he sought was crude, seemingly home-made. Flagstones, much worn by generations of feet and clearly cannibalised from a property much larger and grander than this, formed the steps. Either side of them, wooden slats were loosely nailed to a creaking and rotting frame with a rough wooden railing. The house, like all in the street, was cramped and damp. Within a few years it would be pulled down as part of Perth's urban redevelopment.

Bob knocked on the door and, after a few seconds, it opened and Richard Hamill appeared in the doorway.

'My saviour,' he said, thrusting his hand towards Bob.

'Hardly that,' said Bob, shaking the outstretched hand.

'Come in. I've just put the kettle on.'

The kitchen was cold, peeling wallpaper barely adhering to terminally damp walls. An ageing range was against the wall to the side of the window. Beer mats had been folded over and placed beneath two of the legs of a round wooden table in the middle of the room. Richard Hamill took two cups from a cupboard and placed them on the draining board beside the sink. The room was dark despite bright sunshine outside. Bob sat at the table. The living room was through an open doorway and Bob had the sensation that there was somebody there. He chose not to say anything.

'I just wanted to see how you were,' he said. 'I remember Madge, after the trial, was a bit down for a while.'

'She didn't get the right verdict, though.'

'Aye, true, but I think there was more to it. When you go through somethin like that, it changes you. It did me, even, and I wasn't in the dock. When I'd done my bit on the stand, afterwards I felt strange. Out of sorts. I think Madge was the same.'

'You have this huge build-up of energy to keep you

going, and then when it's over, you don't need it anymore. Makes you feel restless.'

'Aye, something like that. And you've been thrust into this position where you're no in control. Anything can happen and you cannae do anything about it.'

'That's just life, if you think about it. But honestly, my only feeling is one of relief.'

'I can understand that. Though, in the cold light of day, they didnae hae much of a case against you.'

'No, they didn't, but that's not really the point.' He filled the teapot from a large kettle on the range and placed it on the table. He poured milk into the cups. 'Sugar?'

'Two.'

He took a bag of sugar, clearly old, from the cupboard and tipped some into one of the cups and placed them beside the teapot and sat down. 'Courts,' he said, then halted, as though trying to find a way to express himself, 'they can be very dangerous places ... For people like me.' He studied Bob's expression as he poured the tea. 'If you know what I mean.'

'I think so.'

'Hamish.'

Bob looked in the direction of the living room. 'Aye.'

'And if that makes things difficult for you, I totally understand.'

'And the same wi me and Annie.'

Richard frowned. 'What's Annie got to do with anything?'

Bob cocked an eyebrow but said nothing. Richard smiled.

'Thank you,' he said. 'But you must see what I mean about a courtroom being dangerous for someone like me. Once the jury knew I was homosexual, it could have coloured their judgement.'

'It didn't.'

'Because it was an open and shut case. But if it hadn't been? If there genuinely was doubt, on either side. Would

160

they have used that against me?'

Bob knew he was right. It seemed to him a hellish deal, making choice a matter of decency, and then turning decency into a question of morality and taking a moral high ground that was nothing short of bigotry. All the while stoked by a national press that was looking for scapegoats and a political class that was oblivious of the changes happening to the society around them.

'It's going to get worse,' said Richard.

'Aye,' said Bob.

*

'Right,' said Sergeant Petrie, 'now that the trial's done, the solicitor for Smithson's estate wants possession from Monday, so we need to go through the entire house, make sure there's nothing of value to the investigation.'

'What investigation?' said PC Macrae. The vituperation of Sergeant Braggan, encamped back in the City Police Station for the duration of the trial and railing now at the injustice of the court's verdict, still rang in his ears. 'The poofter did it and got away with it. There's no point investigating this anymore. We know who did it and now we can't charge him for it again.'

Sergeant Petrie knew this too, knew the case was destined to lie unsolved forever. 'Officially,' he said, 'this remains an open case and will continue to be so. I accept it's difficult to see us doing any actual investigation, but we must follow procedure. So, check the house, top to bottom.'

Macrae set to work upstairs, opening the wardrobe and chest of drawers in the bedroom and checking under the bed. At least Smithson was a man of few possessions so it wouldn't take long. George shuddered at the thought of having to do this at home, with all his mother's knick-knacks and ornaments and his father's extensive file of communications with and complaints against every form

161

of officialdom going back thirty years. There was nothing to record upstairs and he trudged downstairs to the kitchen. Most of the cupboards were half empty, a few tins and jars of food, some mismatched crockery, jars of buttons and thread. He opened the cutlery drawer and rattled the cutlery in a desultory fashion, as though persuading himself this was somehow a worthwhile undertaking. On a whim, he lifted the box in which the cutlery was stored. Beneath it, wrapped with string, was a bundle of letters.

He untied the string. There were four letters, all in identical, cheap envelopes and written on identical paper. The address was printed in a neat, precise hand. *Female*, Macrae thought. The postmarks were years apart. 1929, 1927, 1922, 1919. He opened the most recent.

"Your sins will be found out. I will make sure of that. When the time is right the world will hear of your guilt."

The other three were variations on the same theme. The letter writer knew a secret about Smithson, threatened to expose him. The handwriting was the same as on the envelopes, scrupulously neat, a beautiful, cursive script. What was this secret? And why had it never been exposed? There were ten years between the first letter and the last, and another six years until Smithson's murder. There was no indication that Smithson had responded to the letters. So, what was the secret?

Macrae finished searching the house and found nothing else of interest. He hurried back to the Station and left the key to Smithson's house with Sergeant Hamilton and sought out Sergeants Petrie and Braggan. Braggan was clearing his desk and was not happy to see this new evidence.

'Should we investigate?' said Macrae. He had hopes of a few days off normal duties in favour of an exciting investigation, some proper detective work, but Braggan's glowering expression quickly disabused him of the notion.

'What's the point? We know who wrote them. It even

looks like a nancy boy's handwriting. What can we do? Even if we proved – again – that he did it, we can't charge him again. Double jeopardy. It's a waste of time.' He thrust a couple of folders into a brown leather satchel and pulled it shut. 'No offence, but I'll be glad to see the back of this bloody case.' Without a word of goodbye, he strode out of the office and through the reception and onto Tay Street.

'Well,' said Petrie, 'he's got the manners of a barbary ape, but he's right enough. There's only one man ever going to get charged with this murder and we've already done it and he got off with it.'

'What d'you want me to do with these?' Macrae gestured forlornly at the letters.

'File them.'

'Yes, Sergeant.'

\*

Even though it had been eight years since he was first introduced to the Conoboys, after he came to live with Gran following his father's suicide, and he knew them to be the kindest people he had ever met, Bob still felt hesitant in their presence. Tonight would be even more difficult, with Lord Kellett also in attendance. Indeed, Victor had told him it was Lord Kellett himself who suggested Bob should join them, and Bob had no idea why that should be but he was nervous all the same. It wasn't the fact that the man was a Lord that intimidated Bob. He simply found him unnerving. The confidence. The ease. He seemed to swallow the energy of a room and, in his presence, Bob's confidence seemed to diminish proportionately.

Annie answered the door in her maid's uniform and kissed him quickly and led him through to the dining room, where Victor and Bella and Lord Kellett had already gathered.

'Sorry I'm late,' he said, although he knew he wasn't. He took a seat at the table next to Bella, opposite Lord Kellett, and smiled nervously. Bella patted his lap.

'Hasn't that been a grand day?' she said.

'It was, aye. I was up Kinnoull Hill at dawn. Watching the sun on the Tay. It was braw.'

They ate soup and roast pheasant, followed by a cheese board, and retired to the living room with brandies. Bob would have preferred to join Annie in the kitchen to help with the washing up. Lord Kellett sipped from his brandy.

'I understand you were the star of the trial once more?' he said.

'Well,' Bob replied, staring into the fire, 'I have mixed feelings about that, to be honest. I'm delighted Mr Hamill was acquitted, of course, but I fear the City Police didn't come out of it very well.'

'And why should that bother you? You don't work for them any longer.'

'No, but I feel some loyalty.'

'I can't imagine why. They never showed you any, and it seems to me they underestimated you constantly.'

*They're not alone in that*, thought Bob. He didn't reply.

'How would you like to swap uniforms? Come over to the County force? I'd see to it you were better appreciated there than you were by the City boys.'

'I don't think so ...'

'Policing is changing. In the past, it used to be about keeping the peace. We didn't have the technology or the wherewithal to do proper detection. There's a new world approaching. I saw that when the Glasgow force helped us last year. I know I was adamant I didn't want them and they didn't help, but what I saw impressed me. Fingerprints. Scientific analysis. Forensic study. That's the way policing has to move. The days of little forces like ours are numbered. I'm lobbying in the highest places to have the Perth City and County forces merged. Those Glasgow people – Sillitoe and the like – they know what they're about. The future looks very exciting. And we need young men with ideas and open minds to help us. I could see a real future for you.'

'It's not really ... '

'If it's Braggan that's bothering you, don't. He's been transferred. I signed the order last night. Uniform sergeant in Lochearnhead. As far away as I could get him. He's the past, he's everything we need to get away from.'

'It's not that.'

'What employment have you now?'

'Alexander's Bus Company. Office Manager ...'

Kellett shook his head vigorously and Bob trailed off. 'That's not a career for an able young man like you. No future in it. The future is the motor car. Soon, everyone will be able to afford a motor car. There won't be any need for buses.'

'Goodness,' said Bella, 'if everyone had a car, where would they all go? There aren't enough roads.'

'Precisely. Which is why the Government's just passed the Trunk Roads Act. All the main routes in the country are now the responsibility of the Ministry of Transport. We'll see the network improving all the time. New, straight roads. Perth to Edinburgh in forty minutes. Who needs buses? There's no career there, my boy.'

'I don't want a career there,' said Bob. 'This is just to tide me over.'

'Until when?'

'Until I can open up my new business.'

Kellett inclined his head. 'Really? And what business have you in mind?'

'I'm goin to open up a café. And in the back I'm goin to teach music. Two jobs in one, to make sure it'll pay its way.'

'Pay its way? Good God, man, how do you ever propose to make money from such a venture? Tuppence a time for a cup of tea and how many people are going to want to learn music? Learning music's for schoolchildren. Adults haven't

165

got time for fripperies like that.'

'I wouldn't say that music was a frippery,' said Bella.

'It damn well is if you're starving and you've nothing to put in your belly and no job to go to.'

Bob bristled at being lectured on poverty by a peer of the realm. 'We'd nae money when I was growin up,' he said, 'but first my faither and then my Gran taught me to play music.'

'But your father and your grandmother were in employment ... '

'And I dinnae see why one should preclude the other. Poor people shouldnae hae culture, is that what you're sayin? They should wallow in their misery? Let me tell you, when you're poor, that's when you need culture maist of all. Tak you out of yoursel. Why d'you think our music is handed doon generation to generation by the common folk and no the Lords and the gentry?'

Bob sat back, embarrassed by his outburst. Bella tried to conceal a smile. Victor frowned. There was an awkward silence, broken when Lord Kellett laughed.

'Quite right,' he said. The living room door opened and Annie bustled in to replenish their brandy glasses. 'Now then,' said Kellett, 'let's ask the young lady her view. How would you feel if your husband opened up a cafeteria? Don't you think he should be looking for a good job?'

Annie, caught unawares, opened her mouth but no words formed. She looked at Bob, saw the strain in his expression, knew things weren't going well.

'I think, perhaps,' she said, 'a good man is more important than a good job, my Lord.'

Bella Conoboy clapped her hands. Victor sat tight-lipped. Bob wanted to jump up and kiss Annie. Kellett smiled.

'The innocence of youth,' he said.

Bella recognised the need to change the subject. 'I hear the planning for the coronation is gathering pace?' she said.

'Indeed,' said Lord Kellett. 'But whose coronation?' He gave an enigmatic smile and sipped his brandy.

'What do you mean?' said Victor, biting at the hook Kellett had floated in front of the gathering.

'There has been some speculation, I understand,' said Bella. 'In the foreign press.'

'How do you know that?' said Victor.

Bella smiled. 'I have my methods.'

'It's no mere speculation,' said Lord Kellett. The others looked at him expectantly and when he was satisfied he had an audience, he continued. 'I was at the Derby on Wednesday. My horse was a runner, *Yellow Broom* ... '

'Did it win?' asked Victor.

'Alas not. The Aga Khan was first. And second. Officially, the King wasn't there. The court is technically still in mourning. But, of course, he *was* there. And in the evening he held a dinner at St James' Palace to which I was invited.'

'You had dinner with the King?' said Victor incredulously.

'I did. And a very odd occasion it was, too. Strangest assortment of people I've ever dined with. There was the Prime Minister and Mrs Baldwin, Mr and Mrs Duff Cooper, Lady Cunard, Lord Wigram. Charles Lindbergh the aviator. If ever you want to meet a charlatan, look no further than him. That man will come to a bad end, make no mistake. And a couple of Americans called Ernest and Mrs Simpson.'

'Who are they?' asked Victor.

'You may very well ask. Ernest Simpson is a disreputable little man, oily, deeply unpleasant. Wallis Simpson – well, I can't go into details, but remember the name.'

'You fear some scandal?'

'Victor, if we can get to Christmas without all hell breaking loose, we'll be lucky. Frankly, it's nothing short of a disaster. At the very point this country needs stability and leadership we appear to have a feckless neer-do-well on the throne. There's all these dissenters, people like Churchill, lobbying for us to prepare for war ... '

'And so we should,' said Bella.

'Germany are intent on empire, I grant you,' conceded Kellett, 'but they're no threat to us, unless we threaten them. And that's ... '

Bella slapped her hand on the arm of her chair. 'That's hogwash, Reginald.' Lord Kellett was surprised by the urgency of her outburst. 'You know my family's history,' she went on. 'We lost our son in the War, and I'm a pacifist to the core, but if you imagine for a second you can appease Hitler or Mussolini or Franco, or even our own tinpot lunatic Mosley, then you're living in a dream world.'

'But peace ... '

'It's not about peace anymore. We've gone too far for that. Herr Hitler isn't interested in peace. All he knows is destruction. It's not about peace, it's about freedom, and if we're not careful we'll throw that on the rubbish tip, egged on by Rothermere and the *Daily Mail*. Surely you remember that disgusting article they ran when Hitler came to power? "No one will mourn the loss of German democracy" Really? And will we also fail to mourn the loss of British democracy? Because that's what's coming if we don't stand up to these lunatics.'

Lord Kellett raised his hands, palms outwards. 'Bella, you always were the wise one. In some respects, you don't know how right you are. Again, the dinner on Wednesday was illuminating in that respect. Some of the most important people in the country are flirting with danger.'

'You mean the King?'

'I do.'

'What sorts of danger?'

'All sorts.'

*

Bella stopped Bob as he was leaving at the end of the evening.

Lord Kellett had already departed, his driver arriving at ten-thirty. They stood in the hallway.

'Well done for standing up to Reginald Kellett,' she said.

'I hope he didn't think me rude.'

'What you said was quite right. Reginald was being patronising. Paternalistic. Typical Tory, assuming they know what's best for everyone.'

'People need music. They need peace. Music gives you that.'

'I know it does.' She studied his face. Tired eyes. Strained. 'How are you managing?' she said. 'Without your gran?'

'I'm fine, ma'am. I miss her, of course, but I get by.'

'If you need to talk, you know you can come to me?'

'Thank you.'

'You haven't played music for us for a while. You must come and play some of your ragtime tunes soon.'

'I'd like that.'

She smiled. 'Your café,' she said. 'Have you a place in mind?'

'I think so, aye, in Crieff. I saw it last year when we took Marjory out for the day. It's still on the market. I'd need to look at it properly …'

'Naturally. Is it purchase or lease?'

'Purchase.'

'How much would you require to get the business up and running?'

'It's for sale at £600. I need a 5% deposit, so that's £30. I could manage that, just about, with my savings. I can take out a twenty-five-year mortgage so that would be about £70 a year. And rates on top of that. I think I can manage that. So, the ongoing costs, once I'm set up, I think are fine. It's the set-up costs that bother me.'

'Such as?'

'I'll need to decorate. And buy furniture – chairs and tables. And an oven. I can get second hand, of course, but I still think I'll need about £100. And I haven't got that yet.'

'Very well, I shall lend you £150. Interest free. To be paid when you're in a position to.'

'I couldn't, ma'am.'

'Robert, you and Annie are like family to us. You *are* family to us. I would have liked to help Tom into business one day, but that wasn't to be. My only son died and now you are here for me to fuss over and look after. It would be my pleasure to help you out. You and Annie.'

'I don't know what to say, ma'am.'

'"Yes" will do.' She smiled and stroked his cheek.

'Thank you.'

# Part Three

# December 1936

# Tuesday 1ˢᵗ December

## *A Day of Resolve*

The low early morning sun was dazzling, reflecting against the granite headstones, and Bob had to squint as he walked the now familiar pathway downhill. Gran's grave still had a wooden marker. It was too soon for the granite headstone to be erected, but it was already made, by Beveridge and Son in York Place. *Agnes Kelty 1860 – 1936. Much loved wife of John Kelty. Mother of David Kelty.* The ground was beginning to settle, and Bob thought that in another month he would be able to lay the proper headstone. He closed his eyes. At least he had a grave to mourn beside. His father, a church attendee all his life, was denied consecrated ground because of the manner of his death. His cremated remains were taken by the authorities and disposed of Bob knew not where. That caused an ache, an emptiness inside him, a void where he ought to have been able to grieve. He stood for five minutes, remembering Gran, giving thanks. He did not speak to her or pray for her because she was beyond such things. Death affects only the living. He put his bunnet back on his head and walked uphill into the heart of the cemetery. Beneath a yew tree, he saw a familiar face and walked towards her.

'Hello, Madge, how are you?'

'PC Kelty,' said Marjory Fenwick. Her eyes were red-rimmed, but she smiled broadly. She looked down at the grave of Danny Kerrigan, her sweetheart, murdered on the Cuddies Strip on the night she was raped, eighteen months before, a series of events never to be forgotten. 'I don't often come here,' she said. 'Not now. But yesterday was the first anniversary of the day that man was convicted. It's been on my mind.'

'So it was,' said Bob. 'Last day of November. You look well.'

'So do you. Much happier, I'd say.'

Bob smiled. Marjory was always more perceptive than she realised. 'Probably because I'm no with the polis anymore. I handed in my notice the Monday after the trial ended.'

'Why? Because of the trial?'

'Aye, partly. All those games in court. Trying to baffle the jury. Make us out to seem ...'

'It was horrible.'

'It was, aye. I got scunnered, truth to tell, so I quit. I'm very happy now.'

'What are you doing?'

'I'm opening up my new café in a fortnight. In Crieff. I'm signing it off with the solicitors this morning.'

'That's wonderful. That's what you always wanted isn't it? I remember you sayin that the time you took us down – what was the name of that place?'

'Lady Mary's Walk.'

'That's it. I still remember that as one of the best days of my life.'

'Aye, it was grand. And what are you doin with yoursel? You were goin to start night classes wi Annie.'

'I still aim to. Next year. Mum took ill earlier this year.'

'I'm sorry.'

'She's fine now. But I had to look after her for a while.'

'So where are you workin?'

'I'm still at the confectioners.'

Bob nodded, tried to hide his disappointment. Marjory could achieve more in her life, but she had to be made to believe it.

'I'll ask Annie to speak to the college for you. Put in a good word.'

'That'd be grand.'

But they both knew, as they went their separate ways, that it wouldn't happen.

\*

Richard Hamill tied his apron round his waist and washed his hands in the Belfast sink against the back wall of McKerchar's Butchers. He took the whetstone from the counter and started to sharpen his knives. Mr McKerchar walked through the beaded curtain over the doorway from the back office.

'You neednae do that,' he said.

'I thought, last night, they needed sharpening.'

'Maybe so, but I'll do it mysel.'

'It's no bother.'

'I want you to leave.'

Richard replaced the knife on the counter and studied the old man. He was shifting uncomfortably, not making eye contact. 'Why?'

'I'll pay you for today, but I want you to leave now.'

'Why?'

'I cannae hae this affectin my trade.'

Richard was hit by a sense of resignation. *Here we go again.* 'What is it?' he said.

'I just want you oot of here. That kind of thing, it could ruin our reputation.' Mr McKerchar shuffled past him and picked up the knife Richard had relinquished and started to grind it against the whetstone, all the while staring out the window at Scott Street.

'You have to tell me what this is about,' Richard said.

'I had a letter.'

'Who from?'

'I dinnae ken. Anonymous.'

Richard cursed. This was the third time. The third time he'd lost his job because of anonymous complaints about him.

'And what does this letter say?'

'I'd rather not discuss it.' McKerchar attacked the whetstone with the knife as though it were an enemy. He kept his back to Richard. 'Disgustin behaviour. Perversions. Unnatural acts.'

'The letter accuses me of being a homosexual?'

'If that's the word for it. I'm no even goin to ask if it's true. Just get oot of my sight and never let me see you again.' He pulled a ten-shilling note from his pocket. 'That's what you're owed. Now get out.'

*

Bob leaned forward and lifted the fountain pen from the desk. His hand was shaking. He signed the form and passed it across the desk to Mr Small. This was the most important action he had ever taken. Mr Small studied the signature as though looking for some impropriety. He laid the contract on the table.

'Congratulations, Mr Kelty, you are now the owner of a cafeteria and flat in James Square, Crieff.' Annie, seated beside Bob, squeezed his hand.

'Well done,' she said.

*Well done, Bella Conoboy*, thought Bob. None of this would have been possible without her. She had put up the capital for Bob to develop the business and negotiated a mortgage with her own bank manager. Bob felt sure he could never have done so without her. She had even accompanied him to the first meeting, one of her rare forays out of the house. He looked at the deeds on the table in front of Mr Small and felt a mixture of fear and elation.

174

'What will you call it?' Mr Small asked. '*Kelty's Cafeteria*? That has a nice, alliterative air.'

'Cloudland,' said Bob.

'Cloudland? How extraordinary.'

*Yes*, thought Bob. *It is extraordinary. It will be.*

*

The horse box pulled up outside the North Cattle Loading Bank in St Catherine's Road and Dauvit McCallum opened the rear of the box while his brother Colin went into the Loading Bank. Four Argentine horses, the first from there to be sold in Scotland since the Great War, were to be transported to Macdonald, Fraser and Co. on the Glasgow Road in time for Thursday's mart. They were fine looking beasts, chocolate brown skin, sleek, powerful. They would attract buyers from all over Scotland.

With assistance from a couple of lads from the Loading Bank, the horses were led from their stalls onto St Catherine's Road. There had been a heavy shower an hour before and now the sun, low in the sky, shone brightly, glinting against the cobble stones. The lead horse, spooked by this harsh reflection, faltered and lost its footing. It panicked and bolted, jolting free of Dauvit McCallum's grip, and brayed and bucked a couple of times before galloping down St Catherine's Road. Dauvit shouted and began to give chase and his noise panicked the other three horses. Two of them bolted free from their handlers and sped off in pursuit of their companion, with the McCallums running after them, raising the alarm.

The terrified horses ran the length of Caledonian Road and rounded the corner on to St Andrews Street and Leonard Street. Bob Kelty, back at his desk in Alexander's offices, but his head still whirring from this morning's events, heard the sound of galloping hooves and the neighing of frightened horses, and he looked out of the window with astonishment as the animals ran past him towards Station Square.

'What the hell?' he shouted, throwing down his pen and running outside. The McCallums, out of breath and nearly exhausted, joined him and Bob pointed towards the General Station. 'Come on,' he said.

The General Station was in a state of consternation. The horses had crashed through the entrance into the main concourse and onto Platform One beyond. There, frightened by the darkness and the echo of their hooves, they jumped from the platform onto the tracks and were running along the northbound line.

'Put down the barriers,' Bob shouted. 'Dinnae let any trains through.'

The McCallums sat on the platform and prepared to jump onto the track in pursuit. 'No,' said Bob. 'Dinnae chase them. You'll spook them. They'll start to run and get their hooves caught in the points.'

'What the hell do you ken about it?' said Dauvit McCallum.

Bob knew plenty. His father had been a heavy horseman all his life on the farms of north and east Perthshire and Bob had been expected to follow him into the trade. It was a job for life, Faither said, but when he killed himself Bob was put in the care of his gran in Perth and his life began to spin in a different direction. Bob had never ceased to regret that, never stopped missing the horses.

'Just bide here,' he said. He slid onto the track and walked as slowly and steadily as he could over the rough stones between the sleepers. The horses had slowed, about fifty yards ahead, probably frightened and confused by the St Leonard's bridge looming over the track in the near distance. Bob walked towards them, arms outstretched, making soothing noises.

'All right there, all right boys. Don't be frightened.'

The horses turned and watched him. Bob could sense

they were still agitated, their breathing heavy and head movements swift and erratic, but he was encouraged to see they did not retreat.

'Steady, boys. I'm here to help you.' He was within yards of them, and he stopped to let them study him, smell him, gauge him. Slowly, slowly, he advanced. He raised his hand.

'Good boys. That's it.'

He pressed his palm against the muzzle of the nearest horse, felt it hot on his skin, felt the sheen of sweat. The touch was electrifying, jolting him back ten years to his childhood. He stayed like that for some moments, quiet, calm, while the horse grew accustomed to him. The second horse had nudged closer, and Bob raised his right hand and rested it on the horse's muzzle. Again, he waited, watched, felt for the horse to relax into his care. When both horses were composed, he turned to the third horse, five yards or so up the track, its head lowered, dark eyes alive and staring. Bob laid his hand on it, too, and waited while trust pulsed between them.

Gently, he turned the horse through ninety degrees until it was facing up the track towards the bridge. He went back to the others and turned them, too, and nudged them and began to walk. They followed. The jagged rocks between the parallel rails made progress difficult and progress was slow, Bob praying none of the horses would turn an ankle. He talked all the while in a low and reassuring voice. They passed beneath the bridge and the sudden darkness made the horses restless once more, but Bob patted their flanks and talked and reassured them and they emerged once more into light. The South Inch stretched green and inviting ahead of them. Where the track began to turn southwards, Bob saw a gap in the fence bounding the line and the park and led the horses towards it. The green grass of the Inch attracted their attention and they jumped up the narrow banking, neighing with pleasure at a return of the familiar. Bob followed, scrambling up the banking with less elegance than the horses.

'Fine lads,' he said. 'Brave lads.' He stroked them and patted them and smelled their flesh until the McCallums arrived with halters, and for those few precious moments Bob Kelty was transported to the life he had lost, to the time when he was complete, before his dreams began to unravel.

*

'My, that was impressive.'

Bob was lost in contemplation as he walked across the Inch to King's Place. He turned at the sound of the voice and saw Richard Hamill smiling at him. 'Quite the hero. Again.'

'Hardly,' said Bob. 'I winnae shake your hand. I stink of horses.' They walked uphill towards the General Station, passing the McCallum's horse trailer. 'So how are you?' said Bob. 'Havenae seen you in a while.'

'Honestly?'

Bob sensed immediately that something was wrong. Richard, normally so ebullient, seemed downcast. Bob shifted into his professional demeanour. He wasn't sure what that was, exactly, or how he produced it, but he could always recognise when it happened. It was like a switch being pressed in his head.

'I lost my job. Again. Third time since the trial.'

'What did you do?'

'What did you do when you lost your job at the library?'

'Nothin.'

'Precisely.'

'It was the polis that got me sacked from the library.'

'Precisely.'

'The polis are gettin you the sack? I don't understand.'

'Not the police per se. One policeman.'

Bob thought for a moment. 'Braggan?'

'I think so.'

Bob took out his pocket watch. 'Aye, well,' he said. 'I

178

bought a café today and it's near as damnit knockin off time. Let's have a drink. Celebrate and commiserate.'

In the Corner Bar, they sat in the same seats they had ten months before, on the day Richard was arrested. This time, Bob bought the drinks.

'Congratulations on the cafeteria,' said Hamill.

'Thanks. I've that much to do, I cannae think straight. But first, tell me all about you. What's goin on?'

'I've been working at McKerchar's about a month. Mr McKerchar said this morning he'd had an anonymous note. "I just want you out of here," he said. "That kind of thing, it could ruin our reputation."'

'What kind of thing?'

'That I'm a homosexual.'

Bob shook his head. 'I'm sorry.'

'So that's me sacked again. Third time.'

'Where were the others?'

'First time was Nicholls' bakery on the Old High Street. Opposite Rattrays'. Anonymous phone call that time. "I saw him stealing from the till." Second time, Tyler's brickies. "Heard him and another man talking about carrying off a load of bricks in the night." I wasn't sorry to be sacked from that one, mind. Too much like hard work.'

'And you think it's Braggan?'

'Who else?'

'But he's in Lochearnhead.'

'I expect even Lochearnhead has telephones and postboxes.'

'But why?'

'I suspect partly because he *is* in Lochearnhead. Which he no doubt thinks is my fault. He didn't come out of the trial well, did he? Got transferred to Lochearnhead almost immediately, I believe. Back into uniform. He's a man who's going to bear a grudge, wouldn't you say? People like him always do. If anything bad happens to them, it must be someone else's fault. Never theirs.'

'Do you want me to speak to Lord Kellett?' Bob wasn't at all sure how he could speak to Lord Kellett, but he felt he ought to offer some form of assistance.

'There's no point. I've realised I may have to leave Perth. Even then, I expect he'll find me. Trouble is, as well as the humiliation of the trial, I think he still believes I'm guilty.'

'Why d'you think that?'

'George Macrae told me. After the trial. Braggan was livid. Said I'd done it and got away with it. So, I ruined his career, and I'm still a murderer.'

Bob took a sip of beer. 'Well, in that case we're goin to have to prove him wrong.'

'How?'

'Find out who really did kill Hugh Smithson.'

\*

Bob reckoned that if George Macrae was on duty, he would be on the Muirton beat, Ainslie Gardens, Carnegie Place. He whistled a ragtime tune as he sauntered down Balhousie Street. He stared up at the Castle as he always did, studying its strange turrets and profusion of ivy. Despite its name, it was a convent and Bob had always been curious about how it looked inside. An old woman approached, carrying a shopping basket over her right arm, her hair covered by a chequered headscarf. She scowled at him.

'You havenae seen a bobby?' he asked her.

'Aye, doon yonder. Why, what's happened?'

'Nothin.'

She watched him suspiciously as he carried on walking and turned onto Florence Place. In front of him was Muirton Park. In the distance, he saw PC Macrae.

'Geordie,' he shouted.

George Macrae waited until Bob caught up with him and they shook hands. 'Well, stranger,' George said, 'been wrestlin any swans recently?'

'Roundin up three horses, actually. Frae the Argentine.'

Macrae laughed uncertainly, not sure whether Bob was being serious.

'You'll see it in the *PA* on Friday, I expect. I was wonderin, the Smithson murder. When Richard Hamill was found not guilty, did you investigate it any further?'

'Nah. Braggan came back durin the trial, but he told the Chief it was a miscarriage of justice and Hamill had got off wi it. There was naebody else to look for, he said.'

'And the Chief Constable believed that?'

'I think it was convenient, like. Meant we didnae have to own up to gettin it wrong.'

'Meanwhile, there's a real murderer still out there? Who could do it again?'

'I suppose so.'

'D'you no think that's wrong?'

'What can I dae aboot it?'

Bob swore. He told Macrae Hamill's story about Braggan's harassment. 'I want to find out who killed Smithson. Put an end to all this.'

'The trail's goin to be gey cauld by now, man.'

'Maybe so. All the same, I'm goin to try. Was there anythin else came in after I left? Any other leads?'

'There was, aye. After the trial, we were shuttin up Smithson's hoose to return it to the solicitors and I came across some threatenin letters in the bottom of the cutlery drawer.'

'What did they say?'

'"I know your secret. I'm going to turn you in." That kind of thing.'

'How many?'

'Four. Sent years apart. First ain was just efter the War.'

'All sayin the same thing?'

'Mair or less.'

181

'And you never investigated it?'

'What was the point? They thought Hamill had done it. They couldnae charge him again. He'd got off wi it.'

'You dinnae really believe Hamill did it?'

Macrae walked on, scuffing his boot on the pavement. 'No. I never did. The guy's harmless. That's why ...' He paused for a moment as though deciding whether or not to continue. He blinked slowly. 'That's why I kept ain of the letters. I was told to put them in the files, but I kept one. I was never happy the case wasnae re-opened either, I'll be honest wi you. Thought I'd hang on to that, just in case.'

'Could I see it?'

'I can bring it round the night, if you like.'

'Grand. Seven?'

'Seven.'

*

Richard Hamill and Annie were sitting on the settee when George Macrae arrived at quarter past seven, breathless and red-faced.

'D'you run all the way?' said Bob.

'Sorry I'm late. Mam made me clean out the pantry.' He followed Bob into the living room and gave a start when he saw Richard, but he smiled and said hello. 'I've the letter here,' he said, handing a crumpled envelope to Bob. Bob studied the postmark. Edinburgh, July 1929. More than six years before the murder. He unfolded the letter. The writing was neat and regular, full of loops and whorls. '"Your sins will be found out. I will make sure of that. When the time is right the world will hear of your guilt."' He looked at the others. 'Strong stuff.'

'I wonder why he never carried out the threat,' said Annie.

Bob studied the handwriting. He showed it to Annie. 'I'd say that was a woman's writing, wouldn't you?' Annie nodded her agreement. 'Maybe she didnae have as much evidence as she was lettin on?'

'Or she was tryin to smoke him out?' said Annie.

'Aye, could be.' He turned to Macrae. 'I cannae believe the polis never bothered investigatin this?'

Macrae shook his head. 'Though, in all fairness, what would there be to investigate? The letters are so old they'd be useless. Nae fingerprints or nothin by now.'

'Well,' said Annie, 'at the very least, it suggests for the first time an actual motive for the murder.'

'Aye,' said Bob, 'that's always bothered me. Why would anyone kill an old hermit who'd barely set foot out of doors in donkeys' years?'

Annie turned to Richard. 'Was he always reclusive like that?'

Richard thought for a moment. 'No, I don't think so. I seem to remember, when I was a boy, he used to come round the house to see my father. And obviously he worked in Bell's with dad.'

Bob nodded as though that made sense. 'They said, in court, your dad and Smithson had an argument. What was it about?'

'I don't know. I was only young. It was just grown-ups squabbling.'

'Can you remember when it was?'

'Fifteen years? A couple of years after the War, maybe.'

'Was it around the same time Smithson became a hermit?'

Richard stopped still. The others watched him. 'It could have been,' he said. 'But you don't think my father was involved in anything, do you?'

'I don't know what I think yet.'

'Well, even if dad was involved in something, it wasn't him who killed Smithson. He's been dead five years.'

'When did the threatening letters stop?' Annie asked George.

Macrae nodded, following Annie's train of thought.

183

'About five years,' he confirmed.

'But it's a woman's handwriting,' said Richard.

'Maybe,' said George.

'It's certainly not my dad's handwriting. That was almost unreadable.'

'Anyway,' said Bob, 'we need to know more about what caused the argument. Are there any of their old workmates still around?'

'Fred Hammond and Archie McCarthy. They both drink in the Burns' Bar in County Place most days.'

'Right, I'll pay them a visit the morn.'

'Good luck with that.'

'Are there any friends of your mother still around?' Annie asked. Richard shrugged. 'I'm just thinking, if something happened between the menfolk, the women would likely know what it was aboot, too.'

'Beryl Black, I suppose. Lives in Bank Street.'

'I'll go and see her tomorrow.'

'See and leave yourself plenty time then.'

'She likes a blether?'

'Something like that.'

'Grand,' said Bob, 'we've got somethin to be gettin on with. The main thing is to figure out why Smithson was killed. What was the motive?'

# Wednesday 2nd December

## A Day of Detectives

As he ate a slice of toast, an article in that morning's *Courier* attracted Bob's attention. The report was brief, only a single paragraph, covering a speech given by the Bishop of Bradford the day before on the subject of the new King Edward VIII. "The King holds an avowedly representative position. His personal views and opinions are his own, and as an individual, he has the right of us all to be keeper of his own private conscience. But in his public capacity at his Coronation he stands for the British people's idea of Kingship. It has for long centuries been, and I hope still is, an essential part of that idea, that the King needs the grace of God for his office." The language was opaque, but Bob sensed that something important was being said here. He recalled the dinner party at the Conoboys' in May and Lord Kellett's prediction: "If we can get to Christmas without all hell breaking loose, we'll be lucky." And what had he said about the King?: "a feckless neer-do-well". Now the Bishop of Bradford seemed to be suggesting something similar. Elsewhere, news around the world was grim. The old ways were unravelling. Politicians were proving, time and again, not to be up to the task. Bob had no affection for the monarchy, but he wondered, if hell really was about to break loose, what might emerge in its place. The ugly suspicion could not be ignored that, whatever it was, it might be wearing a black shirt.

*

'Well then, if it isn't Bob Kelty.'

'Afternoon, Pete. How's business?'

Pete Arnold gestured towards a largely empty Burns' Bar as the former police constable approached. The lad was no use when trouble broke out, as it generally did on Friday nights, but he was a canny soul. It was impossible not to like him. 'Business would be just grand,' he said, 'if folks would spend a bit of money now and then.' He nodded towards two men at the rear of the pub, playing dominoes with a baffling intensity, cigarettes hanging from their mouths. Half-drunk halves of heavy sat in front of each of them. 'Hour and twenty minutes they've been drinkin those.'

'It might be them I'm here to see. Is that Fred Hammond and Archie McCarthy?'

'It is indeed. You're no after speakin to them, are you?'

'Aye.'

'Good luck wi that.'

'You're no the first to say that. What do they drink?'

'Are you payin?'

'Aye.'

'In that case, it'll be a half and a wee half.' Bob noted the lack of whisky glasses on the men's table but nodded. 'Aye fine, and a pint of mild for me.'

'Drinkin durin the day?'

'Special occasion.' Still, he felt the ghost of Gran sitting on his shoulder, disapproving.

'May I join you, gents?' he said as he sallied across the room with a quivering tray of drinks. The men watched him warily, conflicted. A free drink was a free drink, but what did this wee laddie want? Bob placed a half pint and a glass of whisky in front of each man and pulled up a chair.

186

'Cheers,' he said. Fred Hammond poured his whisky into the beer and drank half of it and grimaced. Archie McCarthy took a sip of whisky.

'Doms?' said Fred, gesturing at the dominoes on the table.

'Aye,' said Bob, hoping he could remember the rules. Dominoes was something else Gran hadn't approved of. Games bred idleness. Idleness led to wantonness. Everything, for Gran, could be turned into a one-way journey to perdition.

'Tanner pot,' said Fred.

Bob looked at the table and saw no pot. 'Where's yours?'

'We've paid already.'

Bob fished a sixpence from his pocket and placed it on the table. Archie turned the domino tiles face down and shuffled them expansively. Everyone could tell he never relinquished hold of the double six. When he had finished, Fred leaned over and pressed his finger on the domino and, covering his actions with his other hand, shuffled its position again.

'You missed a bit,' he said.

'So, what is it you're after?' said Archie, scowling at Fred and pulling six dominoes into a huge fist and studying them. Bob and Fred selected their tiles.

'Were you no a bobby?' said Fred.

'Aye.'

'Thought so. You were useless.'

'I was, aye.'

'So where are you bein useless now?'

'Alexander's.'

'Ah, that'll be why my bus is aye late.'

'Nae doobt. You were friends o Hugh Smithson, were you no? And Henry Hamill?'

'I wouldnae say friends. Shuggy Smithson was a right cunt.'

'Was he buggery,' said Archie. 'Nothin wrong wi the man. Henry Hamill, though, he could be a right shite.'

'How?'

'Stand-offish, ken? Thought a lot o himself. Too good for the likes o us.'

'Keech, man,' said Fred. 'Henry Hamill was salt of the earth. Christ, the man was a member of the Communist Party.'

'And what kind of recommendation is that? Bloody Communist Party? Dinnae bring politics intae this, you clapped-oot socialist nyaff. You got a thick lug the last time you tried it, mind?'

'And you baith got barred for a week,' shouted Pete Arnold from the bar.

Fred ignored him. 'Are you goin to play?' he said to Archie, 'or are you keepin they doms as a memento?'

Bob tried to keep the conversation on track. 'They used to be good friends, aye? Hamill and Smithson?'

'Thick as thieves,' said Archie.

'Thieves is right,' said Fred. 'They had a scam goin. Helped themselves to a few cases of whisky when they were on late shift thigither. I'm bloody sure o it.'

'You've nae proof of thon. That's slander.'

'You cannae slander the deid.'

'Aye, you can. It's just they cannae dae onythin aboot it.'

Fred rolled his eyes. 'Just play, will you?'

'Chappin.'

'Christ, could you no have said that five minutes ago? There's only an hour till closin time. I'd like to get the game finished ... '

'Wait till you're chappin. You could mak yersel a cup of tea in the time it takes you to admit it.' He paused. 'And drink it.'

'And when was the last time you drank onythin that wasnae alcoholic?'

'Says the chairman of the Temperance Society.'

Fred turned to Bob. 'Come on, son, it's your turn. Or are

you as slow on the uptake as him?'

Bob laid down a five:three. Fred stared at it incredulously.

'What in the name of Christ did you play that for?'

'What?' Bob looked at his hand of dominoes. It was the only tile he could have played.

'Bloody kids. Nae idea.'

'Too busy wenchin at the picters to learn how to play properly,' said Archie.

'I heard they had a fallin out?'

'Who?' said Fred.

'Smithson and Hamill.'

'Aye. Years ago.'

'It wasnae years ago,' said Archie.

'It bloody was. Would have been no long after the War.'

'Was it buggery. Couldnae have been more than five, six year.'

'Listen tae the auld fool. Five, six year? When did you retire?'

'1929.'

'Seven year ago. So how could it be five, six year? Answer me that, arsehole.'

'Have you any idea what it was aboot?' said Bob.

'What?' said Fred.

Bob was certain the man was playing with him, but he tried to remain cool. 'The fallin oot.'

'How the hell should I know? Was I there?'

'No, but you're aye stickin your bloody nose in where it isnae wanted,' said Archie.

'I was the gaffer. I was paid to ken what was goin on.'

'You were not the bloody gaffer. Jumped-up wee storeman, that's all you were.'

'I was the gaffer.' He paused. 'When the gaffer was aff.'

'And when Edward's shaggin his Yank I'm the King o England.'

'Now,' shouted Pete from the bar. 'Nane of that talk in

here. Even if it is true.'

'So, the fallin oot. You've nae idea what it was aboot?'

'Stop askin questions and play.'

Bob laid a one:one on the table. Fred stared at him witheringly. 'What?' said Bob.

'You might look glaikit, but by Christ there's depths of stupidity in you that's never been plumbed.'

'Was it no aboot the same time Smithson's wife left him?' said Archie.

'What?' said Fred and Bob in unison.

'The fallin oot.'

'Aye, it could have been, now you say. Mind, accordin to you, that was probably only six month ago.'

'Aboot 1919, 20.'

'Just efter the War. Which is what I said all along. Welcome to the party.'

'D'you think there was a connection?' Bob asked.

'How should I ken?'

'Were they haein an affair?'

'Who, Hamill and Smithson?'

'Hamill and Smithson's wife.'

'I wouldnae hae thought so.'

'How?'

'Did you ever see her?'

'No.'

'Absolute minger. Christ, she was ugly. One look could turn milk intae butter.'

'She was nothin of the sort,' said Archie.

'"Face like Kaiser Bill's arse", you used to say aboot her.'

'That was you.'

'I never said that.'

'No, it was you had a face like Kaiser Bill's arse. Any time you had to part wi some money.'

'Funny you should say that. Is it no your round?'

'The puppy'll buy us another. Won't you, lad? If it's

information you're efter.' He nodded at the table. 'Your turn.' Bob added a one:three.

'Christ, would you look at that!'

'Pete,' shouted Archie, 'Same again. Just a half for the laddie, though. Looks like he cannae handle the drink. Look at the colour o him. He'll be needin put tae his bed after this.'

Fred pocketed the sixpence Bob had put on the table. 'If you want another game, you'll have to put up another tanner,' he said.

'We havenae finished this ain yet.'

'We have. You just dinnae ken it yet.'

Bob stared at his remaining doms. He hoped Annie was having more luck.

'If you think I'm carryin these drinks over there, you've got another think comin,' said Pete. 'I'm a barman, no a fuckin waitress.' Bob sighed and went to the bar.

*

The house on the end of Rose Lane, next to the corner shop on Longcauseway, was dingy and run-down, window frames rotting, roof bowed, door and windows filthy. Annie took a moment to compose herself before rapping the door knocker.

'Mrs Black?'

'Aye?' The old woman peered suspiciously from behind her front door.

'My name's Annie Maybury. I'm ... '

'Betsy Maybury's lassie? Feus Road?'

'Aye.'

'Och, come away in, hen. Heavens, I mind when you were a wee bairn. D'you remember that time you shat yoursel at the Sunday School picnic on the North Inch? Your mother was black-affronted.'

Annie had no memory of this and was certain no such event had occurred, but she smiled politely and followed the woman into a sparse, freezing living room. A coal fire was almost out, a single plume of smoke, more a thread, rising from it.

'I've coal in the yard,' Mrs Black said, 'but I cannae lift it. No wi my sair arm.' She eased herself into a threadbare armchair.

'Would you like me to fetch you some?'

'Would you, hen? That'd be awfae kind o you. It's ben the yard. When you're done, I dinnae suppose you'd mind choppin me an ingin and peelin some tatties as well? My rheumatics is playing up the day. It's the damp.'

Annie hesitated. 'Aye,' she said. 'The rheumatics is a terrible business, I mind my gran gettin it.'

'You've nae idea, lassie.'

Annie gathered a bucket of coal from the bunker in the yard and left it on the hearth. 'Would you like me to put some on the fire for you?'

'No, no, no the noo. It's fine as it is.'

Annie shivered as she retreated to the kitchen to chop the onion and peel some potatoes.

'Make sure and chop the tatties nice and wee, so they bile better. I can't abide a firm tattie.'

When she was done, Annie asked if Mrs Black would like a cup of tea.

'Oh, that would be grand, hen, if it's nae trouble.'

'None at all.' She went back to the kitchen and found the tea caddy and boiled some water on the range. She searched the cupboards but could find only one cup, bone china, much stained and lightly chipped.

'Have you another cup?' she shouted through the wall.

'No, I just have the one.'

'Right.' She filled the teapot and carried it and the single cup through to Mrs Black and sat opposite and watched as the old woman poured her tea, sat back and sipped it.

'That's hot.'

*Which is more than I am,* thought Annie, shivering in her

swagger coat. 'I wanted to ask you about Hugh Smithson,' she said.

'He's deid.'

'Aye, I ken. Did you ken him? When he worked at Bell's?'

'Aye, he made my Jim's life a misery, jumped-up little arsehole.'

'He was a bit of a loner, was he no? Never left the hoose. Was he aye like that?'

'Nae idea.'

'And he was friends wi Henry Hamill. Did you ken him?'

'Stuck-up shite. Thought he was better than aabody else.'

'Did they get on well? Hamill and Smithson.'

'I couldnae tell you, hen.' She sipped her tea and stared at it suspiciously. 'How much tea did you put in the pot?'

'Two teaspoons.'

'Hell, lassie, d'you think I'm made o money?'

'Sorry.' Annie sighed. This wasn't what she'd anticipated at all. Last night, lying in bed, she'd gone through this over and over again, what she was going to say, what Mrs Black might say. She had crafted the conversation like one of her mother's detective novels, Annie slowly revealing the truth.

'But I tell you who might ken.'

'Aye?' Annie's heart lurched with sudden anticipation. Maybe it would work out after all.

'Gladys Comer.'

'Who's she?'

'She was best friends wi Maisie Smithson. Aye thigither, that pair.' She sniffed.

'Where does she live?'

'Spends maist of her time in St John's Kirk. Unpaid skivvy for the meenister. Right enough, she's plenty guilty secrets she needs to atone for. She'll need all the help she can get, that one, come judgement day. You'll find her there.'

'Thank you.' Annie made to rise.

'Afore you go, lassie. The blankets on my bed are in a

193

richt fankle. And wi my back ...'

'Aye, of course. Leave it to me.'

'You're a credit to your mither. I'll mind and tell her that next time I see her.'

*

'Mrs Comer?'

'Miss.'

'Sorry.'

'Who are you?'

'My name's Annie Maybury. Mrs Black gave me your name.'

'Beryl Black? No doubt some idle tittle-tattle as well.'

'No really, no.'

'Well, I'm busy, so if you have something to ask, ask, but I'll carry on wi my work.' She carried a filthy duster and swept desultorily at the chairs in the church hall. Annie saw another duster on the side table beside a brass collection plate and took it and started wiping the chairs at the opposite end of the row from Miss Comer. Gladys Comer saw what she was doing but said nothing.

'You were a friend of Maisie Smithson?'

'What's Beryl Black been sayin aboot me now?'

'Nothin. Just that you were friends.'

'Aye. What of it?'

'It's Hugh Smithson I'm interested in. When he was murdered, he was a recluse. Never left the house. Was he aye like that?'

'Och, no. Quite the opposite. Always gaddin aboot. He used to do a bit o poachin. Oot Callerfountain way. And he was a one for the cuddies. Aye in the bookmakers, wastin his money. Maisie never saw him. No that she was complainin, she liked it that way.'

'So, what happened? What made him become a recluse?'

Gladys kept wiping the chairs in an exaggerated fashion.

She remained silent. Finally, she spoke, her back to Annie. 'I think it was around the time Maisie ran away.'

'I heard she'd done a bunk.'

'Aye. Made off one Friday, never came back.'

'And that's what turned Hugh into a recluse?'

'I've nae idea. I never spoke to the man aboot it. But it's an awfae coincidence, is it no?'

'I suppose it is, aye. D'you ken why she ran away frae him?'

Gladys Comer sat heavily on the chair she had just dusted. She gripped her left thumb tightly in her right hand. 'She didnae run away frae him.'

'Aye she did. You've just said ... '

'No, I didnae. I said she ran away. I didnae say she ran away frae him.'

'So, who did she run away from?'

She turned and faced Annie. 'Me,' she said. She registered the shock on Annie's face and laughed. 'You werenae expectin that, were you?'

'No ... Sorry, I don't understand.'

'Maisie and me ... One time we ... More than one ...'

'What?'

Gladys took out a cigarette and lit it. 'Maisie, she couldnae deal with the shame o it. Two women, together. It's not natural. It's obscene.'

Annie knew her face and neck had flushed with embarrassment. 'You mean you two were ...?'

'Aye. I asked her to leave him. Come and live wi me. She couldnae. It wasnae that useless lump she ran away from. It was me.'

'D'you know where she went?'

'No. I've never seen her again.'

'Did you ever try to find out?'

'No.'

'Could I? If I wanted to find her? Is there any way?'

'What are you so interested in Hugh Smithson's murder for? He's no a loss to anyone.'

'I'm a friend of Richard Hamill. He's the man who was tried for Mr Smithson's murder.' Gladys nodded. 'He was acquitted, but there's still folk who think he did it. No smoke without fire, ken? Mud sticks. And so, there's still all this gossip aboot Richard ...'

'Poor laddie. People talk, all right. I ken all aboot that. Talk, talk, talk. It's poisonous, what these people do.'

'So, I just want to set the record straight. Find out what really happened. Find the person who did kill Hugh Smithson. Prove it wasnae Richard.'

'Well.' Gladys stood up. 'I dinnae care a jot what happened to that man. He deserved everythin he got. But I mind Richard Hamill. He was a strange laddie, but he was a gentle sowel. Better than his faither. I dinnae like to think of him bein the subject of tittle-tattle like me. Aye, well, there was another friend around that time. There was the three o us. Me, Maisie and Leslie Redford. We were aye thigether. If Maisie kept in touch wi anyone when she ran away it'd be Leslie.'

'Is she still around?'

'No, not for years.'

'D'you ken whaur she went?'

'No. But I ken whaur she lived afore. She was frae Aiberdeen. I can even mind the address.'

'You can?'

'Sixty-nine Leslie Road. I mind laughin that her first name and street name were the same. And I mind sixty-nine because – well, sixty-nine, ken?'

Annie had no idea what the significance of sixty-nine might be. She nodded uncertainly.

Gladys Comer looked at Annie's left hand and saw no wedding ring. 'That's maybe no something you're acquainted wi yet, hen. You'll like it when you get there. Trust me.'

'Aye, thanks.'

'I imagine Leslie's parents'll be long deid. But she had a brother. Malcolm. Malcolm Redford.'

*

Bob placed the teapot on a mat on the side-table in the living room. He sat next to Annie. 'Well,' he said, 'we're no Hercule Poirot and Miss Marple.' They laughed as they shared their respective experiences, tried to establish who had suffered the greater indignity.

'You should have seen that bed,' Annie said. 'It hadnae been made in weeks, I'm sure of it. It took me twenty minutes to get it sorted.'

'If I ever play doms with that pair again, I'll be bankrupt.'

They agreed that nothing of much use came from the conversation with Pete and Archie, but both were intrigued by Leslie Redford.

'Bertie Hammond telt me the key to the murder has to be in the past,' said Bob. 'It must, because nothin happened in the present.'

'We need to find Leslie.'

'We do. The mcrn, we're goin to Aiberdeen. See if we can find the brother.'

'What about your work?'

'I finish on Friday anyway. There's nothin much left to do.'

'Will we tak the bus?'

'God no, that would tak all day. We'd have to bide overnight.'

'Can we afford a train?'

'We'll manage.'

'Are you sure?'

'This is important.'

'D'you really think we can find Leslie?'

'Probably not. But we can at least try.' He poured the

tea and switched on the wireless. '*Para Handy*'s on in five minutes,' he said.

'Grand. I love *Para Handy*.'

'Me too. Sunny Jim's the only man more feckless than me.'

Annie laughed. 'He's no that bad,' she teased.

'Watch it, madam, or I'll no take you to Aiberdeen with me.'

'You wouldnae dare, Bob Kelty.'

'No, I wouldnae.'

# Thursday 3<sup>rd</sup> December

## A Day of Visitations

The rhythm of the wheels on the tracks during the two-and-a-half-hour train journey to Aberdeen was hypnotic for both Bob and Annie, neither of whom had ever been on a train before. In early December, the service wasn't busy, and they had the second-class carriage to themselves. They sat either side of the window and watched the Scottish countryside pass by, Dundee, Broughty Ferry, Arbroath, Montrose. By the time they reached Stonehaven, the railway line was skirting the coast, high above the water, and for both of them this, too, was their first view of the sea.

'Gosh, it's wild,' said Annie. Waves were cascading onto the shore in formation, white foam and agitation. Even from this distance, without sound, the power of the elements was palpable.

'I dinnae think I could live by the sea,' said Bob. 'It's wonderful, right enough, but I'm no sure I could ever relax.'

'Aye, gie me the hills any day.'

At Aberdeen, they exited the railway station into a crisp and cold day, Bob clutching a plan of the city, Annie looking round in wonderment. Ahead of them was the steepest and longest stairway either of them had ever seen, the Back Wynd Steps stretching high into the distance.

'My,' said Annie, 'I'm glad we don't have to go up those.'

Bob checked his plan. 'Sorry,' he said, grinning. 'We do. Union Street's up there. That's where we're headed.' He took her hand and they made the fifty feet ascent slowly, both gripping the rail tightly, neither daring to turn and look back. At the top, Union Street was thronged, trams and cars and even horses pulling carts on the wide thoroughfare, the pavements bustling with women in headscarves and men in bunnets.

'Good grief,' said Bob, looking at the width of Union Street, 'you could fit three Perth High Streets side-by-side on this.' To their left, the road stretched in a straight line uphill. To their right it dropped to what looked like a large square in the distance. Bright sunshine glinted on the granite stonework of the austere buildings lining the road. The noise of human activity was almost overwhelming. Opposite was a large graveyard, clearly old but in good condition. This juxtaposition in the centre of the city of the living and the dead, of commerce and remembrance, struck Bob as odd.

'This way,' he said, heading downhill. They turned on to George Street and, after about five minutes, the road began to rise steeply and they climbed free of the hustle of the city. The fine granite facades of the city centre were replaced by cheaper sandstone, by rows of tenements and town houses, and the road narrowed until the buildings on either side, dark and tall, seemed to press in on them. They reached a bridge, below which ran a railway line. On the wall opposite them, in white paint, was written: "Down with the American harlot".

'What does that mean?' asked Annie.

'The rumours aboot the King, I imagine.' The morning paper had contained a clarification from the Bishop of Bradford, saying he had not intended his speech to be interpreted as a rebuke to the King, and when he wrote it he was unaware of the rumours surrounding the King's private life. But the consequence of this was that those rumours were now circulating freely, rumours that the King had proclaimed his love for an American divorcée. Even Fred and Archie had been talking about it yesterday in Burns' Bar.

This was the scandal Lord Kellett had mentioned in May and, as he predicted, it seemed that it was about to explode.

'However did they manage to write that?' Annie asked.

Bob pondered. The writing was far enough down the wall to make it impossible to have been written from above, but below was a drop of around twenty feet to the railway line. 'It must have been a feat, right enough,' he said.

They walked on, the road becoming steeper, and Annie began to slow. 'Are we nearly there yet?' she asked.

'It didnae look that far on this plan I've got,' Bob said, waving his map. 'I think they've missed some streets oot.' He felt his brow flush as he concluded they might be walking in the wrong direction but, just as he was about to stop to re-assess, he saw in the near distance a split-the-winds, the Northern Hotel occupying the space between the Great Northern Road and Clifton Road. He recognised it from the map.

'Nearly there,' he said. Ten minutes later they arrived at Leslie Road and found number sixty-nine on the corner of the Inverness Road. It was a grand looking house, large and spacious, better than most they had passed on the way up George Street. Bob swung open a painted, wooden gate and walked up a short path to a clean, white front door. An expansive bay window stood to the right. The square front garden was laid to lawn and surrounded by narrow flower beds. Roses, winter-skeletal, predominated.

The man who answered the door was perhaps in his fifties, bald and plump, wearing a gaudily-patterned cardigan.

'Mr Redford?' The man nodded. 'My name's Bob Kelty. This is Annie Maybury. I wonder, sir, if we could talk with you for a few moments? About your sister.'

'Leslie? What about her? Is she okay?'

'I was hopin you might tell us. We're tryin to get in touch with her.' Bob tried to decipher the expression that overtook Mr Redford's face. Concern? Fear? Hope? The older man gave a lop-sided smile and Bob wondered if perhaps he had had some kind of stroke.

'You'd better come in.' He retreated into the house, limping heavily, and Bob and Annie followed.

They were led into a large, high-ceilinged living room overlooking the street. A coal fire was raging, so hot nobody could sit near it. Malcolm Redford brought tea and biscuits and laid them on a table against the back wall. Bob and Annie balanced their cups and saucers on their thighs and made small talk for a few minutes.

'Anyway,' said Mr Redford, 'what is it you'd like to know?'

Bob explained the story of Smithson's murder, Richard's arrest, the trial, his subsequent travails.

'What does any of this have to do with Leslie?'

'Maybe nothin. She left Perth years before any of this happened, but, to be honest, we've nothin else to go on. We've no idea why Mr Smithson was murdered. Especially so viciously. It doesn't make sense. The man was a hermit, never left the hoose. How could he have made enemies?'

'That's why we started to look further back,' said Annie. 'He wasn't always reclusive, so maybe if we could find what caused it, we could shed some light on the murder.'

'And at the time it happened,' continued Bob, 'Leslie was a close friend of Mr Smithson's wife.'

'You're not suggesting Leslie's mixed up in the murder?'

'No. As I say, she hasn't been in Perth in years, as far as I'm aware. But what was really strange was that Mrs Smithson did a bunk and left her husband. And about the same time, so it seems, Leslie left as well.'

'Did they leave together?'

'We've no idea.' Bob thought it best not to mention Gladys Comer's comments about their private liaisons. There was no proof, and what did it matter anyway?

'Leslie wouldn't harm a fly. She was too trusting of

people. She was a bit … you know? Soft? She couldn't judge people, took everyone at face value. Some people took advantage. So, if there was something going on, something related to this man or his wife, she could easily have got herself involved without realising it.'

'D'you have any idea where she is? Have you heard from her?'

'I used to get a letter once a year. But then they stopped.'

'When?'

He shrugged. 'About six years ago.'

'You dinnae ken why they stopped?'

'No.'

'Did she say where she was?'

'Not really. I think she's in England, maybe the Lake District. She talked about lakes in her letters. The postmarks were usually smudged but you could sometimes make out Carlisle.'

'And she never said why she left Perth?'

'No.'

'Are your parents still alive?' asked Annie.

'No. Dad died in twenty-four. Mum two years ago in March.'

'Did Leslie no come to the funerals?'

'She won't even know they're dead. I'd no way of getting in touch with her.'

'I'm sorry. That must have been hard.'

'I just miss her.'

'Do you have any idea how we might track her?'

'None. Sorry. If I did, I'd have done it myself years ago.'

'Of course.' Bob and Annie exchanged glances. They felt a shared disappointment, a sense they were running out of ideas. Malcolm Redford was a lovely gentleman, but it was obvious he was as clueless about the whereabouts of his sister as they were.

'Will you tell me if you find anything?' he said. He stared

at them imploringly. 'Good or bad. I want to know.'

*

On their way back to the railway station, they passed a
Lipton's Tea Rooms on Union Street. Its lights gleamed in
the dullness of the afternoon like a beacon for the restive.

'Shall we have some tea and a scone?' said Bob.

'Have we time?'

'Aye. The train's no for an hour.'

'Can we afford it?'

Bob was less sure of that. The train tickets had left a dent
in the money he had set aside for doing up Cloudland. He
was trying to save as much of Bella Conoboy's grant as he
could for the inevitable quiet days ahead before he could
build a clientèle. 'Think of it as research,' he said. 'See if I
can get some tips for the café.'

They ordered a pot of tea and two scones and looked
around the tearoom. The furniture and fittings were all oak
and the floor was a chequerboard of black and light brown.
Tiling and marble covered the walls. Bob contrasted the
opulence with what he could afford. He was hoping to find
a few nearly matching tables and chairs in Neil's salerooms.
This was a different class from anything he could procure.
The grand vision he had of Cloudland began to feel a little
less grand.

Their scones arrived and Annie split hers and spread it
with butter. 'We didnae really learn anythin,' she said.

'No really. I'm no sure where to go from here.'

'I do. We'll ask Mrs Conoboy when we get back. She'll
know.' Bob smiled in agreement. Bella Conoboy always
knew. He spread marmalade on his scone and raised it to his
mouth. A middle-aged couple settled themselves at the table
next to Bob and Annie. The man, bald beneath his flat cap,
laid a copy of the *Press and Journal* on the table.

'The chickens are comin hame to roost,' he said.

'Aye,' said the woman, presumably the man's wife. 'The harlot's got him twisted around her little finger.'

'Excuse me,' said Bob, 'is that the King you're talkin aboot?'

The man eyed Bob cautiously, weighing up whether he might be a monarchist looking for an argument. He saw nothing that frightened him. 'Aye,' he said.

'There's rumours aboot him and an American? A married woman?'

'And divorced as well.'

'They're no just rumours,' said the woman. 'We've kent aboot it in Aiberdeen since September. The King was meant to open the new Infirmary, like, but he cried off at the last minute so he could meet his Yankee floozy.'

'A bloody insult,' said the man.

'A bloody disgrace,' said the woman.

'We'll be well rid of him.'

'You think he'll have to go?' said Bob.

'Fit dae you think? An American divorcée for our Queen. I dinnae think so.'

*

A wall of books framed Bella Conoboy in her favourite chair, novels and poetry and literary criticism. Victor, smoking a cigarette, sat upright in a matching armchair, newspaper folded over at the crossword page. He was a man comfortable with his lot. Bob smiled at Annie, wondered whether one day they, too, might be sitting in such domestic bliss.

'How's the work on the cafeteria coming on?' Bella asked.

'Slowly at the moment. But I've handed in my notice. I finish tomorrow, so that'll give me time to work on it. I'm aiming to get opened week after next.'

'Heavens. That's optimistic.'

'Aye, it is, but the sooner I'm open, the sooner I start making some money. I'm havin Gran's piano transported tomorrow. And there's a sale comin up at Neil's auctioneers in Crieff. I'm hoping to pick up some furniture.'

Bella smiled at his earnest expression. 'Play us something.' She inclined her head towards the baby grand piano. 'One of your ragtime tunes, perhaps?'

Bob crossed to the piano and raised the lid and flexed his fingers to stop them shaking. 'This is something I've been practicing,' he said. '*St Louis Blues.*'

'WC Handy?' said Bella.

'Aye, maybe, but I learned it from Fats Waller.' He spread his fingers on the keys and started to play, a vibrant and energetic piece, full of longing and loneliness but oddly uplifting, something to do with the stridency of the rhythm. When he finished, Bella and Victor clapped. Annie smiled.

'Do you sing it as well?' Bella asked.

'I didn't know it had words.'

'Oh yes, it's a marvellous song.' She asked him to stand and lifted the lid of the piano seat. Inside was a stack of gramophone records and she flicked through them until she found the one she wanted. 'This is Bessie Smith,' she said as she wound the gramophone and carefully placed the needle on the record. Immediately, the most magnificent voice filled the room, deep and resonant, almost untamed, yet utterly compelling. Bob listened in silence.

'That was amazing,' he said when it was finished. 'I've been playing it all wrong.'

'No. What you do is excellent. But there's more than one way to play a song.' She carefully returned the record to its sleeve and replaced it in the piano chair. Victor picked up the day's *Courier* and turned to Bob.

'Did you read Mr Eden's comments yesterday? "There's no proof there's a triple alliance".'

Bob shook his head in exasperation. 'I always thought

he was the sensible one, but I just dinnae think any of these politicians understand what's going on. Of course there's no proof there's a triple alliance. They're hardly going to admit it, are they? But can you seriously trust Germany, Italy or Japan? It's naive. And that wasn't all. He also said there's a good chance of peace in Spain. I mean to say ... '

'I know,' said Victor.

'The Germans have just landed 600 soldiers at Cadiz. What does Eden think they're there for? It's as though he's just saying what he thinks people want to hear.'

'A politician's trick,' said Bella, 'shielding us from bad news.'

'Exactly. But the bad news is there, and we're going to have to deal with it some time. Germany's just made the Hitler Youth compulsory. He's created a child army, for goodness sake. Doesn't that frighten you?'

He carried on without waiting for a reply, agitation coursing through him. 'And Roosevelt's no interested. He's too busy courting the South Americans. Says America won't join the League of Nations. It was them who created it in the first place, and they won't even join their own organisation. What's the point of a League of Nations if the most important nation in the world isnae part of it? America's the only country who could stand up to Germany.'

'The trouble with Britain,' said Victor, 'is that our politics is so divided. Last year's election was a disaster. Labour almost wiped out. The Liberals fatally split. There's no proper opposition to right wing views, and the right wing are either appeasers like Eden or warmongers like Churchill. Where's the statesmen? Where's the voice of reason?'

'And extremists are getting a foothold,' said Bella. 'Fascists and communists, one as bad as the other.'

'I'll admit,' said Bob, 'I used to think Russia might be the answer. Communism. Total revolution. But it's pie in the sky, that's what I've come to realise. Look at what they've just done in Russia. They've brought in this new constitution. They say it gives complete freedom of thought, freedom of speech, freedom to write what you want, say what you want, vote for who you want. But only if it's *communist* opinion. No other parties are allowed because they would bring back capitalism. So, you can think what you want, vote how you want, say what you want, as long as it's communist. They've used the banner of free speech to completely obliterate free speech. It's obscene.'

Annie was smiling at him. 'Sorry,' he said. 'I get a bit worked up sometimes.'

'I like it,' she replied. 'I like that you have convictions. My dad never did. Just wanted a quiet life. He would never have got involved in Richard Hamill's case. Taken us to Aiberdeen on a hunch.'

'Aye, well, I'm thinkin maybe we've hit a dead end on that. I don't know what to do next.' He looked at Bella.

'I do,' she said. 'You're struggling with the "why" question and there's nowhere to go with that at present. But there's still the "how" question. How did he get in?'

'And out.'

'Exactly.'

'So you need to work on that next. I believe Mr Hamill insists there was only one key for each door. I'm not doubting him, but if it's true, it's impossible to see how the killer got in and out. So that's what you need to investigate.'

'How?'

'That bit's up to you.'

## *Friday 4th December*

### *A Day of Evidence*

Annie waited in Carcary's while Mr Carcary dealt with Mrs Moon from Aberdalgie House and Billy, the apprentice lad, attended to Miss Greensmith. The conversations yesterday replayed in her head, poor Mr Redford fretting about his sister, probably blaming himself for her walking away from her family. She was convinced the death of Hugh Smithson was tied up with whatever happened all those years before. What motive could there be otherwise, with Smithson never leaving his house to make potential enemies?

'Miss Maybury,' said Mr Carcary, 'a pleasure to see you, as always.'

'Likewise, Mr Carcary. And isn't it nice to have a break from rain and snow? May I have a pound of stewing steak, a pound of mince, two pounds of potatoes, half a dozen carrots, a turnip and a packet of loose tea, please?'

'Of course.' He asked after the Conoboys, and then Bob, and he was delighted to hear news of the impending opening of the café in Crieff. 'I'll be sure to drop by some time.'

'That would be wonderful. He'd like that. I wonder, could you recommend a good locksmith?'

'In Crieff?'

'No, not for Bob.'

'Are you having a problem?'

'No, I'm just lookin into it.'

'There's Adam Watters in South Street.'

'Has he been established a long time?'

'No, only a couple of years. Young chap. Pleasant though. I knew his faither.'

'I'm sure. But I'd prefer a longer established firm.'

'Archie Duncan, then. St Paul's Square. Been here longer than I have.'

Annie smiled. 'That sounds grand. Is Mr Duncan among the more economically priced companies in town?' She tilted her head. 'Truth to tell, it would be important to me that they offered *very* good value for money.' Or, at least, that presumably would have been important to the skinflint Hugh Smithson.

'Quite right, too. You'll get a fair price from Archie Duncan.'

Annie arranged for the lad to deliver the messages that afternoon and said good morning. St Paul's Square was round the corner, and she walked briskly, aware of the admiring looks of sundry young – and not so young – men as she passed. The clock of St Paul's Kirk struck the hour just as she passed beneath, and she shrieked with surprise.

'Aye,' said an old man, winking at her, 'someone should put a sock in they bells, eh?' Annie laughed politely. 'Ain of the few advantages of gettin old, hen, is that sudden noise doesnae gie you such a fleg cause you can barely hear it.' He cackled, revealing a largely toothless mouth, and walked on.

Annie took a breath as she entered Archie Duncan's shop. It was narrow and cramped, the walls filled with plain cardboard boxes of assorted sizes, all adorned with neat handwriting. The place smelled like an ironmonger's, that sweet smell of oil and dust and polished metal. Behind a plain wooden counter stood a man in brown overalls. He was probably about sixty, with a startling head of hair, pure white and seemingly exploding from his skull. She returned his cheery greeting.

'I was wonderin whether you remember ever doin locks for a house in Barossa Street? It was a long time ago ... '

'Smithson's hoose?'

Annie was startled by the speed of his response. 'Aye,' she said.

'D'ye ken, I've been waitin months for someone to come and ask me aboot that, ever since he was done in. Wasnae expectin it tae be a lassie, right enough.'

'Why?' she replied, ignoring the hint of condescension in his voice.

'Just cause of the way he deed. An him bein so security-minded.'

'He was very concerned about security, then? I'd heard that.'

'Christ aye. Obsessed. He came in ae day, fifteen year ago maybe, and he was fair vexed, I could tell. Somethin had given him a real fleg. Said he wanted new locks front and back. Nae bother, I said, and I went for my diary tae find a date. "Right noo," he says. "I want you to come back wi me now tae cae it." "I cannae leave the shop," I says. "Yer missus'll be ben the back," he says, and she was, so I called her through and off we went.'

'There and then?'

'Aye, that's what I'm tellin you. And when we got tae the hoose, he was still actin strange. Didnae want to let me in. "It's goin to be gey difficult changin' the locks frae the ootside," I says. And he let me in, but he was standin ower me the hale time.'

'What did he think you were goin to do?'

'Nae idea, lass. I just got on wi the job and left him tae it.'

'Am I right in thinking there was only one key for each door? That's what they said at the trial.'

'Aye, that's the truth o it. He was adamant, like. I says they come wi twa keys and he says to me, well I want you to cut ain of them in half. In front of me. So, I did. He even made me leave the halfs wi him.'

'And this was fifteen year ago?'

'Aye, thereaboots.'

'Did he say what was botherin him?'

'Naw. I tried tae make conversation like, askin if he'd had a break-in or somethin, but he wouldnae say onythin. That man was petrified, though, I'll tell you that for nothin. The locks he got fitted, they were the maist heavy duty in the shop. Bloody expensive. They were mair for commercial buildings, ken? Five lever mortice deadlock. As secure as you get. Thon man was scared bloody stiff.'

*

'So how did the killer get in?' Annie twirled a lock of hair round her finger as she stood in Bob's living room. Boxes of crockery filled the settee and chairs and there was nowhere to sit. Bob shook his head.

'There's somethin that's aye bothered me,' he said. 'When we went through the Conoboys' garden we found the back door key under a stane at the door.'

'Lots of people do that.'

'No for a back door you cannae get to. There's no passage intae that garden. It's totally enclosed.' He looked at the boxes into which the latest chapter of his life had been packed. He'd borrowed a car from Jimmy Wright at Alexander's to take them through to the café in Crieff to start the new adventure, but now that could wait.

'Come on,' he said.

'Where are we goin?'

'The Conoboys'.'

'But I'm not due back till three.'

'This isnae work.'

The Conoboys were listening to the afternoon concert on the wireless when they arrived. Bella was reading TS Eliot, Victor frowning over the crossword. Bob explained what he wanted to do and why.

'Of course,' said Victor, 'although I can't imagine there's

212

anything to see after all this time.'

'Aye, probably not, but it's worth a try.'

'There's no way he could have got in through the front door?' Bella asked.

'Not unless Smithson let him in, which seems unlikely. We now know for certain there was only one key, and it was in the door. I'm more and more convinced of that the more I think about it.'

'Let's go, then,' said Victor, leading them out to the garden and the shed at the bottom. Bob collected the ladder and propped it against the wall in the same spot he had months earlier. The cold of the December afternoon was equally as chilling as that January day. He wished he'd brought gloves. He climbed the ladder and sat on the top of the wall and waited for Annie. Victor consciously walked away as she started to climb and, when she reached the top, she swung her legs round while Bob lifted the ladder and pushed it over the other side.

'You go first,' he said, and she descended carefully. Bob followed and took her hands and kissed her. 'Well done,' he said.

'Och, climbin ladders is nothin to me. I used to use one for pickin apples.'

'You took a ladder to go spoolyin? Crikey, that's organised.'

'No spoolyin. Mr Joyner's orchard, oot the Dunkeld Road. He paic me one and six a tree.'

'I never knew that.'

'I didnae tell anyone. Didnae want anyone else musclin in on my territory.'

Bob laughed. 'I didnae ken you were such a business-woman.'

'You just watch me.'

They looked at one another for a moment, each thinking the same thought about Cloudland and whether Bob could make the business work.

'Right,' said Bob. He showed her the stone where the key had been hidden. 'Someone must have come out of the house and left it there, trying to pretend it was normal. So, if they came out here, where did they go?'

They looked round the untidy yard. The grass was more than two feet long but lying flat to the ground, exhausted under the weight of water and snow. Bounding them on all sides were walls, ten or twelve feet high.

'There's no way there,' said Bob, gesturing to his left. 'And that's the Conoboys' in front of us.' He pointed to the wall they had just climbed. 'So he can't have gone that way or he'd have had to go through their house.'

'So, the only option would be here,' said Annie, striding towards the far end of the back wall, beyond the line of the Conoboys' demesne.

They bent over and studied the ground. A rough bed had been overtaken by weeds, now died back for winter, leaves slimed against the cold soil. Bob had a sudden memory of the Cuddies Strip case, when he discovered ladder imprints beneath the laundry of Aberdalgie House. That had been the catalyst for a quickly unfolding chain of events that led to the arrest of John McGuigan for murder and rape. Now, he felt a similar surge of hope. He felt among the undergrowth with both hands.

'Here,' he said. 'Is that a hole?' He estimated the width of a ladder and felt either side of the mark he'd found. 'Yes,' he said, his voice rising with excitement. With two hands he felt what was undoubtedly the marks of a ladder. He brushed the weeds away to reveal two indentations.

'You're sure it's not from when you came over the last time?'

'Can't be. The Conoboys' garden ends over there.' He pointed to a spot a couple of yards further down the wall.

'What's over this bit?'

'It must be the Old Academy building. The County Library have it now.'

'We need to get in there.'

'We do, aye.'

They reported their discovery to Victor and Bella. 'Do you know how we can gain access?' said Bob.

Victor looked at the clock on the mantelpiece. 'The Library Headquarters finishes early on Friday. They'll be gone for the day by now. Wait a moment.' He stubbed out his cigarette and went to the telephone in the hall and asked the operator to be put through to Eck Harrold.

'Eck?' he said when the connection was made, shouting as though speaking to someone in a distant field. 'Victor Conoboy next door. Are you in right now? Excellent. Two acquaintances of mine are going to come round in a moment. I'd be obliged if you'd let them in. They have something to discuss with you. It's police business. Police business,' he repeated, yelling at the top of his voice. He put down the phone and coughed. 'Eck's the caretaker,' he explained. 'He lives in the flat above the library but he's deaf as a post. He'd never hear you knocking.'

They thanked the Conoboys and went next door and Bob knocked on the grand, arched doorway that was once the entrance to Perth Academy. It creaked open and Eck Harrold appeared, seventy years old and long past retirement age but still working because what else would he do with his time?

Bob explained his business, twice, the second time so loudly it hurt his throat.

'Aye,' said Eck. 'That makes sense.'

'What does?'

'Come wi me.' He led them through a passageway, the first half of which was inside the building and the second half outside, into a large, empty courtyard. From there he proceeded to a set of outbuildings and entered one of them, a wooden construction in need of repair.

'There,' he said, pointing to a wooden ladder, relatively new, in excellent condition. 'I found that ae mornin ahint the bushes ower there.' He pointed through the shed wall towards the garden beyond.

'When was this?' said Bob.

'Earlier this year. Around the time the King deed.'

'And Hugh Smithson?'

'Aye, that would be right.'

'Did you tell the polis?'

'They never asked. I dinnae see the relevance.'

'That's Hugh Smithson's hoose oer the wall.'

'Is it? Christ, would you credit that? I'd never hae thocht it.'

'Did you see anythin else?'

'Well, I'll tell you the queerest thing. When I found it I felt someone or somethin rush past me and race back doon the passage. It came frae the side, so I never saw it as such. Not to see what it was, onyway. I went to check and the front door was open.'

'And it wasn't before?'

'Hell no. I'm maist particular aboot that. This is the Library Headquarters, laddie. There's all sorts of valuable books here, ken?'

Annie and Bob stared at one another. 'Right,' said Bob. 'And this was when, first thing in the morning?'

'Efter my breakfast. Seven o'clock, aye.'

Bob's eyes were shining with excitement. Finally, something was making sense. 'He must have waited all night until you turned up to work and then made his escape. So,' he turned to Annie, 'now we know how he got out.'

'Aye,' said Annie, 'but we still dinnae ken how he got in.'

'One step at a time.'

# Saturday 5th December

## A Day of Discovery

Bob parked Jimmy Wright's DeLuxe Ford outside Muir's Ironmongers on James Square and sat for a moment, looking at the café – *his* café. Jack McOmish, the joiner, would be here at eleven to erect the sign over the front window. Cloudland.

'Well, Gran,' he said aloud. 'You aye said I lived in cloud-cuckoo-land and here's my ain version o it.' He had known since he first decided to run a café he would call it Cloudland, a tribute to Gran and a way of making the place his own. 'This is whaur I'm goin to spend my life, for good or ill.'

He spent an hour unpacking crockery and cutlery and then he walked down King Street and cut through an odd, twisting passage that emerged at Galvelmore Street. He banged on the door of Neil's auction house and stepped through a narrow door built into a much bigger and wider pair of doors which could be opened in full to let cars or even vans inside the building.

'Mr Neil?' he called.

'That's me,' came a voice from inside. A man appeared, neat in a tweed suit, smoking a pipe. 'You're Kelty?'

'Aye. Lookin for tables and chairs.'

'What is it you want them for again?

'I'm openin a café. James Square.'

'Where Urquhart's used to be?'

'Aye.'

217

'Nothing ever lasts there.'

'Well, here's hopin that's no true, or I winnae need to be spendin any money wi you in the sale.'

Mr Neil laughed. 'We've a good selection at the moment, as it happens. Place in Comrie we had to clear. Owner got in debt, did a bunk.' He laughed again. 'And here's hopin that's no an omen, eh?' He took him deep into the cavernous building, past dozens of lots ready for the next sale, until they reached a dingy room offset from the main building. A dozen tables and perhaps thirty chairs were crammed into this space, some smaller tables perched on the larger ones. The furniture came in a variety of styles, shapes and types of wood. Memories of Lipton's Tea Rooms, with its pristine, matching furniture and finely decorated walls and flooring, resurfaced in Bob's mind. Cloudland would be an altogether couthier affair, he realised. And none the worse for that.

'When's the sale?' he asked

'Wednesday. Ten o'clock.'

'Grand.' On his return to Cloudland, he walked along Commissioner Street and up King Street. He regretted it, the one in three gradient forcing him to stop for breath outside the Police Station.

'I'll be needin to get fitter if I'm to goin live here,' he said to an old woman dragging a trolley behind her. She looked him up and down as though confirming his assertion and walked on. 'Aye,' said Bob. 'Welcome to Crieff.'

Jack McOmish was waiting for him when he turned onto James Square and Bob gave him a wave.

'Mornin,' he said.

'Afternoon,' said Jack McOmish.

'Am I late?'

'You're here now.'

Bob opened up, once more getting that thrill of anticipation as he crossed the threshold. 'Welcome to Cloudland,' he said. 'My first visitor.'

McOmish looked round the empty building. 'A café, is it?'

'Aye, oot front. And ben the back I'm teachin music.'

'Oh aye. What d'ye teach?'

'Piano, guitar, fiddle, bagpipes.'

'Pity the poor bugger that lives ahint you, then.'

Bob rapped his knuckles against the nearest wall. 'Auld building,' he said. 'I'm sure the walls are right thick. Soundproofed, ken? If you could put oot the word, I'd be very grateful.'

'Aye. There's a rare demand for pianists nooadays, so I hear. What wi the recession an a ...'

'Would you like a cup of tea?'

'Would you be chargin me for it?'

'No.'

'Two sugars. Plenty milk.' McOmish went outside and fetched the sign he had made from his van. It was wood, painted white, with Cloudland written in red in a distinctive, cursive script. It looked very modern. Chic. Bob watched McOmish work, the deft way he manoeuvred it into place and screwed it at each corner until it was sound. He took about twenty minutes to complete the job, including a couple of descents of the ladder to drink his tea. Bob would have taken hours and would still have not finished the task. He'd probably have hung it upside down. Or the wrong way round.

'That looks grand,' he said.

'Aye. Well, I cannae say I'm keen on that design but if that's what you want ...'

'Looks modern, d'you no think?'

'I do think. That's why I'm no keen on it. This isnae a modern toon, ken?'

Bob went inside and pulled his Beau Brownie camera from his coat pocket and handed it to McOmish. 'Would you mind takin my picter? Wi the sign?' He showed McOmish how the camera worked and McOmish took it in his huge, gnarled hands. It looked suddenly tiny.

'Come on, then,' McOmish said. 'Gies a smile.' Bob relaxed and let his satisfaction show and smiled broadly as McOmish took the photograph. He handed the camera back and looked up at his handiwork again. 'Aye, it looks grand, right enough. Good luck wi it, son. When d'you open?'

'A week on Monday, probably. I need to buy some tables and chairs.'

'Aye, it wouldnae be awfae welcomin withoot them, right enough.'

'Ye'll hae to come in. I'll gie you the first cuppa free.'

'I'll maybe do that.' He turned towards his van, taking out a cigarette and lighting it. 'I ken someone,' he said. 'His wee lassie's been after gettin piano lessons. I'll let him ken.'

'That would be grand. Thanks.'

*

'Where have you been?'

Annie was practically skipping with excitement on the step outside Bob's house when he arrived home. She was wearing a pair of brown corduroys and it was the first time Bob had ever seen her wear trousers. She looked right bonnie.

'Takin the car back to Jimmy Wright. You cannae get away without a wee blether. He loves to have a moan, does Jimmy.'

'Never mind that! I ken how he did it.'

'Did what?'

'Get intae Smithson's hoose.'

Bob unlocked the front door and swung it open, but he turned to Annie before stepping inside. 'How?'

'Mum telt me. I was explainin aboot it to her this morning. How we kent how the killer got oot, but no how he got in, and she said: "But that's easy".'

'Come on, then. Oot wi it.'

'These old houses, Mum said, mid-Victorian, they usually have a shared loft space. The builders never bothered to divide them up. Saved money, I expect.'

'So you can get to Smithson's loft space ... '

'From any hoose in the row.'

'There was a hatch in the landing, right enough. I mind seein it.'

'Come on, then.'

'Where?'

'Where d'you think? Barossa Street.'

'We're no actually goin to ... '

'Yes, we are!'

'We need to call the polis.'

'And what'll they do? They dinnae care about this case, you ken that. They're happy to go on blamin Richard.'

'Let me get oot of these work claes, then.'

'Dinnae be daft. It's goin to be filthy up in thae lofts. Keep them on.'

Bob was desperate to tell Annie about Cloudland, the new sign, the furniture he'd seen in Neil's, but he could see her excitement. He put his own on hold. That could wait. 'Let's go,' he said.

Twenty minutes later, they stood on the pavement opposite the block of houses on Barossa Street. There were four two-storey town houses and then a patch of bare land and a series of smaller cottage-like dwellings which comprised the rest of the street until it joined up with the tenements on Atholl Street.

'This hoose has been empty for ages,' said Annie, pointing to the last house in the row. 'Old Mrs Barratt lived here. She died the middle of last year but they cannae find her next of kin. There's nothin they can do wi the place until they do.'

'So, it's just lyin empty?'

'Aye.'

'What a waste.'

They looked up at the house. Paint was peeling from the windowsills and some of the wood was rotten. There was a triangular break in the lower-left pane of the upstairs left window. The door was filthy, a year's worth of grime and city living beginning to obscure the dull black paint.

'This is the only hoose with rear access,' Annie said. 'Because of this yard.' She walked into the yard, a peculiar expanse of barren land bounded by Rose Terrace to the rear and the two separate rows of houses on Barossa Street. It seemed like an oversight. Annie marched towards it and Bob followed. Just as he had on Bank Street when visiting Richard Hamill, he felt as though dozens of pairs of eyes were watching although, as he looked around, he could see no sign of life.

'Here,' said Annie, pointing to the rear-right window. 'It's been broken. The latch has been left unlocked.' She looked at Bob, startle-eyed. 'This really is how he got in, isn't it?'

'Just be careful.'

'Push the windae up.'

Bob stood before the window and gripped the bottom sill, his fingers splayed. At first nothing gave, but after a couple more attempts, he felt the window shift in its frame. He managed to prise his fingers underneath and push upwards. When the window was opened wide enough for them to enter, he stopped and they looked at one another in trepidation. Theirs was meant to be a quiet life. Not this.

'Come on, then,' said Bob, 'afore anyone sees us and calls the polis.' He clambered inside and landed on the stone flag floor of the kitchen. Annie pulled herself through and he gripped her waist and helped her down. She pulled the window shut behind her and they looked around the kitchen. It was cold and musty, that lonely smell of a house that was no longer a home. A brass kettle sat on the range and a box of loose tea was on an open shelf above. Dust and memory.

Bob shivered.

They went into the hallway. The layout was identical to Mr Smithson's house, two little rooms either side of the front door and a central stairway running upstairs. There were family photographs in a neat line the length of the hallway, Victorian sepia and formal poses, formidably moustachioed men and severe, expressionless women, children dressed like miniature adults, some blurred by a juvenile inability to sit still for long enough. A different world, time interrupted.

Bob gripped the banister and started to climb, feeling that same sense of dread he had when he climbed Mr Smithson's stairs. His heart raced. *Why?* he thought. There was no danger here. The killer was long gone. The house was empty. Still, the tension made his muscles tighten. They were walking in the steps of a killer. The last person to climb this stairway was the man who stabbed Hugh Smithson twenty-nine times. Traces of that evil hung in the air, and ever would while there were people alive to remember what had happened. On the landing he could see the square hatch into the loft space. It was still open, the way the killer had left it. As he looked up, he realised they would not be able to reach it.

'The killer must've brought that ladder with him. The one Mr Harrold found in the bushes.'

'There's a sideboard in here,' said Annie, standing in the doorway of the main bedroom. They dragged it into the landing and set it beneath the hatch. Bob climbed on top.

'You come up as well,' he said. 'And you can gie me a bunk up as I pull mysel up.' He helped her onto the sideboard, and they stood together, balanced precariously, arms around each other, Bob bent and kissed her. He still thrilled at the sensation of holding another human being. That was something his father and gran had never done. The intimacy, the longing.

'On we go, then.'

He reached up and tried to secure a hold on the frame of

223

the hatch and heaved himself upwards, while Annie pushed on his thighs. Slowly, he rose until his head and chest were in the loft and he settled where he was for a moment before heaving again and twisting his right leg up and into the loft. He rolled over and pulled himself all the way in. The floor was filthy, years of dust and detritus in a layer half an inch thick. He could see daylight through dozens of cracks and holes in the slates. Half a dozen shards of light penetrated the darkness from larger holes, revealing dust circling hazily in the air.

'You ready?' he shouted through the hatch. He reached down and Annie gripped his hand and he pulled as hard as he could. When she could reach it, Annie gripped the ledge and, as Bob continued to pull, she dragged herself up and into the loft beside him.

'It's freezin up here,' she said.

'Dark as well.'

'That's why I brought this.' She turned on a torch and a thin beam of light shone into the darkness. Oddly, it seemed to make everything not in its line seem darker still.

'Right, tread carefully and be quiet, or the people next door'll hear us.' He took Annie's hand and together they walked towards Smithson's house. The space above Mrs Barratt's was completely empty, but as they crawled over a ceiling joist that marked the boundary between two houses, the space above the adjacent house was brimming with stuff, bags and boxes, an empty bird cage, a three-quarter size guitar. Bob picked it up and strummed the strings. Apart from the high E, they were almost in tune.

'"Be quiet", he says,' said Annie, rolling her eyes and laughing.

'Sorry.'

They picked their way through the jumble with care, Annie's torch revealing their route. The space above the third house was also empty, and finally they reached the loft above Hugh Smithson's house. Annie trained her torch on the floor and located the hatch into the hallway.

'Here we are, then,' she said.

'Aye.' The moment felt oddly anticlimactic. 'I'm no really sure what I was expectin to find,' he said.

'No, me neither.'

There was a smell in the air, sickly sweet, or perhaps acrid. Like air that had gone stale. Like varnish. They stood above the hatch and Annie swept the torch beam across the loft. Bob thought he saw something lying in the far corner.

'Shine your torch back over there,' he said. Dust motes flickered in the light as she swung her torch beam around the loft space. The sudden screech of a crow in flight outside gave them a start. Bob was becoming increasingly aware of the smell, as though it was somehow growing stronger. He felt suddenly uncomfortable.

'Further over,' he said. As Annie trained the torch on the rear of the building, they saw there was, indeed, an object, square and flat, lying against the wall.

'What is that?' said Annie.

'Probably just rubbish,' said Bob, but he was dubious. If it was rubbish, why had it been placed so far away from the hatch? All on its own? It was as though it had been moved as far out of sight as possible. Something felt wrong. He walked towards it.

'Don't.'

'It's fine,' he said, but he felt far from fine.

Annie followed, training her torch on the object the whole time, as though making sure it couldn't escape. Close up, they could see it was an old tin case, maybe four feet long. Bob knelt beside it and felt it. It was cold. He held his breath. Although the case was closed, the two clasps which should have held it shut were open. He looked up at Annie. The fear in her expression matched his own. He turned back and gripped the lid of the case and lifted it. Annie shone her torch on the contents.

The mummified remains of a woman.

# Sunday 6<sup>th</sup> December

## *A Day of Resolve*

Bob woke himself up moaning. His blankets lay heavily on him, twisted under his left side so that as he came round, he panicked, thinking he had been tied up. He struggled to free himself, kicking his legs and pulling the blankets from the bed. Immediately, December cold penetrated and he lay back as still as he could to allow the warmth to return. He stared at the coving around the walls, then at the whiteness of the ceiling. Superimposed was that image, the body in the case, dead staring eyes, screaming grimace, the smell of it, like leather, like despair. A wizened homunculus who once was a woman. A woman murdered and left to mummify in a loft. A life exchanged for what? Why? He had slept only fitfully, alternately too cold and too hot, turning in the bed and failing to settle, to forget, to relax. Morning found him agitated and irritable. He got up, shaved, cooked breakfast. There was a note posted through his door, instructing him to report to Chief Constable Chadwick at Police Headquarters at ten. He checked his pocket watch. Ten o'clock.

\*

If Bob slept fitfully, Annie did not sleep at all. She kept a candle lit all night. She sat upright in bed, arms folded, staring at her reflection in the wardrobe mirror as it contorted in the shivering candlelight. The image she saw returned was of a frightened girl, and that was how she felt. She had come closer to evil than she could bear, and the sight of it and the

227

smell of it and the thought of it was in her head now and ever would be. She thought of Bob, witness of the violent death of his own father and of Danny Kerrigan and Hugh Smithson, now witness of this monstrosity. She wanted to hold him. Help him. Help herself.

'Please let me sleep,' she said. 'Dream nothing.'

*

Sergeant Hamilton rolled his eyes as Bob entered the City Police Headquarters, shaking snow from his overcoat. 'Here he comes, Sexton Blake.'

'Morning, Sergeant. I was asked to call in.'

Hamilton checked the clock on the wall opposite. 'Forty-five minutes ago. The Chief Constable wishes to speak with you personally. On a Sunday morning. And you're late. So don't go imagining he's here to congratulate you.'

Bob shrugged. The thought of speaking to the Chief Constable would once have filled him with terror, but this morning he felt strangely untroubled. The memory of his discovery was still too vivid for any other fear to supplant it. Technically, he'd broken into several domestic dwellings. He'd found – and disturbed – a crime scene. He'd uncorked a story the police had been happy to keep bottled. They could conceivably charge him with the first and second of those misdemeanours, but Bob suspected they wouldn't because of the third. And, if they did, he knew a defence advocate in Edinburgh who would no doubt be happy to lend his support.

Chief Constable Chadwick was writing on foolscap as Bob entered the office and stood to attention in front of a mahogany desk. Sergeant Petrie sat to the side, his hands clasped on his lap, his face a study in seriousness. The merest twitch of his eyebrow suggested to Bob, though, that he was possibly on Bob's side. Charlie Petrie was a decent man, old school, honest.

'You may sit,' said the Chief Constable. Bob took a seat

228

in a rickety wooden chair and waited for the Chief Constable to begin.

'The investigation must now be re-opened.'

'I would have thought so, aye.'

'The body you discovered has been there for many years, between fifteen and twenty in the view of Dr Murphy. It has been sent to Professor Anderson in Glasgow for further tests. Forensic science has taken remarkable strides in the past few years and we expect to uncover much more information. But we are currently working on the assumption that the dead woman is Maisie Smithson, Hugh Smithson's wife. She was reported to have left him about fifteen or sixteen years ago. We're now making enquiries to see if she has been seen since then. We now suspect not.'

Bob nodded. 'There was somethin, fifteen year ago, that changed Smithson. Turned him into a hermit. Made him stop leavin the hoose. Stopped him lettin anyone in the hoose. The body in the loft would make sense of that.'

'It would '

'So, whoever killed Smithson is probably someone from that period. Fifteen year ago.'

'It would seem so.'

'Which means Richard Hamill is innocent. He'd only have been a bairn then.'

'What's Richard Hamill got to do with anything?'

Bob faced him down. *You won't intimidate me. Not today. Not again. I've seen too much in this world.* 'When Richard was acquitted, you made no attempt to resume the investigation. You said you werenae lookin for anyone else in respect of the crime. What people took that to mean – whether that was your intention or no – was that Richard did it and got off wi it. He's lived wi that for six months. Suspicion. Rumours. Bad-mouthin. Anonymous letters gettin him the sack. Three times. He didnae deserve that.'

Chief Constable Chadwick lit a cigarette and leaned

forward. 'I can't be held responsible for what people believe,' he said. 'However, the investigation will now resume. And I need you to keep quiet about all this, Kelty. The papers are going to be hounding you, wanting your story, offering you all sorts of inducements. That can't happen.'

'I dinnae work for you any longer.'

'I could have you arrested. For burglary.'

'You ken as well as I do that would never stand up in court.'

'Breaking and entering.'

'In a guid cause.'

'That's debatable. Interfering with a crime scene.'

'Discoverin a crime scene. Because you didnae bother lookin.'

Chadwick glowered at him. 'I'm disappointed in you, Kelty.'

'Likewise.'

Behind the Chief Constable, out of eyeline, Petrie stifled a laugh.

'Don't be impertinent,' said the Chief Constable.

'Don't overstep your authority. Remember the Cuddies Strip case? The Home Office gave it a week before they brought in the Glasgow police to take over – sorry, "to assist the Perthshire force". How long d'you think you'll get now that this has blown up again? With another body lyin right above the murder scene all this time? It smacks of incompetence. And what d'you think the Glasgow boys'll say aboot me and Annie – civilians – havin to do your job for you?'

'You're a nasty piece of work.'

'No, I'm not. But I'm no a doormat anymore. I won't be told what to do.' He slid his chair back. 'Was there anythin else, sir? Only, I'm moving to Crieff and openin my new café next week and I still have a lot to do.'

Bob spent the remainder of the morning and early afternoon clearing the house. Gran had hoarded for years, rubbish of all sorts overbrimming every cupboard and drawer. The more the recession had deepened through the twenties and early thirties, the more she had felt the need to stockpile, buying anything that was cheap on the basis that it was a bargain and she would find a use for it one day. Mr Neil was coming to take some of the furniture next week, the larger pieces for which there was no room in the small flat above Cloudland. Bob was relieved about that. It offered a break from the past. These daily reminders of Gran in a house where she'd lived for over twenty years made it hard for Bob to let go. He whistled as he packed. He liked the mindlessness of the work. Outside, snow continued to fall and by the time he left to visit Richard Hamill, there was an almost total white-out. Last winter had been severe. This one was shaping up the same. On Longcauseway, he heard someone calling his name and turned to see George Macrae approaching.

'Sergeant Petrie's been tellin aabody what you said to Chadwick. You're the toast of the Station.'

'Well, that's a novelty.'

'The investigation's bein opened up again.'

'Who's in charge?'

'Petrie.'

'Aye, well. I like Charlie Petrie, and he's a grand bobby, but he's no a detective, so they'd be as well shuttin it straight back doon again.' Bob raked snow into the gutter with the side of his boot. 'If you want my guess, he'll footer about for a month or two, say all the leads have gone cold, it was all too long ago, and that'll be that. Aabody happy, job done.'

'You're probably right.'

'You ken I am. Meanwhile, there's still a murderer oot there. Someone killed Hugh Smithson.'

'Aye, but at least there's a motive of sorts now. I mean, Smithson was the target, like. It wasnae just random. Before, folks were nervous because there was nae reason for the killin. If it was random, they could have been next, ken? But now, it means there probably isnae goin to be a next.'

'So that's all right then? You just let someone get away wi murder?'

'I dinnae make the decisions.'

'No, but you implement them.'

*

'Man, these steps are lethal.' Bob had approached Richard Hamill's house through the back entrance again and the stone steps were covered in a layer of ice beneath the new snow fall. He had saved himself from going full length with his left forearm. He waved it at Richard to demonstrate his near miss.

'Sorry. I wasn't expecting company, or I'd have salted them. Come away in and have some tea.'

'Have you got a job yet?' Bob asked as he took off his coat and folded it over a kitchen chair. He sat down.

'No, but I have an interview next week I'm hopeful about.'

'Aye? That's good. Whereaboots?'

Richard measured three teaspoons of tea into the pot. 'I don't want to say yet. In case I jinx it. You take sugar, don't you? Two, is it?'

'One. I'm cuttin doon.' Bob patted his stomach which, in truth, was taking on an unwonted portliness. 'I wondered if you'd be goin to the lecture the night? Rosita Forbes?'

'The explorer?'

'Aye.'

'She's speakin here?'

'County Hotel.'

'Well, that would be interesting, right enough. She's quite

a woman, but I don't think I could stomach her politics.'

'Aye?' Bob had no idea about her politics. The suggestion had come from Victor Conoboy. *"An extraordinary woman"*, he said. *"An inspiration"*.

'If you get a chance, ask her about her relationship with Mussolini. Or Stalin. Or even Herr Hitler.'

Bob looked at him in amazement. 'She kens them?'

'So rumour has it.' He placed the teapot on a trivet on the table and sat opposite Bob. 'Not that I allow idle gossip to influence me, of course.' They both laughed. 'It's just that in her case, some of the gossip isn't so idle.' He poured their teas and Bob studied his face, thought he seemed ill-at-ease.

'You had any more anonymous interference?' he asked.

'No. But I haven't got a job to get run out of at the moment. I'm sure when I do it'll all start up again.'

They both thought of Sergeant Braggan, his vindictiveness, his downgrading to a rural Station, his need for vengeance.

'Anyway,' said Richard, 'to what do I owe this pleasure?' Richard was trying to sound full of bonhomie but, again, Bob had the sense that he was somehow uncomfortable. He looked in the direction of the adjacent living room and jerked his head.

'Is your pal Hamish ben there?'

Richard faltered. 'He is,' he said.

'Well, invite him through. He might want to hear this, too.' There was a shuffling sound from the other room and a man emerged, short and nervous-looking, unprepossessing. He wasn't how Bob had imagined. 'Hamish?' he said. Hamish nodded. 'Nice to meet you. I've heard all about you.'

'Have you?'

Bob laughed. 'Well, no, not at all, to be honest. But at least I have heard *of* you. Glad to finally make your acquaintance.'

'I owe you a debt of gratitude,' Hamish said. 'If it hadn't been for you at the trial, things could have gone badly wrong.'

'It wasnae just me ... '

'It was. Your testimony was so persuasive. Honest.'

'You were there?'

'Of course. If the love of my life is going to be hanged, I want to be there to hear the news myself.'

'Aye, well, thankfully it didnae come to that. It's the murder I'm here aboot, though.'

'Really?' said Richard.

'They've found a body,' Bob said. 'Well, me and Annie found it.'

'How? Where?'

Bob explained their journey through the lofts of Barossa Street, the discovery of the body in the case.

'Who is it?'

'Maisie Smithson.'

'Smithson's wife?' Bob nodded. Richard exhaled heavily.

'So, you're in the clear. That's what I wanted to tell you. Smithson's murder must be linked to the death of his wife. And that was fifteen year ago. You'd have been a bairn.'

Richard sat for some moments, pondering. 'For the first murder.'

'Eh?'

'I'm not sure it exonerates me at all. I didn't commit the first murder. But I could still have killed Smithson.'

'Why?'

'Well, obviously I didn't, so I can't answer that. But it won't stop people like Braggan saying I did. Or trying to prove it.' He took Hamish's hand. 'We *are* a danger to society, after all.'

Bob studied them both. He knew that this was how hatred gained the oxygen it needed to thrive. Point out something isn't impossible. No more than that. Don't try to prove anything, just declare that something hasn't been *dis*proved. Jewish people or gypsies or homosexuals are different. They aren't like *normal* people. Like you and me. Maybe they're acting against the state. Maybe they're dangerous. That's all it takes. Sow that seed of doubt. Leave it. Watch it grow. Spread. Then, and only then, start to fulminate against them. The others. Those people who are not like us, so must be against us. Look what they're doing. It's not right. It's not decent. They're disgusting. We need to rid ourselves of these people. Society is better without them. And what easier way to get rid of them than to pin a crime on them, any crime? Richard was right. This wasn't over yet.

'I may pay our friend Sergeant Braggan a visit,' he said.

'I wish you the best of luck with that.'

*

Rosita Forbes strode onto the stage to a generous round of applause, waving at the audience seated beneath her. The County Hotel function room was almost full, the audience a roughly fifty-fifty gender split, here to listen to the famous and intrepid lady explorer. Bob took Annie's hand. He was pleased they had this to attend tonight – it would take their minds off what happened the day before. As the day had progressed, he had been able to shut out the memories, but with darkness they had returned. That moment, the discovery, confrontation with death, a woman discarded in that tiny space, leathered skin, the obscene way her body had folded over and the skin had sealed around the folds, the rictus grin of her fallen jaw, all this was imprinted on his memory, never to be forgotten. He knew that Annie would be thinking the same and he reflected that he should have spent time with her today. He felt for her hand now and squeezed it.

'I must say,' Rosita Forbes began, 'I'm more used to heat and sand than cold and snow. I had a deuce of a job getting here tonight without falling on my behind.' The audience laughed. 'I want to tell you,' she continued, 'about the Forbidden Road to Samarkand from Kabul in Afghanistan into the provinces of Russia. It is a place where they have only one word for "stranger", and that word also means "spy". I was accompanied on the first stage of my journey by Captain Galloway of the Indian Army and by three native soldiers. The native soldiers perished when their truck plunged over the edge of a precipice and exploded in a fireball that took two hours to subside. Captain Galloway took his leave on the Russian border and I went on myself, accompanied only by a Russian guide.'

She was a tall and elegant woman with a long nose, a wide mouth and penetrating eyes. She was a captivating presence, commanding the room with the ease of a woman with total confidence in herself. She spoke in a clipped English accent, her voice deepened by cigarette smoking, and gave an account of extraordinary adventures as though nothing could be more commonplace. She talked of her travels in North Africa, disguised as an Arab woman – the first woman, and only the second European, to visit the Kufra oasis. She talked about the Hindu Kush, about the Sahara Desert. She was accompanied throughout by a lantern show displaying these exotic outposts and the hour passed so quickly Bob could have sworn he had only just taken his seat.

As the audience applauded at the end of her talk, Mr Wilmer, the hotel manager, joined her on stage and thanked her, then called for questions from the audience. The man next to Bob thrust up his hand and started speaking before being asked.

'Templeton, *Evening Telegraph*. Is it true you have met Herr Hitler?'

Rosita Forbes gave a throaty laugh, as though she had been anticipating the question. 'On three occasions. The first time was in 1933, when he had just come to power. The very first thing he said to me, without any introduction, was "I do hate destruction". A remarkable sentiment, I think you'll agree. "I want happiness for Germany", he told me. "Life is too complicated". He is a man who speaks extremely simply. He gives the impression of seeming to be extremely honest. His genius is in the way he brings simplicity and honesty to his handling of complex problems.' She looked around the room, then focused on Templeton. 'All the same, you must be aware that the truth doesn't mean anything to him.'

'Do you believe he is preparing for war?' asked Templeton.

'He told me quite categorically no. But he did say that if there is another war, it will be on a scale nobody has before conceived. He wishes to avoid that. He wishes common sense to prevail. He wishes to reach an understanding with France. In some ways, he reminds me of Mohandas Gandhi. I remember once, in Knightsbridge, Gandhi was sitting at my feet eating celery and I asked him how he could defend the frontiers of India from Bolshevists and Afridi looters. "We shall not need to fight if we are free", he replied. The Chancellor describes his vision of Germany in equally idealistic – by which I mean impossible – terms: the rich should help the poor, imported goods should be restricted, the country should become self-sustaining. In my travel I have seen many mirages, but none so big as that.'

'Does he mean to harm Britain?'

'I believe not. He told me he had no wish to interfere in British affairs. "Let Britain keep its colonies", he said. "Let her muddle along with her empire, half of which is already in upheaval".'

'You've also met Senor Mussolini, I believe,' said Templeton. He turned to Bob and whispered: 'Had an affair, by all accounts.'

'I met Mussolini in 1920. He advised me my mission to Kufra was preposterous for a woman. I'd get as far as Benghazi, he said, where some man would make love to me and I wouldn't want to go any further.' The audience broke into laughter, and Rosita Forbes, an accomplished performer, rode the laugh, smiling broadly. 'The next time I met him I was sure to tell him of my success in reaching Kufra. "I know," he said. "And that journey will be useful to me one day, when I send my army in your footsteps." And he did, of course, in 1931.'

'Committing hideous war crimes along the way,' whispered Bob. Templeton turned to him and nodded. He looked Annie up and down and smiled at her. She smiled back.

When the talk was over, Templeton walked out with Bob and Annie, lighting a cigarette and flicking the spent match onto the slushy snow. 'She's one of the most astonishing women I've ever come across,' he said. 'The people she's met. The things she's done. As a journalist I'd give my eye teeth to interview her.'

'Aye, she is that,' agreed Bob. 'I know I should come away thinking what an inspiration she is.'

'Should?'

'She *is* astonishing, I agree. And obviously very clever. But is there a soul in there? Does she care aboot anythin? Truth doesnae mean anything to Hitler, she says, but then she goes on to defend him. She says he doesnae want war. Of course he wants war. He's been re-arming for two years. He's puttin the country's whole infrastructure into armaments. And Mussolini – the man's committing war crimes every day, crimes the League of Nations is too cowardly to deal with. Should she be tellin stories like that about him for entertainment? Makin him out to be some sort of loveable rogue? And should we really be sittin listenin to it? And Gandhi. "No need to fight if we are free." Forbes was right about that, at least. Idealistic and impossible. What if you arenae free? What if you're a Jew, or a tinker, or a homosexual? What if you're no one of the elite? Freedom, is it? What does freedom mean to the Jews of Germany after the Nuremberg Laws?'

Templeton smiled at the younger man's outburst of passion. 'You haven't lost your idealistic fervour, I see,' he said.

'Do I ken you?'

'No, but I ken you. I was in court every day for the McGuigan trial. You were very good.'

'No good enough.'

'I hope you don't blame yourself for the jury's cowardice.'

'I'm still disappointed.'

'Of course. The verdict was disappointing. As to your question, what freedom means: freedom means the manifestation of the true self.'

'I dinnae understand what that means. Freedom means making choices. Choosing sides.'

'And have you chosen?'

'I have, aye.'

# Wednesday 9ᵗʰ December

## A Day of Changes

'Lot seventy-one, a set of nine tables and twenty-nine chairs, not matching but similar in style. In very good condition for the most part. Who'll start the bidding? Two guineas?' Mr Neil looked round the auction room for the shy lad he'd met the week before and saw him standing at the back. He nodded at him encouragingly. Bob waved back.

'Two pounds then,' Mr Neil said. A gentleman clutching a bowler hat in the first row raised a finger. 'Thank you, sir. Do I hear two pounds one shilling?' A woman near the side window waved her hand and for the next minute these two bidders went head-to-head while the bidding rose towards three pounds. Bob watched in panic. This was so fast. He'd set his heart on these tables, but the bidding could get out of control and he still hadn't entered the fray.

'Three pounds,' said Mr Neil. The man at the front ticked his finger again. 'Thank you, sir. Three pounds one shilling?'

Bob raised his hand and Mr Neil acknowledged him. 'New bidder at the back. Welcome, sir. You can put your hand down now.' Laughter arose around Bob and he lowered his hand, feeling himself start to blush. 'Against you,' Mr Neil said to the man at the front. He nodded and Mr Neil accepted another bid. 'I have three pounds two shillings,' he said, looking at Bob. Bob raised his hand again, and again he kept it raised as the bidding war between him and the man at the front proceeded at pace, rising past four pounds towards five pounds. Laughter rang round the auction room and the

240

man in the front row turned round to see Bob with his hand permanently raised. He turned back to the front and raised an eyebrow at Mr Neil.

'I think we have a very determined bidder in the room,' Mr Neil said. The man in the front row shrugged and shook his head. 'Madam at the back, are you done?' The woman nodded and Mr Neil looked round. 'Any further bids?' he said, and waited a few seconds before clapping his gavel against the wooden table. 'Sold.' He smiled at Bob. 'I thought for a moment you might start bidding against yourself there, young man,' he said, and the crowd laughed once more. Bob beamed.

'Five pounds well spent,' he said to no one in particular.

*

Lochearnhead Police Station looked more like a domestic dwelling than a public building, and Bob walked past without spotting the sign. Snow was thick on the ground and falling heavily from a doom-grey sky, much thicker here than it had been in Crieff. The weather front was travelling eastwards, so what Lochearnhead was getting now would be in Crieff within the hour and then Perth not long after that. Despite still being elated after his success in the auction, he was starting to worry about getting home again and he resolved to be ready for the three-thirty bus. He climbed the steps of the Police Station and breathed deeply before entering.

'Well, well, well, if it isn't the conscience of the western world.'

'Morning, Sergeant.'

Sergeant Braggan had put on weight. He looked odd in a uniform anyway and the way it stretched across his belly didn't help his appearance. He looked like the Laughing Policeman, except he wasn't laughing.

'Just passing, were you?'

'No, I wanted to speak to you.'

Braggan looked at the swirling snow out of the window. 'You must want to speak to me really badly to risk coming all the way out here in this weather. If this keeps up, you'll be stranded. You wouldn't want that, believe me.'

'I'm sure it's a grand place. Plenty to keep you busy.'

'There's plenty poaching. Bugger all else. Sandy Moncur booted his dug up the arse on Auchraw Terrace last Friday. Isa McNeill complained. Wanted him charged with assault and battery. That took a bit of sorting.'

'Paperwork.'

'Aye. So, what's the occasion? I don't suppose you're here to reminisce about the good old days?'

'The Smithson murder.'

'I vaguely recall something about that, aye.'

'They found another body. Maisie Smithson.'

'I know. I'm still in the police, you know.' He gestured at the office in which they were standing. 'We do get the news out here.'

'Aye. It's just … Well, the murder of Mrs Smithson probably happened fifteen year ago. And it was probably Hugh Smithson that done it.' Bob stared at him.

'What d'you want, Sherlock? A medal?'

'So, it's likely the death of Hugh Smithson was related to Maisie's death. Revenge maybe, I don't know.'

'Listen,' said Braggan, 'as you can see,' he gestured once more at the office, 'I'm very busy keeping the streets of Lochearnhead safe for people to walk, so I'd be grateful if you'd come to the point. Assuming you have one.'

'And if the motive is fifteen years old, that probably rules out Richard Hamill …'

'Yes.'

Bob stopped. 'You agree?'

'Richard Hamill had nothing to do with Hugh Smithson's murder.'

'But … How …'

242

'The man's a tink and he's a pansy, and I don't know which is worse, but he's not a murderer. That much was obvious in the trial.'

Bob shook his head. 'So why the anonymous letters?'

'What anonymous letters?'

'Every time Richard gets settled in a job there's anonymous letters ruinin his reputation.'

'And you think they're coming from me?'

'Well …'

Braggan laughed. 'The saintly detective Kelty. Right then, where's your evidence? Or have you not got any? Are you just making assumptions? "Braggan's a wrong-un, he must have done it." Isn't that what you accused me of doing with your precious Richard Hamill?' Braggan stared at him and Bob felt instantly intimidated. 'Hypocritical little bastard.'

'I'm sorry.'

'Maybe you're not so smart after all.'

'I never thought I was.' Bob looked out of the window. Snow was whirling, whipped up by a fierce wind. The sky was grey and lifeless. 'You said, after the trial, there was no point lookin for anyone else. He'd got off with it.'

'Aye, immediately after, I thought that. Thought it was a miscarriage of justice. But when you think about it, which I did in the days after, it was pretty obvious he had nothing to do with it. But, even so, there was still no point looking for anyone else. Because there's no evidence that points to anyone else. There's nothing to go on.'

'Except a body in the loft.'

'And what's that going to tell us? Fifteen years on?' Braggan lit a cigarette and flicked the match into a circular glass ashtray. 'Listen,' he said, 'I'm as disappointed as you are we never solved that case. You haven't a monopoly on caring, you know.'

'I'm sorry.'

243

'You keep saying that. You're not. You don't like me. That's fine. I can't stand you. I want to punch your sanctimonious bald head in every time I see it. But don't make me into something I'm not. I'm a good policeman and I care about my job. Don't make out otherwise. Don't set yourself on a pedestal.'

Bob studied the older man. There was nothing pleasant in his demeanour. He made no attempt to be sociable. Not now, not then. *Take me or leave me*, his expression said. Bob envied the self-sufficiency that lay behind such arrogance.

'I need to get back for my bus,' he said. 'Could I use your toilet first?'

Braggan gestured behind him and swung open the counter and stepped aside to let Bob pass. 'Down the corridor, first left.'

Bob walked through the office into a narrow corridor and into the toilet. As he washed his hands afterwards, he looked at himself in a chipped mirror above the sink. *Not as smart as you think you are. Don't set yourself on a pedestal.* Did he? He unlocked the door and stepped back into the corridor.

'Hello.'

The voice was a child's. Bob followed the sound into the room opposite. The cells were at the far end, and in them, locked, was a boy of no more than five, sitting on the stone floor and drawing on a large sheet of paper.

'Hello,' said Bob. 'What's your name?'

'Davey,' said the boy. 'Are you a baddie?'

'I hope not. What are you all locked up for?'

'I'm not locked up, silly. You are.'

'Right.' The boy resumed his drawing, crouching so close to the paper his shock of blond hair was brushing against it. Bob returned to the office.

'You arrestin bairns now?' he said as he passed back through the counter into the reception.

'That's Davey.'

'Aye, he telt me.'

'He's my laddie.'

'I didnae ken you had a bairn.'

'What would I tell you for? He starts school after Easter. Thank Christ.'

'D'you bring him to work every day?'

'Mostly.'

'What d'you do if you have to arrest somebody?'

'I'll worry about that when it happens.'

'Why do you lock him in?'

'Because the little bastard keeps wandering off. Found him paddling in the loch a few weeks ago. Mile and a half away.'

'Where's his mother?'

Braggan reached for his packet of Player's and slid one out. He didn't make eye contact. 'She left me. When I got posted here. Ran off to Belfast with a carpet salesman.'

'I'm sorry.'

'There you go again.'

'I really am.'

'Why? What do you care about me?'

'I was thinkin of the bairn.'

Braggan laughed. 'He'll be fine. He's going to be a bobby, like his father.'

'I hope he doesn't get too used to bein behind bars then.'

'No, he thinks he's on the right side. He thinks he's the policeman and it's us who's under lock and key.'

'That's why he asked if I was a baddie.'

'Either that or he's a good judge of character.' He raised an eyebrow sardonically.

'I'm not a bad man.'

'Neither am I.'

Bob thought. 'No,' he said. 'Maybe not.' He pulled the collar of his coat up and fixed his bunnet on his head. 'I'll see you around.'

The bus journey back to Perth, which usually took two and a half hours, took three and a half. The Comrie bends outside Crieff were almost impassable. So, too, the Gilmerton bends. By the time they reached Fowlis Wester the scene outside – a white-out of swirling snow – was reminiscent of that January day when they had rescued the schoolchildren. Bob shuddered at the memory, at how close to death he had come. It was past seven when he saw with relief the downhill stretch of the Crieff Road towards the Dunkeld Road. He turned and paid homage to Muirton Park as they passed. A few moments later, on Atholl Street, he jumped up.

'Just here's grand, Jamesie,' he said to the driver and waved as he stepped off the bus. He had arranged to be at the Conoboys' at half past six for tea and he hurried through the snow to Rose Terrace. Victor waved away his apologies.

'It's fearsome weather,' he said. 'What a year it's been for snow.' Bob greeted Bella and took his seat at the dining table as Victor served the roast beef that Annie had made earlier. 'Have you heard today's news?' he said.

'No,' said Bob. 'I've spent most of the day in auction rooms and on buses.'

'The affair of the King has taken a turn,' he said. 'It's looking more and more like he will abdicate.'

'Quite right, too,' said Bella. 'That woman could tear apart the country. People would never accept her as Queen.' Bob said nothing, but Bella saw doubt on his face. 'You don't agree?'

'I do,' he said. 'But … Well, I think this could tear the country apart whatever happens.'

'Perhaps,' agreed Victor. 'There have been demonstrations in favour of the King. In London. Glasgow. All over. Mostly young people, right enough.'

'And that's what bothers me,' said Bob.

'Yes,' said Bella, 'I understand your concern. A generational divide. That's not healthy.'

'It isn't, no. Divisions aren't good. People take advantage.'

They finished their meal and retreated to the living room. Victor poured three sherries. Talk turned to politics, the League of Nations, Bob's fretfulness about imminent war.

'The Germans downed a French Embassy plane in Spain,' he said. 'Can the Government still believe Hitler wants a solution with France? That he doesn't want war?' He looked at the Conoboys and shook his head in resignation. 'Why does nobody tell the truth? Why is everyone frightened of talkin about war?'

'You have to understand the trauma our generation went through,' said Bella. 'The war to end all wars. Over by Christmas. In the name of democracy. All those lies we were told. The effect on our generation was indescribable in its cruelty. It's understandable if we shy away from any more of that kind of talk ... '

'But not talking about it won't make it go away.'

'Neither will talking about it. It'll just drive you mad.' Bella felt a pang of affection for this troubled young man. He always took the cares of the world on his shoulders. 'You have to make time to enjoy yourself in this life, Robert. It's the only one you get.'

'I ken. It's not always easy though.'

'No. But try.'

'I will. I had some good news today, anyway.' He started to tell them about the auction that morning and his triumph with the tables and chairs when they were interrupted by the telephone ringing in the hallway. Victor went to answer and returned a moment later.

'It's for you,' he said to Bob. 'George Macrae needs to speak to you urgently.' Bob looked at the Conoboys in confusion.

'Go,' said Bella. 'It must be important.'

247

He thanked them for the meal, put on his overcoat and stepped back into the freezing night. The sky was lighter, the clouds that had delivered so much snow now dissipated. There was a crispness in the air that was refreshing after such a heavy meal and so much sherry. He walked slowly.

George Macrae's mother opened the door and Bob fancied he spotted a disapproving look in her expression. She had a brown streak in her grey hair caused by nicotine. She held a cigarette in her mouth. The house reeked of tobacco. George greeted Bob animatedly.

'Where have you been all day?'

'Lochearnhead. Visiting Sergeant Braggan.'

George never could tell when Bob was joking, and he didn't know now.

'So, what's your tearin rush to see me?'

'We've had some forensic results from Professor Anderson. On the body in the case.'

'And?'

'It's not Maisie Smithson.'

'How?'

'They've done tests. God knows how. This is a younger woman. Still in her twenties. Maisie Smithson was in her early forties when she was last seen.'

'Are they sure?'

'Aye. It's the same people who did that work on the Ruxton murders last year. I tell you, these guys are magicians.'

'Have they found anythin else? Do they ken who she is?'

'Naw. Nae way of tellin that frae the body. What they need to do, they say, is trace someone they think it is and then link her to the body. No the other way round.'

'And how can they do that?'

'Well, one way they said was that on the body there's evidence she broke her leg. Right tibia. An old break, they said, from when she was a lassie, likely.'

'So, they need to find someone who once broke her leg?'

'Aye.'

'Do they ken the cause of death?'

'Stabbed. Once through the heart. Either a good shot or lucky.'

'Well.' Bob stood up. 'I hope that means the polis are goin to take this more seriously now. There's an unidentified woman dead. You have to find out who she is, so you can put her family at rest.'

'How the hell are we goin to do that? We cannae just put a picter of her in the papers. She looks like King Tut's sister.'

'Geordie, you're a grand lad, but sometimes you can be a right arse.' He headed for the living room door.

'Alright, Mr Clever Clogs, how do we find out who she is?'

'I already ken.'

# Thursday 10ᵗʰ December

## A Day of Acknowledgement

Montrose represented the half-way point in their journey and, as the train clacked through the town into countryside once more, Annie stared out of the window. Snow still lay in drifts on the fields and more was falling, but it was sleety stuff now. It wouldn't lie. Bob read that morning's *Courier*. The headline declared: "No Decision Yet In The Crisis". Annie read over his shoulder.

'Will he ever make a decision?' she asked.

'I suspect he already has. They'll be arguing over how much public money he'll be gettin. Abandon your country, get a new title and an annual allowance for the rest of your life.'

'And leave your brother to pick up the pieces.'

'Remember all those reports in January sayin what a fine man he was. Sense of honour, purpose. Professional manner, progressive ideas. All of it fawning rubbish. And now we know all of it lies as well. They must have known, even then, what was goin on, but they fed us all that tripe and we believed it. And now we've got Winston Churchill leadin a troop of MPs who've written to the King sayin they'll do anything to defend him. Set up a King's Party. Bring down the Government. And we call this a democracy.'

They disembarked at Aberdeen station and, in the face of a howling gale, made the expedient decision to go to the adjacent bus station and enquire which route included George Street. They were directed to the number eighteen

250

bus and Bob paid the conductor and they took their seats at the front. Bob was pleased to note the buses weren't as comfortable or as clean as those of Alexander's in Perth.

They drove uphill to Union Street and onto George Street and climbed uphill once more. As they crossed the railway bridge, Bob pointed out the graffiti on the back wall. "Down with the American harlot".

'And the King with her,' he said.

They got off the bus a stop too early and had to walk the last couple of hundred yards uphill. Neither minded. This was not an engagement to look forward to. They held hands outside sixty-nine Leslie Road and Bob opened the gate and walked up the path.

'Come on, then,' he said, as much to himself as to Annie. He knocked on the door.

Malcolm Redford smiled with surprise when he saw them but, when he discerned their sombre demeanours, his smile faded.

'Can we come in?' said Bob.

They waited while the tea-making ritual was re-enacted, a ceremony to bring civility to any occasion, affording a compassionate pause before action.

'I didn't expect to see you again,' Malcom said when they were finally settled with tea and biscuits.

'No. Neither did we, but somethin happened the other day. Which I think might be important.' He faltered. He had rehearsed this, but he was still troubled. Giving bad news was a part of the job he had hated when he was a policeman, and this was no different. 'This might seem an odd question, but do you know if Leslie ever broke her leg?'

Malcolm looked confused. 'Yes, she did. When we were bairns. Fell off the swings in Duthie Park. It was my fault. I was pushing her and she went too high. Broke her leg.'

'Where?'

'Bottom.'

'Tibia?'

'Aye, if that's what it's called.'

'Left or right?'

'Now you're asking.' He looked into the fire for a moment. 'Right.'

Bob bit his lip. 'I'm very, very sorry,' he said. 'I have some terrible news. I'm afraid Leslie is dead.'

Malcolm put his cup on the table beside him. His hands trembled and the cup shook in its saucer. He looked up at Bob, and Bob despaired at the disappointment he saw in the older man's expression.

'Annie and I, we went back to Hugh Smithson's house on Saturday. Something never felt right about the murder. How the killer got in and out. We found the answer to that – through the loft. So, we went up there. And we found a body. In a tin case. The police assumed it was Maisie Smithson – the dead man's wife – because she supposedly ran away years ago and naebody's seen her since. But then, yesterday, they discovered the body was a much younger woman. And she had an old fracture. Her right tibia ... I really am sorry. I'll have to inform the polis. They'll need to speak to you.'

'You haven't already told them?

'I wanted to talk to you first.' Bob knew Malcolm had no conception of what was coming, the intrusion, the prurience, the public clamour for news. Grief was impossible in such circumstances. It had to be put on hold, to overwhelm you all over again at some later date.

'How did she die?'

'She was stabbed. Through the heart. It would have been quick, if that's any comfort.'

Malcolm stared into the fire once more. His head shook minimally. He closed his eyes. 'I don't really know what to say,' he said. 'I think part of me – it's been so long – I think I suspected something may have happened to her, but you don't want to believe it. And as long as you don't hear anything, you can convince yourself. Carry on ... Do they know when it happened?'

'Not for certain. They're still doin' forensic tests, but they're assumin it was about fifteen year ago. The last time either Maisie or Leslie were seen.'

'But that can't be.'

Malcolm sat upright and gestured towards them. Bob saw a resurgence of hope in his expression and felt a wave of pity. Renewed hope was the hardest thing of all to cope with.

'I've had letters from Leslie,' Malcom said. 'More recent than fifteen years.'

'How recent?'

'They stopped about five or six years ago.'

'Do you still have them?'

'Of course.' He jumped up from his chair and went to the mahogany sideboard that filled the back wall of the room. Annie and Bob exchanged glances, smiled ruefully at one another. Malcolm opened a drawer and rifled through it. He pulled from it a bundle of letters, all in thin, cheap envelopes and written on a variety of paper sizes. He handed them to Bob.

'Is this all of them?'

'Aye. They prove it don't they? She isn't the dead woman.'

There were about twenty, ranging from 1920 to 1930. The last was postmarked Carlisle, January 1930. Six years before Hugh Smithson's murder. And ten years after Leslie Redford, the woman who had supposedly written them, had been murdered. Bob studied the handwriting and realisation dawned on him.

He had seen it before.

He passed the topmost letter to Annie and she inspected it. Bob could tell that she, too, recognised the handwriting from the threatening letters sent to Hugh Smithson.

'I don't know why, Mr Redford,' he said, 'but someone

253

was impersonatin' your sister in these letters.'

'She didn't write them?'

'She was already dead. I really dinnae think there's any doubt. I'm sorry.'

Malcolm took the letters back from Bob and clutched them as though they were holy relics. His eyes were growing glassy. He sniffed loudly.

'Is there anythin in them,' Bob said gently, 'any sort of message, any news, anythin unusual?'

'No. They were – I guess you'd say bland. They're all short, as you can see. They usually say something like "I'm fine, don't worry about me" and that's about all. They never really said anything useful, but I liked to get them all the same. A connection, you know?'

'I do know, aye. Listen, somebody went to a lot of bother to do this. I've no idea why. But it wasnae oot out of malice. Not if there's nothin nasty in them. So, carry on thinkin aboot them as Leslie's. Keep that connection. It might help.'

'Aye.'

*

The train back to Perth was full of bawdy talk about the King and Mrs Simpson, strangers regaling each other with scabrous and slanderous notions. Even in the course of the day, the atmosphere had seemed to shift. The dignity of the monarchy was being trashed. Bob wondered whether it could even survive such a calamity. A British republic? Could it happen? Even though he hoped it might, Bob was certain this was not the right time. The mood in the country was tense, talk of war and nationalist propaganda and populism running rife. This was no time for upheaval.

'So why d'you think the letters stopped?' Annie asked. 'D'you think whoever wrote them died?'

'Could be. Or they might have got bored. Or they might have been stopped from sendin them.'

'Stopped? How?'

'I dinnae ken, yet. But I have a hunch. I'm goin to need help. And another day trip.'

'Where?'

'Embra.' He sighed and shifted in his seat. 'I tell you this, I dinnae ken when I'm goin to get Cloudland finished. I'm cuttin it fine for openin next week.'

'This is important, though.'

He took her hand and held it. His newspaper dropped to the floor, yesterday's news consigned to history. 'It is, aye.'

*

He sat on his own in the living room. Thin light from the gas streetlamp opposite pulled the centre of the room out of shadow. Everything else lay concealed. He preferred not being able to see. He picked up his guitar and began to play the *79ᵗʰ's Farewell to Gibraltar*. The tune had been one of Gran's favourites. She loved a pipe band. Almost the only time she showed Bob any warmth was when he played the pipes. Love yes; warmth no. Hers was a world of discipline, duty and dourness. Showing emotion was such a difficult thing for the Calvinist Scot. Bob fought against this weakness in his character, something inherent, part of his blood, his upbringing, the Scots' way of life. Like mother, like father. Like father, like son. Bob had been starved of love his entire life and he was terrified he'd be the same when his time came, when a son or daughter needed him. What would he do? What would he say?

He slowed the tune from a quick march to a lament, picking each note in turn, letting it ring into the darkness. What had been jolly became sombre, a trick of rhythm, of time, of thought. He thought of Leslie Redford, a young woman now dead, fifteen years locked in a metal box, slowly mummifying while the world revolved oblivious, her parents dying in turn, her brother waiting, hoping, wondering whether one day his younger sister might return. He began to improvise around the tune, sliding into A minor, letting melancholy wash over his playing and over the night. There was no rest he could offer Leslie Redford. Finding her killer would bring her no release from where she was, because she was nowhere, her spirit gone and her life ended. There was no afterlife, no predestination, no ineffable mystery. All there was, was the here and now.

And that had to be dealt with.

He went into the hallway and picked up the telephone and waited for the operator. He asked to be put through to Mrs Macrae on the High Street and, when Mrs Macrae answered in a voice unrecognisably posh, he asked to speak to Geordie.

'George, it's for you.'

Bob waited a few moments and heard footsteps growing gradually louder and then George was on the line.

'Geordie, how d'you fancy bein the one who finds Leslie Redford's killer?'

'Who's Leslie Redford?'

'That's a long story. Are you off the morn?'

'Aye.'

'Grand. I'll tell you all aboot it on the bus.'

'What bus?'

'Tae Embra. You'll need to wear your uniform, though. And bring your warrant card.'

# *Friday 11ᵗʰ December*

## *A Day of Judgement*

On the bus to Edinburgh, Bob explained his thinking. The threatening letters received by Smithson and the letters to Malcolm Redford were written by the same person, that was certain. The handwriting was identical. Both stopped suddenly around January 1930. Bob thought it unlikely that someone who had sent them so assiduously for ten years would stop without good reason. They could have died, of course, but how could you explain the murder of Hugh Smithson now, after so many years?

'So,' he said, 'for some reason, around January 1930 the killer stopped sending the letters. Why?'

George shrugged. 'You tell me.'

'Because he was in the jail.'

'Right.'

'Must have been for something serious. A hefty sentence. At least five years.'

'And he got out at the start of this year?'

'Or back end of last, aye.'

George swore. 'And the moment he got out ... '

'He came for Smithson. If the letters stopped January 1930, that's probably when he was arrested. It would have taken a while to come to trial, though, so we need to check all sentences during the first six months of 1930. If he got out in January 1936, that meant he probably served about five and a half year. So, we need to find everyone who was sentenced to between five and ten years. Any more than that, he wouldnae be oot yet.'

'There must be thousands of them.'

'Not thousands. The whole prison population's less than 2,000. Most folks get much lighter sentences than that. There winnae be that many get a sentence between five and ten year. Couple of hundred maybe.'

'You really think we can find him?'

'Dunno. But we have to try.'

At Edinburgh Bus Station, they walked downhill to Princes Street. In the run-up to Christmas, even with a bitter wind and sharp cold, the wide pavement was crammed with shoppers. Trams and buses ran the length of the street. A young man, seeing George's uniform, stopped and asked for directions to the castle. George looked around and pointed up at the Castle Rock dominating the skyline. 'There,' he said.

'Aye, but how do I get there?'

'Climb.'

They turned east and the crowds gradually thinned until they reached a huge Victorian building proclaiming its importance with the grandeur of its facade. It was separated from the street by a run of imposing steps and in the front was a statue of the Duke of Wellington, his horse Copenhagen ready to charge. Bob wondered why an Englishman should be celebrated in front of the building that housed the repository of Scotland's history and heritage.

'Mind,' he said, 'I'm your assistant.'

'What if they ring the Station to check?'

'What would they do that for? You've got a warrant card and a uniform. What's dodgy about you?'

'The person I'm wi?'

Bob cuffed the back of his helmet playfully. 'Just say what I telt you, you'll be fine.'

They walked up the steps to the National Archives and George introduced himself as PC Macrae of Perth City

Constabulary.

'I'm needin the records of all male prison sentences handed doon between January and June 1930.'

'In Perth?'

'No, the whole of Scotland.'

The receptionist, an ascetic-looking man of around fifty, stared at him through thick, round-rimmed spectacles as though deprecating what he saw. He called over a custodian and whispered the request to him. The two men turned and fixed George with a glare that was unmistakably hostile.

'It'll take a bit of finding,' the receptionist said. 'The information won't all be in the same place.'

'Aye, well,' said Bob, 'I'm sure you've got the right man on the job.'

They were escorted through two sets of double-doors and down a long, marble-lined hallway into a gallery-shaped room with a dozen rows of tables, each able to accommodate up to ten people. It was less than a quarter full. Bob and George alternated between watching the researchers and staring out of the window at Princes Street for about twenty minutes before the custodian arrived, carrying an armful of papers, the court records of various sheriff, high and burgh police courts and the Scottish Court Books.

'Jings,' said George. 'I thought you said there wouldnae be many?'

'You can ignore the burgh police courts. They never deal with anything serious enough for a five-year sentence. Make a note of everyone who meets the criteria. Five-to-ten-year sentence. Name, age, last known address.'

'Ssh,' said a bald man in a fading tweed suit, frowning over a bundle of court papers.

'Ach, away man.' said Bob, 'we're investigatin a murder.' He pulled a pile of the papers towards him and made a show of reading them for a couple of minutes. He watched George, the way he used the tip of his finger to trace every record on the page, stopping and making notes in his pocket book every few lines. A complete waste of time and Bob felt sorry for duping his friend this way. But needs must. He set his bundle of papers aside and stood up.

'What you doin?' said George.

'Carry on. I'll be back in a minute.'

He got lost on the way back to reception and was rescued by a sour-faced secretary as he stumbled into a staff area. The receptionist was busy with another enquiry and Bob waited, hopping from one foot to the other. 'Come on,' he muttered under his breath. When the receptionist was free, Bob strode up to the desk.

'I'm with PC Macrae,' he said.

'I remember.'

'He's asked, could we also have the records of sentences on women for the same period.'

'Could you not have asked at the same time?'

'Aye, sorry. He forgot.'

The receptionist fixed Bob with a furious stare and called for the custodian and explained the request.

'Could he not have asked at the same time?'

'Apparently not.'

The custodian glowered at Bob. Bob smiled back. 'You'll be lookin forward to some time off at Christmas?' he said. The receptionist made no reply. 'I'll make my ain way back,' he said. 'I wouldnae want to be any bother.' He took the same wrong turn as before and ended up in the same office as before and the same sour-faced secretary escorted him to the reading room.

'Is everyone in Embra as rude as this, or do you take special lessons here?' The secretary turned on her heels and clacked away.

George was still hunched over his papers, his back to the door, and he didn't spot Bob's return. Bob took a seat nearest the door and waited. He waved when the custodian appeared, and sat back as the files were dropped on the table with ill-grace. As Bob expected, there weren't many names, no more than twenty-five, a roll call of mostly desperate women driven by circumstance into drastic action. Bob read through the list slowly, looking for anything which might identify a suspect. And, near the bottom of the list, he found what he was looking for.

"Leslie Comer, aged 42, Edinburgh. Nine years for manslaughter." He read it half a dozen times. Leslie Comer. A combination of Leslie Redford and Gladys Comer, the two closest friends of Maisie Smithson. If you wanted to change your name, you'd choose something memorable. Meaningful. And, these three women – and their relationship – were certainly meaningful. Leslie dead, murdered years before. Gladys ticking down her life in the service of the church, seeking atonement, trying to forget. And Maisie? Where did Maisie fit into all of this? How? He noted the last known address – Belhaven Street, Edinburgh. That was six years before, though, a prison sentence ago. What chance was there she'd still be there? All the same, excitement coursed through his body. He looked over at George, who was still oblivious of his presence. 'Sorry, Geordie,' he said. He left the papers on the table and returned to reception, this time without mishap.

'I need to locate the address of somebody from these lists, please.'

'We're not the telephone exchange.'

'PC Macrae and I are investigatin a case of murder. A particularly violent murder, as it happens. Your cooperation would be greatly appreciated.' The receptionist stared at him, and his surly expression remained, but finally he nodded. 'The name is Leslie Comer, last known address Belhaven Street, Edinburgh. That would have been 1930.'

'Leave it with me.' He retreated to the office behind, calling for an assistant to man the desk. A few minutes later he appeared with a slip of paper.

"44 Balcarres Street, Edinburgh," it read.

'Is that far?'

'Ten minutes up Lothian Road.'

'Where's Lothian Road?'

'Other end of Princes Street.'

'Could I walk?'

'If you were a teuchter.'

'I'll cherish the memory of the service I've had here.'

'We aim to please.'

'Listen, when PC Macrae comes oot, can you explain I got called away suddenly. Tell him to make his ain way back to Perth. I'll see him the morn and explain.'

'So, we're a messaging service as well now?'

'Just tell him.'

Bob ran outside and hailed a taxi on Princes Street and gave the driver the address. Half an hour and a mini-tour of Edinburgh later, he stood outside a long row of grey tenements with filthy windows and grime-blacked stonework, deep, forbidding passageways punctuating the facade every twenty yards or so. He found the right block, entered and climbed four flights of stone stairs. There was no paint on the upper portion of the walls. His footsteps echoed. The cold was chilling, even colder than outside. A bare light bulb hung from the ceiling. It offered little to brighten such a space. Bob stood at the doorway of 44 Balcarres Street and bit his lip and knocked on the door.

The woman who appeared was haggard, her skin grey, her hair lank. There was no lustre in her blue eyes. Her cheeks were sallow. She looked in need of a good meal.

'Maisie Smithson?'

Her face crumpled. She lowered her gaze, steadied herself by gripping the door.

'Can I come in?'

She said nothing, but turned and retreated down a straight

passageway and Bob followed. The living room was long and narrow. A meagre sprinkling of coal burned in the fireplace. Green curtains were drawn to keep in what heat there was, although in truth, there was precious little. The room was clean and tidy, but the furniture was old, the chairs sagging and well past the end of their useful lives. Maisie Smithson went into the adjoining kitchen and poured a hefty measure of Old Tom gin into a tumbler. She waved the bottle at Bob.

'No, thanks.' He stopped. 'Aye. Just a wee one.' He didn't like to see people drink alone. His father had done that when the mood came on him, whisky on whisky into the night, erasing memories of debt and failure. Bob eased himself gingerly into the chair nearest the window, as though fearing it might collapse under his weight.

'You found me, then,' Maisie said as she handed him his drink and sat in the chair opposite.

'Aye.'

'How?'

'The letters. That you sent to Leslie and your husband. You kept it up for years, but then they just stopped. I didnae think you were deid, not with what happened to Mr Smithson. And you'd done it so regular, I couldnae see you just stoppin of your own accord. So somethin must have stopped you. And I thought – the jail. That's the only reason I could think that you'd have stopped. So, I checked who was sent to the jail in early 1930 and there it was. "Leslie Comer". The names of your two friends.'

'I kent it was a daft name to choose, but once I'd done it, I was stuck wi it.'

'Why did you go to the jail?'

She had the guarded expression of someone used to concealing such information, but she blinked slowly and responded.

'Manslaughter. Nine year.'

'Right.'

'My man.'

'What? Another man? No Mr Smithson?'

She gave a sour smile. 'They do say women keep fallin for the same types of man. It's true. It's a form of madness. Tommy was just like Hughie.'

'How?'

'Couldnae keep his fists to himself.'

'Hugh Smithson used to hit you?'

'Aye.'

'I'm sorry.'

'And Tommy Smith did an a.'

'What happened?'

'Ae day, Hearts were playin Hibs at Tynecastle. Hearts lost.'

'He was a Hearts man?'

'Aye.'

'Took it out on you?'

'Aye. I was in bed when he got hame. He telt me tae get up and mak him a piece and jam. "Mak it yersell," I said to him, and he belted me across the face and then he punched me three or four times. Nothin unusual. But then he grabbed my hair and dragged me oot the bed and along the landing. I was screamin for him to stop, but he punched me in the gut and I went flyin backwards, the wind knocked right out of me. I mind lyin against the toilet door, starin up at him. And I could tell, the look on his face, he was goin to kill me.'

She stopped talking and drank her gin, her head twisted away from Bob, her eyes staring at a spot on the carpet beneath the window.

'He was standin at the top of the stair. He leaned down to grab me again and I just thought "No, I cannae do this, I cannae do this". I swung my leg and caught him ahint the knee and he buckled and ...' She turned and stared into Bob's eyes. 'He went backwards doon the stairs. Landed on his heid. Broke his neck.' Her face was devoid of emotion, drained by the memory. 'Deid.'

'You got nine year for that?'

'Aye.'

'No mitigatin circumstances?'

'The day I was charged I had two black eyes. Looked like a bloody panda. Bruises on my throat, chest. So, aye, they kent it wasnae me started it. That's why I only got nine year instead of the drop.'

'How long d'you serve?'

'Five year. Guid behaviour. I only kill husbands.'

Bob sipped the gin. It was vile. Maisie laughed at his expression. 'If you dinnae like it, dinnae drink it. I cannae afford to waste any. That's my last bottle.' Bob handed the glass back to her.

'I've been to see Malcolm Redford.'

'Aye? I never met the man, but Leslie aye went on about him, what a kind-hearted soul he was.'

'Why did you write to him? Why pretend you were Leslie?'

Maisie looked round the room as though in search of the answer. 'It was a stupid thing to do, but once I'd done it that first time, I felt I had to keep doin it. I used to go every year to the Lake District for my holidays. Walkin in the hills. No chance of meetin anyone I kent. And on the way back the bus aye stopped in Carlisle so I thought it would be a good way of sendin a letter without any chance of bein found out. And I wanted to do that. The thing wi Leslie is that she was kind too, like her brother. But for all she was a gentle crater, she could be awfae stubborn. That's Aiberdonians for you. She had a terrible fallin oot wi her parents. I never kent why, but she wouldnae hae anythin to do wi them. So, I kent that wherever Leslie went after she left Perth she wouldnae write to him. And if he really was that kind, he didnae deserve that. So I wrote the letters. Onyway, it was a way of keepin Leslie close to me. I missed her that much, ken? I wanted her

265

to still be part of me. That's why I called myself Leslie when I started ower. To keep the connection. When I wrote those letters, I *was* Leslie and that made me feel good. A better person. Because she *was* a better person than me. And I thought ... Well, I thought it might cheer Malcolm up, hearin frae his sister.'

'But she was deid.'

'I didnae ken that.' A look of bafflement overtook Bob's face. 'If I'd kent he'd killed her, I'd have done him in there and then in 1920. I just thought he'd frightened her off.'

'How?'

She gulped the rest of her gin and picked up Bob's glass and drank half of that. 'What d'you ken about me and Leslie?'

'Nothin much.'

'Or me and Gladys Comer?'

'Gladys said the two of you were haein an affair.'

Maisie laughed. 'In her dreams. We had a ... a dalliance, I suppose. A couple of times. When I was feelin low, when Hughie hit me or I just needed someone to no hate me. That was all it was for me, but Gladys got it into her heid it was much more serious. She convinced hersel I was goin to leave Hughie for her.'

'And you wouldnae?'

'No.'

'But then you left him for Leslie?'

'No. But I wanted to. I loved her. Totally, madly. And she loved me an a. She was fifteen year younger than me. And I was aboot ten year younger than Hughie, so there was such big age differences, ken? I kept tellin her it was daft, but she said no, we were goin to run away thigether. A new life, just the two of us.' She finished the second gin. 'Christ, I used to lie in bed, next to him snorin and stinkin, and dream aboot that. I wanted it. I started savin every penny. I'd got a hundred pounds put by.'

'What, frae working as a cleaner?'

'There's mair ways than one to mak money, son. Onyway, I hid it in an old wartime chocolate tin under the floorboards in the spare room.'

Bob remembered the last time he'd seen that tin, in Hugh Smithson's wardrobe.

'You didnae take it wi you, then?'

'I didnae get the chance.'

'How?'

'One night, I got hame frae work and he started layin into me the second I got in the door. It wasnae unusual for him to hit me, but this was somethin else. Brutal, ken? He just started beltin me, punchin my face, kickin my stomach. He beat the shit out of me. And *then* he telt me why.'

'Why?'

'Someone telt him I was haein an affair.'

'D'you ken who?'

'No.'

Bob nodded. It would have been Henry Hamill.

'He telt me he'd have forgiven me if it was wi another man. But it was ...'

'Leslie.'

'Aye. "The shame of it", he said. It would destroy him. He'd never be able to show his face in Perth again. And then he said, "tell me it's no true". I kent if I'd just said what he wanted to hear, he'd have gone along wi it. But I couldnae. I said I loved her wi all my heart and I wanted to spend the rest of my life wi her. He laid into me again. I didnae even feel it that time. He said he'd already dealt wi Leslie that afternoon and I'd never see her again. "She got a bloody good hidin, just like you", he said, "and now she's fucked off out of town. I put her on the Aiberdeen bus mysel and she'll no be back".'

'Did you believe him?'

'Aye. Thing is, I was used to bein beaten, but Leslie

267

wasnae, so I wasnae surprised that she'd run oot and leave me. I would have, too, if I was her.'

Bob screwed up his eyes in concentration. 'So, you genuinely believed Leslie was alive?'

'Aye. Hughie was violent, but I didnae think he'd kill her.'

'So why the letters? To him? Threatenin him?'

She sat back and raised her eyes to the ceiling. 'Them? I did that what four, five times?'

'Four.'

'When I got blind drunk and in a rage. I hated him. I hated that he was probably livin the life of Riley. So, I sent those letters to frighten him. Stupid, I ken, but I've done stupid things all my life.'

'You didnae hae any evidence?'

'I didnae even ken he'd done anythin. I was just tryin to frighten him.'

'Why did you go back? In January?'

'To get the money. The £100.' She gestured at the poor living room. 'I'm hardly livin it up, am I? I cannae get a job – no one'll employ a woman that killed her man. I used to turn tricks to get by, but who'd want to fuck this old cow?' She stared at the floor. She lit a cigarette and went to the kitchen and poured another gin.

'And there was that money just sittin there. It burned me up, thinkin aboot it. I was pretty sure it'd still be there. Who would look under the floorboards? No Hughie, onyway. He was a lazy bastard. He'd never clean the hoose, so I figured he'd never find it. I went back to Perth and heard he'd become this recluse. I was quite pleased aboot that because at least his life was fucked up an a. But how was I goin to get in the hoose? I kent what the loft was like, that it ran the length of the row. And then I read in the papers about Mrs Barratt dyin. Auld witch, never had a decent word to say about anyone. So, I made my plan ... '

'But when you got there, you found Leslie?'

'Aye.' Her voice was little more than a whisper. She sucked heavily on her cigarette.

'You'd no idea?'

'No.'

Bob tried to picture the moment. When he and Annie had discovered the body, that was bad enough. But for Maisie? Finding the body of the woman she loved? A shiver went through him.

'Christ. I'm sorry.'

'I flipped. I got into the hoose wi the ladder I'd brought. I went to the kitchen and grabbed a knife. Hughie was asleep. Drunk as a skunk, no doubt. I ... I'm no makin excuses, but I dinnae really ken what happened ... Aye, I do, I ken what I did, I winnae pretend otherwise, but the moment I actually did it, I cannae really bring it to mind, ken?'

'Aye.'

'It's like I wasnae there.'

'Aye.'

'Afterwards, I couldnae go back through the loft. Couldnae see that again. So, I shut the hatch and went oot the back. I kent that over the wall was the library because I was the cleaner there. So, I hid there overnight and when Eck Harrold came in next morning I ran oot.'

'Why didn't you go oot the front door?'

'Jimmy Randall and Hammy Johnston were havin an argument ootside. Aboot whether there was ice on the road, if you believe. Pair of bloody wallopers. They aye was. They went on and on, wouldnae let up. And I just needed to get oot of the hoose. Get away. I was goin oot of my mind.'

'And you didnae find the money?'

'I never even looked. I was that crazy I forgot all aboot it.'

*If only she'd looked in the wardrobe*, Bob thought. It was there all the time, within reach.

'So, what happens now?' she said. She stubbed out her cigarette and lit another. Her hands were shaking, just like Malcolm Redford's. Victims both. *Don't I ever bring anything good*, Bob thought. 'Are you goin to take me in?'

Bob shook his head. 'I'm no wi the polis. They're doin their ain investigation, but they're no awfae good at it, so chances are they winnae stumble across you ...'

She stared at him in confusion. 'Why?'

Bob stood up. He took out his wallet. There was £10 which he'd set aside for provisions for Cloudland. 'I'm openin up a new café next week. In Crieff. James Square. If you ever need somewhere to go, someone to talk to, come by. It's a nice place, Crieff. They leave you alane.'

He dropped the ten £1 notes on the table. 'I'll see mysel oot.'

## Saturday 12<sup>th</sup> December

### *A Day of Endings*

At nine the following morning, Bob knocked on the back door of Richard Hamill's house on Paul Street.

'I need to speak to you,' he said. He followed Richard inside and sat once more at the little kitchen table while Richard made tea.

'I've found the killer.'

'I knew you would, Sherlock McHolmes. Who?'

'Well, that's a bit of a problem.'

'Right,' said Richard, his expression clearly showing it wasn't right.

Bob explained about Maisie Smithson, the abuse, the way she was treated, the poverty in which she was now living, the assault, her self-defence, the trial, punishment. Manslaughter. Richard bit his lip.

'What are you going to do?' he asked.

'I dinnae ken.'

'I think you probably do. Otherwise, you wouldn't have come to see me.'

'I cannae turn her in.'

'Then don't. Your choice.'

'But I promised you I'd find the killer. Stop all the rumours about you.'

'Well, maybe Maisie Smithson is more important.'

'She's not more important. Absolutely not that. It's just ... She's mair desperate than you. If it was the other way round ... If you were destitute ...'

271

'I understand.'

'She needs help.'

They drank tea in silence, Bob staring out of the window at the back alley running the length of the houses. There was a pattern in the world. He was coming to see it. No matter what they said, no matter how they dressed up their actions as decency or fair play or democracy, no matter how much they professed to help the ordinary people, if you were a woman, or poor, or homosexual, or different in some way from them, then you'd better be on your guard, because their interests always came first. Them. The system. The state. He looked at Richard, a good and honest man. Richard Hamill would struggle in this life because of who he was. There was no sense to it. No justice. For people like Richard Hamill or Maisie Smithson or Bob Kelty or Marjory Fenwick, justice was a contingent thing, a chimera.

'You seem bothered,' he said to Richard.

Richard appeared to weigh his thoughts, debating whether to air them. 'You,' he said finally. 'I understand what you're saying. What you're doing. But ... Are you not in danger of doing what you criticise others for? Braggan, for example. Acting as judge and jury? Making your mind up? Closing it to other possibilities. Acting based on your opinions. Are you not in danger of thinking you're better than everyone else?'

Braggan said the same thing to him, that day in Lochearnhead. Was it true? Bob shook his head.

'Honestly, maist days I'd just like to be better than *anyone* else.' He saw the confusion on Richard's face. 'You might think I'm confident and in control, but it's all an act. I'm bloody terrified maist of the time.'

Richard leaned forward and patted the back of Bob's hand. 'I think we probably all are. At least you can admit it.'

'Aye, much good it'll do me. Maisie Smithson ...' He chewed his bottom lip. He turned his teacup round in its saucer. 'Thing is, this isnae about Maisie Smithson. Or you. It's no personal. It's the system. The system doesnae gie a hang aboot you or that woman. The system's first thought is to make sure the system continues to work. Take Madge Fenwick. That wee lassie was put through hell because they saw her and judged her and labelled her. Same wi you. A "homosexual". Obviously a wrong un. Not decent. They preside over us, tell us what to do, what to think, they put us through the wringer, and we – puir bloody fools – we think they're doin it in our interests. Even if they get it wrong, like Madge, like you, we still think they were doin it in our interests. They were tryin to help Madge. They were trying to get justice for Hugh Smithson. But it's no true. It's always – always – in *their* interest. Whatever they do. It's the system. I tell you, man, it's fuckin evil.'

Richard sat back. He'd never heard Bob swear before. 'You sound like a communist,' he said.

'Communism's just another system. Communism, capitalism, two cheeks of the same arse.'

'An anarchist, then.'

'Aye, I like the sound of that. Until some bugger decides he knows best and tries to take charge.' He finished his tea and clattered the cup back onto the saucer. 'I'm no goin to turn Maisie Smithson in,' he said, 'because whatever she did to Hugh Smithson, right or wrong, it was forced on her. A lifetime of bein beaten, abused, treated like dirt, bein second-class, worthless. We're all in the same boat. It's a bloody wonder mair people dinnae snap under the weight of it.' He stood and pulled on his coat. 'I wish they would.'

He stretched and shook Richard's hand. 'You probably dinnae understand me, but maybe one day you might.'

'I do,' said Richard. 'I think so, anyway. Enough to accept it.'

'Aye,' said Bob. 'Well, I'll away, because there's somebody else I need to see who probably winnae be quite so acceptin.'

*

'Well, look who it is? The Incredible Vanishing Man.'

George Macrae retreated to his living room without a word and Bob closed the front door and followed him. 'I owe you an apology,' Bob said.

'You do, aye.'

'I got called away.'

'So the man said. How did that happen, exactly?'

'What?'

'How did you get called away? Who called you? How did they ken whaur you were? How did they contact you?'

Bob smiled. 'We'll make a polisman of you yet.'

'You made a right Charlie o me, that's what you did. Could you no have at least come and telt me what you were doin?'

'It was an emergency.'

'You're a terrible liar.'

'I ken.'

'Care to explain?'

'I cannae, really.'

'No, I thought not. I'd mak you a cup of tea but to be honest, I dinnae feel like bein civil.'

'Can I mak you one?'

George gestured towards the kitchen. 'Two sugars, dash o milk. Dinnae expect any thanks.'

They sat in the living room when the tea was made, looking out of the window at rain that had just started falling. George wanted to be angry, but it wasn't easy with Bob. Still, he tried to spin out the silence to increase Bob's sense of guilt. He deserved that, at least.

'Did you find her?' he said finally.

'Find who?' said Bob too quickly.

'When I finally figured out I'd been dumped, I went back

274

to reception. But as I was headin for the door, I saw a bundle o papers on the table. That looked awfae like the ones I'd just spent an hour studyin. So, I had a wee look. Women prisoners.'

'Aye.'

'So, it was a woman you were lookin for all the time, was it? And you left me to waste my time looking through the men. Keep me busy while you did the real detectin.'

'Sorry.'

'Whit was it you said to me the day before? How do you fancy bein the one who catches the killer o somebody I'd never even heard of ...'

'Sorry.'

'But no, I was just the poor bloody sap who got you in there. Wi my uniform and warrant card.'

'Sorry.'

'So you keep sayin. So did you find her?'

'Kind of.'

'Kind of?'

'Well, put it this way, she's no a danger to anybody anymore.'

'She's deid?'

'She's no a danger to anybody.'

'Are you goin to tell me what happened?'

'No.'

'Were you ever goin to tell me?'

'Oh aye. I meant it. If there was an arrest to be made, it would have been you.'

'But there isnae?'

'No.'

'Drink your tea. It'll get cauld.'

*

Annie led the way as they walked into St John's Kirk. 'Hello?' she shouted. They heard activity at the far end of the church and saw Gladys Comer polishing the base of the pulpit. She carried on as though she hadn't heard them, but Annie could tell by the stiffness of her posture she had.

'Hello,' she said again when they were standing behind her. She introduced Bob, but Gladys made no attempt to acknowledge him. 'I wanted to speak to you.'

'Well, here I am.'

'The body. That was found in Mr Smithson's house. You'll have read about it in the paper?'

'Aye.'

'We know who it was.'

'Maisie Smithson.'

'No.'

Gladys stopped dusting and stared at Annie. 'Aye,' she said. 'It has to be.'

'Can we sit doon?' Annie sat on the first pew and patted the cushion beside her. The older woman sat next to her and stared ahead, as though listening to the minister in his pulpit.

'Tell me,' she said. 'Who is it?'

'I think you probably already ken.'

'Leslie?'

'Aye.'

She sat forward and cradled her head in her hands. Bob and Annie waited in silence, allowed her to compose herself.

'She'd been there for years,' said Annie. 'Probably since the early twenties. When she disappeared.'

Gladys rocked on her heels, her fingers splayed across her cheeks, eyes staring fixedly ahead, seeing nothing. 'No, no,' she said quietly, almost to herself.

'Because she did disappear,' said Bob. 'Didn't she? Her and Maisie both. At the same time.' He touched her shoulder. She flinched, but didn't break her gaze. 'Your two best friends. Did everything together. And you never mentioned to anyone they'd disappeared. Why was that, Miss Comer?' Again, Gladys Comer said nothing.

'Did you know what had happened?' said Annie.

This finally provoked Gladys into a response. 'No!' she shouted. The word rebounded around the empty church, echoing into impotence.

Bob leaned forward. 'But you kent *somethin* had happened, didn't you? Otherwise, you'd have been more suspicious. Asked questions. Talked aboot it.'

'You dinnae ken what you're talkin aboot.'

'When I spoke to Fred Hammond and Archie McCarthy, they telt me Henry Hamill and Hugh Smithson had a big fallin out. D'you ken what aboot?'

'How would I ken?'

'Because I think what they fell out over was Henry tellin Mr Smithson his wife was havin an affair with Leslie Redford.'

'And what's that to do wi me?'

'Because it was you telt Henry Hamill aboot it in the first place. You wanted him to tell Smithson. You were angry. Maisie turned you doon. She was playin aboot wi this wee lassie half her age. You couldnae stand it. If Maisie didnae want *you*, you were goin to make sure she couldnae hae Leslie either. So, you made sure Hugh Smithson found oot about them. That way, you could put an end to their affair, is that right?'

Bob expected her to lash out, to shout, swear at him, deny it. She did none of those things. She sat small in her chair, sunk into her herself, a diminished presence in the face of truth. 'Aye,' she whispered.

'Jealousy.'

'Aye. And disgust.'

'Disgust?'

'Disgust. I still wanted Maisie. I couldnae get her oot of my mind. Her body, her touch, her smell. Her taste.' She shook her head. 'It's an abomination. Two women ... I'll burn in hell. I deserve to.'

277

'No,' said Bob firmly. 'And dinnae let anyone in your precious church try to tell you otherwise. There's no a single one of them kens what your God thinks on these matters.'

'Scripture.'

'Scripture be damned. Who even wrote it? When? Maist of it was hundreds of years after your precious Jesus Christ walked the earth. Hell, we cannae even write the history of this bloody year and get it right. The fine and noble King Edward we were telt in January. What are they sayin aboot him noo? Feckless waste of space. So, there's not a single word of your precious scripture that really tells you what your God thinks. Dinnae go torturin yoursel on that score.'

She said nothing. Bob waited. 'I was just angry,' she said finally. 'It was stupid.'

'But you must have known that Hugh Smithson was violent?'

'No. He smacked Maisie a time or two, aye, gied her a black eye, but what man doesnae? Nothing wrang wi that.' She exhaled heavily. 'Was it him killed Leslie?'

'Aye, probably.'

'Sweet Jesus Christ, what have I done? What have I done?'

'You couldnae hae known,' said Annie.

'Maybe no. But if I hadnae spoken to Henry Hamill nothin would have happened. She wouldnae be deid.'

'You cannae blame yourself.'

Gladys gave a hollow laugh. 'What the hell do you know, Miss Hoity Toity? I've been blamin mysel all my bloody life. Even without knowin the worst o what I've done. I drove a wedge between me and the woman I loved. I set out to make her life a misery because she'd made mine a misery. Christian charity? I havenae an ounce o it in my body. I'm a witch.' She stood up and waved her duster as though rousing herself back into activity, but just as suddenly as she stood, she sat down again.

278

'Where's Maisie?' she said.

'I dinnae ken,' said Bob.

'Did he kill her, too?'

Bob shifted uneasily. He wanted to put her mind at rest on that, at least, but he couldn't say anything that might give away the fact he knew where she was. 'I doubt it,' he said. 'If he had, he'd hae left the body in the same place, would he no?'

'Aye, I suppose so.'

Bob could see the thoughts circulating in her mind, made real in the set of her mouth, the way her eyes flickered about the room. 'Do you think it was Maisie killed Hughie Smithson?' she said.

'I doubt it. I mean, why? After all this time? That wouldnae make sense, would it?'

'Maybe no. But she's the only person in the world who'd want to. Who else would be interested in killin that useless waste o space?' Gladys stood up again. She wafted the duster aimlessly over the back of the pew she had just vacated. 'I hope she did,' she said. 'I hope she came back and killed him. And I hope she comes back for me an a.'

'No.'

'I winnae put up a fight if she does.' She dropped her duster on the ground and walked towards the sacristy. Bob and Annie watched her go, trailing pain and torment.

'What world is it,' said Bob, 'where people who love people get eaten up the whole of their life by guilt on account of it? Where women think it's fine for men to beat them? Where lies and deception harm everythin that's good in the world?'

'We'll change the world.'

He took her hand and kissed it. 'We will, aye.' He stood up. 'Right,' he said, 'that's the end of this. Richard Hamill is innocent. We've done oor bit. Now I want to never think about this again. This whole year. It's been hellish.' He

279

embraced her and kissed her. 'In fact, let's end 1936 right here. For us, today is the first day of 1937. Right?'

'Right.'

'Here's tae us.'

'Wha's like us.'

'Lots. But they havenae been born yet.'

# Wednesday 16<sup>th</sup> December

## A Day of Beginnings

Wednesday dawned wet and cold, a constant drizzle through whistling wind. Bob Kelty looked out of the window of Cloudland onto the activity in James Square. Council workers were marking off the bottom of the square with rope, delineating the area where spectators would stand. A loudspeaker system was being rigged up at the Murray Fountain. Beyond, a woman was on her knees scrubbing the steps of the North of Scotland Bank. The proclamation of King George VI was due at eleven o'clock. Bob checked the time on the wall clock. Ten. He unlocked the door of Cloudland to its third day of operation. There had not been an overwhelming response so far, but a few locals had poked their noses in. Some had even bought a cup of tea. He pulled half a dozen scones from the oven and placed them on plates on the display stand. The bell on the front door jangled and he looked up as Richard Hamill entered, followed by Hamish Nesbitt.

'Hello,' he said, bounding towards them. 'Grand to see you again.'

'We had to come and see the new place,' said Richard. He looked around, nodding exaggeratedly. 'Very impressive. Going well, I trust?'

'Aye, steady.' He studied their smiling faces. 'Good to see you two out thigether.'

'We thought it was time for a gad about,' said Hamish.

'We still have to be careful, though,' said Richard. 'I have a reputation to live down to.'

'Aye,' laughed Bob. 'I'm afraid you do. You're fine in here, though.'

'Thank you.'

'Have a seat. I'll get you some tea.' He bustled into the kitchen and filled the urn with water. 'I have to tell you,' he shouted at them, 'I came to a dead end on your anonymous letters. But one thing I do know is they werenae sent by Sergeant Braggan.'

'You're sure?'

'Aye. He kens you're innocent. Still cannae stand you, but he kens it wasnae you.'

'Well, we'll just have to wait and see if it starts again, then. That's one of the things I wanted to tell you about, actually. I have a new job. Starting on Monday.'

'Smashin. Is it the one you mentioned the other day?'

'Yes.'

'Where?'

Richard faltered. 'Actually, it's the Sandeman Library. Sorry. I know that's where you wanted to work.'

'And did, for all of three and a half minutes.' Bob laughed. 'It's absolutely fine. This is where I want to be now. I'm delighted for you. Just watch out for Mr Tait. He's a stickler for propriety.' He took three scones from the display cabinet and the men sat at a table by the window and watched the ongoing preparations.

'You wait twenty-five years for a royal proclamation,' said Richard, 'and then you get two in twelve months.'

'Aye,' said Bob. 'But at least I'm no on duty this time. Dinnae hae to pretend to be excited.'

'You're not a monarchist?'

'I dinnae ken. I take it ill, to be honest, folks born into wealth like that, but I cannae help thinkin we're goin to need somethin to steady the country in a wee while. A King might do it.'

282

'If he's a good king,' said Hamish.

'Aye, seems like we had a near miss wi that last one.'

'I don't know,' said Richard. 'He followed his heart, anyway. Isn't that what Hamish and I are doing? What you and Annie are doing?'

'Mrs Simpson I can put up wi. As you say, they appear to be in love, although it seems a strange kind of love to me. But it's the people they consort wi that bothers me. Von Ribbentrop. Nazis.'

'You think Edward's a Nazi sympathiser?'

'I've no idea, but I think we're better with this new man.'

The doorbell jangled again and Victor and Bella Conoboy entered, followed by Annie. Bob jumped up once more.

'Three teas, please,' said Victor, smiling.

'Comin up. The urn's just about to bile.'

'We thought we'd see how you're getting on.'

'Just grand.' He introduced Richard and Hamish and took Bella's coat and hung it on the rack. 'And how are you doin?' he asked her.

'Apart from telling Victor he was driving too fast about twenty times, I'm doing very well. I shall need to stay in here when the ceremony starts, though. I'm not ready for crowds yet.'

'You'll be safe in here, then.'

Bob laughed, but Bella looked concerned. She looked around. 'It's not going well?'

'Oh, it's grand. Gets busier every day.' They looked at one another. 'I'll get those teas,' he said.

Annie followed him to the kitchen, and they kissed by the urn. 'How's it really goin?' she asked.

'A bit slow, but it's early days. I have someone interested in piano lessons for his lassie. Word'll get roond soon enough. A wee place like this.' There was a sudden burst of children's chatter from outside and they watched as schoolchildren from the Crieff Public School were lined up in neat rows behind the rope on the square. Stern-looking teachers filtered among them. A couple of boys received a clip round the ear and the noise diminished.

'Looks like we'll be startin soon,' said Bob.

'Hope there's no Suffragettes,' said Victor.

'Not in Crieff, I shouldn't think. Not even back then.'

He pulled one of the tables next to the one where Richard and Hamish were seated and the group sat together and waited for the second royal proclamation of the year to begin. One by one, town councillors, burgh officials and members of the clergy took their place on the road by the Murray Fountain. A guard of honour was formed by the Officer Training Corps of Morrison's Academy, flanked by the OTC pipe band, their bearskins drooping in the steady rain. Girl Guides and the Boys' Brigade followed. Provost Hunt took to the steps of the North of Scotland Bank and a trumpet fanfare was sounded by Ernie Jackson and John Watters. Bob opened the door of Cloudland as the Provost began to speak.

'In obedience to an Order in Council, and by Instructions of His Majesty's Secretary of State for Scotland, I have to read to the inhabitants of Crieff the following Proclamation:

Whereas by an Instrument of Abdication dated the Tenth day of December instant His former Majesty King Edward the Eighth did declare His irrevocable Determination to renounce the Throne for Himself and His Descendants, and the said Instrument of Abdication has now taken effect, whereby the Imperial Crown of Great Britain, Ireland, and all other of His former Majesty's dominions is now solely and rightfully come to the High and Mighty Albert Frederick Arthur George: We, therefore, the Lords Spiritual and Temporal of this Realm, being here assisted with these of His former Majesty's Privy Council, with numbers of other Principal Gentlemen of Quality, with the Lord-Mayor, Aldermen, and citizens of London, do now hereby, with one Voice and Consent of Tongue and Heart, publish and proclaim, That the High and Mighty Prince Albert Frederick Arthur George, is now become our only lawful and rightful Liege Lord George the Sixth by the Grace of God, of Great Britain, Ireland, and the British Dominions beyond the Seas King, Defender of the Faith, Emperor of India: To whom we do acknowledge all Faith and constant Obedience, with all hearty and humble Affection: beseeching God, by whom Kings and Queens do reign, to bless the Royal Prince George the Sixth, with long and happy years to reign over Us.'

The Provost looked up for the first time at the crowd of several hundred crammed into James Square. 'God Save the King,' he said, and the crowd joined in singing the national anthem.

'We'll see how long this one lasts,' said Bob.

'I gather from Lord Kellett that the Duke of York is of a rather more sober temperament than David was,' said Victor. 'If we do need to have a king, then it may as well be this one.'

'With a queen to follow,' said Bella. 'The Princess Elizabeth.'

'We were just talkin about that earlier,' said Bob. 'And I said maybe, the world bein what it is, we do need a king to steady things. But you're right. I think if we have to have a monarch, I'd rather it was a queen.'

'Why?'

Bob shrugged. 'Women are mair sensible.' He went into the back and returned moments later with his fiddle. He held it shyly. He would have preferred less of an audience, but this had been his plan since he woke at first light that morning and he knew the time was right. He fixed the fiddle to his shoulder and began to play *Green Grow the Rashes*. He played it through twice as he sought the courage to go through with his plan. After the second run he began to sing:

There's nought but care on evry han,
In evry hour that passes, O,
What signifies the life o man,
An were nae for the lasses, O.

And when he finished, he knelt in front of Annie Maybury and looked up at her and stretched out his hand. In it was a ring.

'Annie, would you do me the honour of marryin me?'

Annie gasped and covered her mouth with her hand. She looked at the others, the delight on their faces. She looked round at Cloudland. Her future. Her life.

'Aye,' she said. 'I will.'

*

Rain continued all afternoon, deterring custom. James Square was deserted. Lights from Muir's Ironmongers cut through the gloom, but the rest of the square sat grey in the settling mist. December indolence. Bob wiped the tables. He felt a curious combination of emotions. Elation, obviously, but for Bob Kelty elation was generally accompanied by a rumbling dread, a fatalistic certainty that, no matter how well things are going now, reckoning will follow. He could feel his heart in his chest. He always could. There was a sudden shift in the gloom outdoors and a shape emerged at the door of Cloudland. The bell clanged. Maisie Smithson walked in, drenched.

'Hello,' said Bob.

'I feel a bit foolish,' said Maisie. 'I know you said to come here, but now I am, I'm not sure if you meant it. I'll go if you want ...'

'I did mean it. Have a seat. Over there by the fire, dry yourself off a bit. I'll mak you some tea. You'll have a scone?'

'I couldnae.'

'I made them fresh this morning. They'll only go off.'

'Thank you.'

'Were you here for the proclamation?' he shouted from the kitchen as he poured water from the urn into a teapot.

'Aye. I saw you were busy ... '

'You should have come in. They were all my friends. Did you see the lassie that was in?'

'Aye, a bonnie soul.'

'That's Annie. I asked her to marry me the day.' He placed the teas and scone on the table and sat beside her. Maisie smiled broadly.

'I hope she said aye.'

'She did.'

'She's a very lucky girl.'

'I'm the lucky one.'

'You both are. You found each other. Look after her.'

'I will.' Bob patted her hand. 'Are you bidin long?'

'I think so. You're right, there's nothin for me in Edinburgh. It's time for a new start.' She paused. 'Polis willing.'

'You've heard nothing yet?' She shook her head. 'Well, that's a good sign. The polis had access to all the same information as me. If they havenae made the connection yet, they probably winnae.' He thought of George Macrae, his manufactured anger, the goodness Bob knew he possessed. Geordie had seen that list of names. There weren't many of them. He could easily find Maisie if he wanted to. Did he? Bob suspected not.

'Why did you no turn me in?'

Bob sipped his tea. 'You're no a danger to anyone.'

'I am to husbands.'

'Well, dinnae get married again, then.' They laughed, but Bob grew serious once more. 'It's a hard world,' he said. 'Life can be cruel. Sometimes you just need to be forgiven.'

'And to forgive.'

Gladys Comer came to Bob's mind, that most unhappy

woman, trapped in her own guilt, unable to forgive herself or anyone else, bound to a religion whose teleology was founded on fear of the eternal, rather than love of the ephemeral.

'Aye,' he said. 'Forgive and live. Live and love.'

\*

At nine o'clock on the sixteenth of December, 1936, Bob Kelty locked the door of Cloudland and shut off the gas lights and walked into the middle of the room and stared into the darkness. The light of the dim gas streetlamps barely penetrated. Here was quiet and calm, the mute centre of his existence. He took his fiddle and played *Banish Misfortune* three times. *The Rowan Tree. Ae Fond Kiss.* Tears rolled down his cheeks. He loved Annie Maybury and he missed his faither and he missed his gran and he wished he could have known his mother, if even for a moment. He was twenty-two years old and finally his life was about to begin. There was beauty in the world after all. There was a purpose. In the silence he could hear all the music and all the conversation that would overflow this place of love through all the years to come. Music and memory, harmony, hope. The love of it all. Jock Tamson's bairns in their glory.

# Acknowledgements

Thanks as always to Colin and everyone at the Local Studies department of the AK Bell Library in Perth, this time for unearthing some fantastic photographs of the proclamations of Edward VIII and George VI.

Paul Adair and the staff of Perth Museum and Art Gallery offered great assistance in tracking down some photographs, including the one which forms the cover of the book and I'm very grateful for their time and expertise. Thanks also to Loll Trevis, who designed the cover.

Alex Gordon provided information on Glasgow Celtic, despite me writing about them losing in the book. Thanks to him for his magnanimity.

Thanks to Alastair Blair and Brian Doyle, the great historians of St Johnstone FC, for help with names and details which brought colour and veracity to the football match scene in this book.

Ellie Goodenough, my editor, diplomatically and graciously pointed out a couple of stylistic tics of mine, and her suggestions have improved the book you are holding.

Thanks to Dr Anne Pettigrew for sharing her medical knowledge.

Ringwood Publishing are a very friendly publishers who look after their authors and I am very grateful to everyone, staff and interns, for their support. My fellow Ringwood authors, with whom I've now shared several (virtual) stages are a source of inspiration.

## *About the Author*

Rob McInroy was born in Crieff, Perthshire but now does missionary work in East Yorkshire. He has an MA in Creative Writing and a PhD in American literature, both from the University of Hull. Neither has proved particularly helpful in his writing career but at least he got a few speaking gigs in the US out of the PhD.

His fiction is all based in and around the Strathearn valley of Perthshire, particularly Crieff, the Knock hill and the River Earn. He has in mind a ten story arc taking Bob Kelty and his friends from the 1920s to the 2010s and his great ambition is to live long enough to finish it. Judging by the speed he's writing the third novel in the series this may require him to live into his one hundred and forties. Hope springs eternal.

# Other Titles from Ringwood

All titles are available from the Ringwood website in both print and ebook format, as well as from usual outlets.
www.ringwoodpublishing.com
mail@ringwoodpublishing.com

## Cuddies Strip

Rob McInroy

*Cuddies Strip* is based on a true crime and faithfully follows the investigation and subsequent trial but it also examines the mores of the times and the insensitive treatment of women in a male-dominated society.

It is a highly absorbing period piece from 1930s Scotland, with strong contemporary resonances: both about the nature and responsiveness of police services and the ingrained misogyny of the whole criminal justice system.

"Cuddies Strip is a wonderful novel. I read it with a tear in my eye. I could hardly bear to read the ending but it was beautiful."
- Cathi Unsworth, novelist

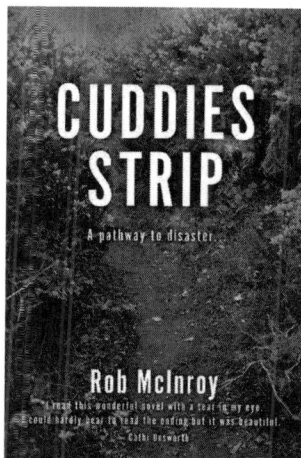

ISBN: 978-1-901514-88-9 £9.99

## Ruxton - The First Modern Murder

Tom Wood

It is 1935 and the deaths of Isabella Ruxton and Mary Rogerson would result in one of the most complex investigations the world had ever seen. The gruesome murders captured worldwide attention with newspapers keeping the public enthralled with all the gory details.

But behind the headlines was a different, more important story: the ground-breaking work of Scottish forensic scientists who developed new techniques to solve the case and shape the future of scientific criminal investigation.

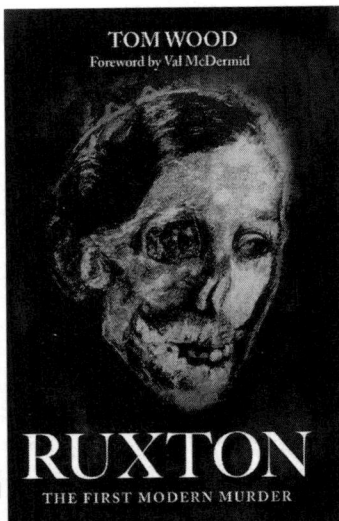

TOM WOOD
Foreword by Val McDermid

RUXTON
THE FIRST MODERN MURDER

ISBN: 978-1-901514-84-1
£9.99

## The Ten Percent

Simon McLean

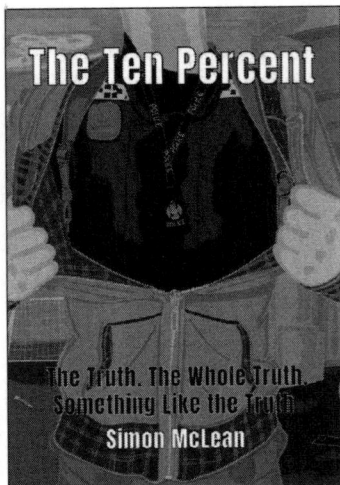

The Ten Percent

The Truth. The Whole Truth. Something Like the Truth
Simon McLean

ISBN: 978-1-901514-43-8
£9.99

An often hilarious, sometimes scary, always fascinating journey through the ranks of the Scottish police from his spell as a rookie constable in the hills and lochs of Argyll, through his career in Rothesay and to his ultimate goal: The Serious Crime Squad in Glasgow.

We get a unique glimpse of the turmoil caused when the rules are stretched to the limit, when the gloves come off and when some of their number decide that enough is enough. A very rare insight into the world of our plain clothes officers who infiltrate and suppress the very worst among us.

## Murder at the Mela

Leela Soma

DI Alok Patel takes the helm of an investigation into the brutal murder of an Asian woman in this eagerly-awaited thriller. As Glasgow's first Asian DI, Patel faces prejudice from his colleagues and suspicion from the Asian community as he struggles with the pressure of his rank, relationships, and racism.

This murder-mystery explores not just the hate that lurks n the darkest corners of Glasgow, but the hate which exists in the very streets we walk.

ISBN: 978-1-901514-90-2
£9.99

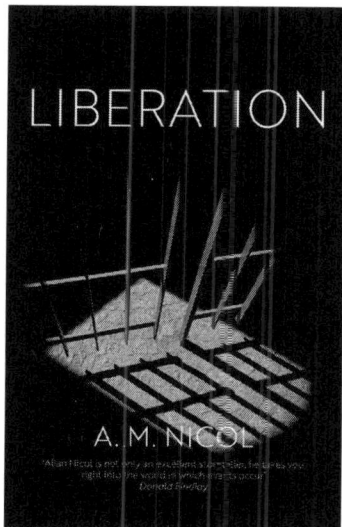

ISBN: 978-1-901514-56-8
£9.99

## Liberation

A. M. Nicol

Midnight in Glasgow, 28th of July 1950: a stolen car drives backwards and forwards, backwards and forwards over a prone, broken body. A mother of two is brutally murdered. Away from her body, on the edge of the pavement, two faux-leather shoes sit innocuously, the first clue for police that this is not just a simple traffic accident.

A family man; a religious devotee, honoured member of the mysterious Plymouth Brethren: more than this, P.C. James Robertson was a man of the law. How can he be connected to a case of this nature?

## Not the Deaths Imagined
Anne Pettigrew

In a leafy Glasgow suburb, Dr Beth Semple is busy juggling motherhood and full-time GP work in the 90s NHS. But her life becomes even more problematic when she notices some odd deaths in her neighbourhood. Though Beth believes the stories don't add up, the authorities remain stubbornly unconvinced.

Is a charming local GP actually a serial killer? Can Beth piece together the jigsaw of perplexing fatalities and perhaps save lives? And as events accelerate towards a dramatic conclusion, will the police intervene in time?

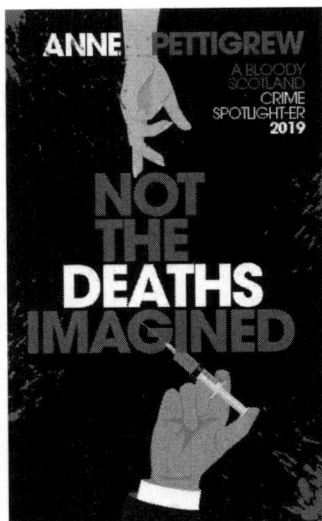

ISBN: 978-1-901514-80-3
£9.99

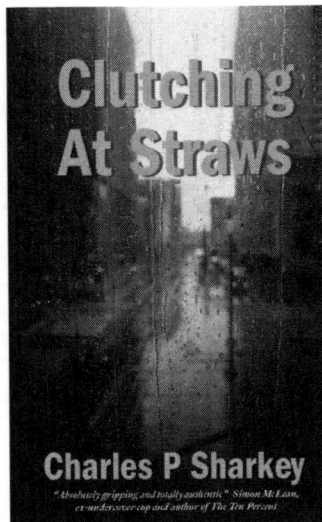

## Clutching at Straws
Charles P. Sharkey

*Clutching At Straws* is a gritty and realistic dive into Glasgow's criminal underworld. The novel follows Inspector Frank Dorsey and his partner DC George Mitchell as they investigate a dead body they believe to be linked to the Moffats, one of the most notorious crime families in Glasgow. However, as they begin to delve further into the case, it becomes apparent that they have a complex web of connected mysteries and murders to make sense of.

ISBN: 978-1-901514-72-8
£9.99